"Readers who delighted in [...] will be rubbing their hand[...] instalment from the coru[...] McCALL SMITH

Miss Blaine's Prefect and the Golden Samovar
Miss Blaine's Prefect and the Vampire Menace
Miss Blaine's Prefect and the Weird Sisters

SHORTLISTED: CrimeFest Last Laugh Award 2019
LONGLISTED: Comedy Women in Print Prize 2019 and 2020

"Audacious ... witty and fun." ALASTAIR MABBOTT, *Herald*

"Effortless ... Smart, funny and all-round good company, wherever Shona goes, readers will eagerly follow." *Scotsman*

"I couldn't wait to be reunited with this character. I utterly love her ... More, more, more, please!" LYNNE TRUSS

"A delightful addition to the ranks of comic crime, mixing sharp observation with a lightness of touch." LAURA WILSON, *Guardian*

"Jane Austen stylings and Stella Gibbons satirical wit." *Scotsman*

"Every bit as light-hearted, level-headed, inventive, hilarious, and altogether enchanting as its heroine." *Kirkus*, STARRED REVIEW

"Marvellous... Readers will appreciate the skill with which Wojtas mirrors Spark's style." *Publishers Weekly*, STARRED REVIEW

"I loved this book ... most entertaining reading." ALEX GRAY

"Knowing, original and very funny." SIMON BRETT

"A carefully and delightfully constructed romp in the tradition of Gogol and of Wodehouse." NORTHWORDS NOW

"*Anna Karenina* written by P.G. Wodehouse." LINDA CRACKNELL

"A thrilling and fast-paced tale ... written with verve, lightness of touch and joie de vivre ... unadulterated fun." SCOTS WHAY HAE

"The crème de la crème of crime fiction debuts." ALLAN GUTHRIE

"Clever, witty, and brain-tickling." RAVEN CRIME READS

"Laugh-out-loud funny ... a real charmer." LIVE AND DEADLY

Published by Contraband
An imprint of Saraband,
3 Clairmont Gardens
Glasgow, G3 7LW

ISBN: 9781913393878
eISBN: 9781916812017
Audiobook: 9781916812048

10 9 8 7 6 5 4 3 2 1

Printed and bound in Great Britain by Clays Ltd, Elcograf S.p.A

MIX
Paper | Supporting
responsible forestry
FSC® C018072

MISS BLAINE'S PREFECT

and the

GONDOLA OF DOOM

OLGA WOJTAS

CONTRABAND

*For Clan Marr, especially healthcare
experts Frances and Rosemary*

ONE

A terrible scream pierced the air.

"Look! It's true!" The woman pointed a trembling finger. "Flee, or we will all die!"

There were more screams now, shrieks of "Come away! Come away!", and in seconds the throng had disappeared into the swirling mist. I wasn't at all sure what I was looking at. To be honest, I must confess I wasn't at my best. I had just time travelled from twenty-first-century Edinburgh, which involves some quite unpleasant abdominal cramping.

This time, I was also feeling uncomfortably overheated, although unfortunately when you're fifty-something, that goes with the territory. And I wasn't entirely sure whether I was actually seeing swirling mist, or if my eyes had gone funny.

One thing I was quite definite about, however: when the woman screamed and pointed, she was pointing at me.

I set about processing what I had seen and heard. I could tell I had gone back several centuries. The woman had been wearing a kirtle over a long-sleeved smock, accessorised with an apron, like quite a few of the other women, although there were some poshos in long fitted brocade gowns showing a deplorable amount of bosom, despite the chilliness of the day. The common blokes were also wearing long-sleeved smocks over knee breeches, but the upper classes were covered in lace accessories, not just round their necks and on their wrists, but also round their waists and on their shoes. None of this helped me to deduce the date, because I know nothing about fashion. There's very little I know nothing about, having had the finest education in the world at the

Marcia Blaine School for Girls. But fashion holds no interest for me, being nothing but a snare and a delusion, a diversion from matters of importance, so I ignore it. I do wear Doc Martens, but that's nothing to do with trying to be trendy; it's because they're comfy and practical. Right now, even though I could see what people were wearing, I would have to find out where and when I was by other means.

I couldn't think of anything I'd done to provoke such a violent reaction from the kirtled woman. I'd only just arrived, after all, and while the abdominal discomfort takes up most of my attention, I'm pretty sure I don't arrive shimmering and with sound effects, like the Tardis or the crew of the starship *Enterprise*. The woman would simply have spotted me as another member of the crowd.

When I time travel, I like to stay out of sight for a while, just to get my bearings. This was the first time I had been dropped straight into a crowded area. But at least it wasn't crowded any more, so I could go on a bit of a recce. I set out into the mist and after only a few metres, found myself teetering on the edge of a canal. One more step and I would have been in it.

A canal. On the basis of this flimsy evidence, most people would assume they were in Venice. But our Founder, Marcia Blaine herself, warned me against making assumptions. Canals could just as easily mean Birmingham, Bruges or Stockholm.

And then I realised that the kirtled woman had been speaking Venetian, a Romance language derived from Latin, and quite distinct from Italian. I had barely registered that she wasn't speaking English, since, thanks to my education, I'm completely fluent in virtually every major language and quite a few minor ones. Again, most people would assume that this confirmed we were in Venice. But the kirtled woman might have been a Venetian tourist visiting Birmingham, Bruges or Stockholm, exclaiming in her native tongue. The crowd had scattered after her warning, but that may simply have been an instinctive reaction to the pointing and screaming, rather than understanding what she had said. True, there had been other shouts in Venetian, but who was I to say they might not also have come from the same bus-load of Venetian tourists?

It's this commitment to assess and evaluate that I believe led Miss Blaine to choose me for her missions. The Blainers' code is to strive to make the world a better place. There are plenty of us around in the twenty-first century, but time travelling allows us to improve previous worlds as well. I say "us", but I have no idea how many of her girls Miss Blaine has sent out into the ether, especially as she herself seems to be several hundred years old. (Not that you would know it – she looks to be a woman in her prime.) But I rather hope I'm a pioneer.

Despite not knowing where or when I was, I knew better than to wish I had had advance warning. That sort of thing would lead to severe pain in my big toe, as though someone in their prime had trodden on it very hard. Discovering my whereabouts and mission depended on acumen, something I like to think I have in significant quantities.

But I've also come to realise that a visit by Miss Blaine to my place of work, Morningside Library, usually contains a clue. This time, she came in on the sort of day we thankfully have very rarely in Edinburgh, the temperature soaring to 21C (70F). I was very grateful to be indoors, out of the blistering heat.

A borrower was browsing through the online catalogue, but I politely ignored her. I believe in letting readers do their own thing, and not intervening until asked. Unless, of course, I see someone looking for *The Prime of Miss Jean Brodie*, in which case I set off the fire alarm and have the building evacuated. Over sixty years since the wretched thing was published, defaming our unimpeachable school, and yet some people still insist on seeking it out. But not on my watch. I will defend to the death an author's right to say whatever they want. That doesn't oblige me to let readers read it.

As I passed the screen for a second time, it was the work being searched for that caught my eye – *De humani corporis fabrica libri septem*, otherwise known as "On the fabric of the human body in

3

seven volumes" by Andreas Vesalius. Arguably the first book on modern medicine.

And then I looked at the person who was browsing. I caught sight of that distinctive profile with its resolute jaw and aquiline nose. Miss Blaine. Should I go and offer to help? That might make her cross. But if I didn't offer to help, that might make her cross, too. She can really be quite irascible.

I hovered, swithering, and as I did so, Miss Blaine suddenly raised a hand to her neck, as though to remove a constriction, and sank gracefully to the ground. It was done with such élan that I wondered whether she was re-enacting *The Dying Swan*.

My colleague Dorothy shrieked, "Borrower down! Borrower down!" and raced across to us, panting, "What are we going to do?"

"*We* are not going to do anything," I told her. "You are going to go back to your desk. I am the first-aider."

I knelt beside Miss Blaine, slightly nervous in case she had actually expired. I'm not sure what the life expectancy is for someone who's several hundred years old, even if they are in their prime. But she was still breathing; she had merely fainted. My training kicked in. Elevate the legs to help the blood flow back to the brain. Here we were in a library, surrounded by books – and what are books for, if not for elevation? Large print volumes and a couple of dictionaries did the trick and, after a few moments, Miss Blaine's eyes flickered open.

"Where am I?" she demanded.

"Morningside Library," I said and then, in case she required more precise information, I whispered so that Dorothy couldn't hear, "in 2024."

She glared at me. "I'm not dottled, girl. I merely felt slightly dizzy because of the unseasonal warmth."

"Let me get you upstairs, Miss Blaine, and I'll make you a cup of tea," I said.

"In this heat?" she snapped. "The last thing I want is a hot drink."

I didn't like to say that having a hot drink lowered the heat within the body, as long as your increased amount of sweat was able to evaporate. Mentioning sweat to the Founder would be an impertinence.

"However," she said, "I think I could manage a wee ice cream."

"There's an ice cream parlour just up the road," I said. "You lie here, and I'll bring you a cone."

"I am not an invalid," she announced. "I am more than capable of going up the road, especially if there is the prospect of an ice cream parlour." With that, she rolled lithely on to her side and got to her feet, smoothing down her skirt in a purposeful manner.

Despite her obvious determination, I was worried about her going out into the searing temperature on her own. I quickly told Dorothy that I was going to take my lunch break early, and followed Miss Blaine up Morningside Road. She was so obviously at home in the area, a venerable Morningside lady in her sensible shoes, sensible tights, sensible skirt and sensible jacket, all of which were geared to a much cooler climate. Even so, she was stepping out briskly, refusing to let something like a small fainting fit slow her down. Admirable. She was even humming a little tune that sounded positively Baroque.

When we were seated in the ice cream parlour, I said, "I can recommend the nut sundae – Neapolitan ice cream with chocolate sauce and chopped hazelnuts. Or the toffee fudgy wudgy ice cream is very nice."

"Great heavens, girl, whatever's the matter with your taste buds?" she said. "A plain vanilla ice cream without ornamentation is what is required."

So that was what I ordered.

She took a spoonful and leaned back, eyes closed, to savour it. "Italian ice cream is the best. It is my favourite."

I was going to protest that there were a number of excellent Scottish brands, but it doesn't do to argue with the Founder.

"Glad you like it," I said.

"Now," she said when she was about halfway through the bowl, "my hearing was somewhat impaired for a few moments in the library, but did I understand you to say that you are a first-aider?"

"Exactly right, Miss Blaine," I said.

"Kindly list the skills you have acquired through that."

I laid down my ice cream spoon and began enumerating them on my fingers. "I can splint broken bones, I can apply a tourniquet, I can treat first- and second-degree burns, I can check for concussion, I can perform CPR – that's cardiopulmonary resuscitation—"

I was interrupted by a woman at the next table half-rising from her seat as she clutched at the table, gasping for breath, her face scarlet.

"—and the Heimlich manoeuvre," I concluded. "Excuse me one minute."

I got up from my own seat, got behind the woman and put my arms round her waist, preparing to thrust a fist into her abdomen.

"What do you think you're doing, you bampot?" she yelled, shoving me away.

"I was saving your life," I said with dignity. "You were choking, and I was trying to clear your airwaves. But thankfully I see you've managed to clear them yourself."

"I wasn't choking," she said. "I was raging. I've just had a text from my boyfriend dumping me."

Amid some tutting from the other patrons over the unseemly to-do, I resumed my seat.

"I thought it might have been a rogue chopped hazelnut," I said to Miss Blaine.

She looked at me in reproach. "You *assumed*," she said.

Since, prior to my first mission, Miss Blaine had made such a point about not assuming, I panicked that she might be about to cancel me. For surely that was why she had turned up, not simply to have a wee ice cream, but to send me off once again to make the world a better place? So it was a relief when the familiar stomach pains started, and soon enough I was on this misty canalside, date and location to be confirmed. The encounter with Miss Blaine had yielded no clues as to what I might be required to do. Perhaps if she hadn't fainted she might have given an indication, but then the ice cream became her key focus.

I assessed my surroundings. The mist still swirled around me. I certainly wasn't anywhere hot. That suggested Stockholm, but I wasn't going to assume. There was also a faint smell of aniseed, which strengthened the Swedish hypothesis, given their festive "aniseed pig" fried doughnuts. Even so, I was keeping an open mind.

I retraced my steps to where the woman had screamed at me, and went in the opposite direction, to find myself crossing a small arched bridge over another canal. It led into a quiet square, on one side of which was a three-storey building with grand columns on each floor, and large arched windows. The heavy wooden door was partially open, so I decided to go inside in search of clues.

It seemed to be almost as misty inside as out. I could hear voices coming from what, had I been in Venice, would have been called the *piano nobile*, the first floor where the main reception area was located. I quietly crept up and found myself outside a doorway covered with a length of richly embroidered drapery. I could still smell aniseed, but I could also now smell cooking, or at least herbs: parsley, oregano, rosemary and marjoram.

"Who would have thought it?" came a man's voice. "Here we are in 1650, for goodness' sake. We thought we were quite safe, and it's happening all over again."

This was an excellent start, knowing that it was 1650. On my very first mission, I found myself in something of an embarrassing situation when there was no immediate clue as to the date. I know some people will think I should just have asked, but that would have completely destroyed my credibility. It's important to maintain professionalism at all times. I did, however, feel it was a bit disappointing simply to be told the date at the outset, as though Miss Blaine had no confidence in my deductive skills.

I racked my brain to remember what had happened in Sweden in 1650. The coronation of Queen Christina, the monarch memorably portrayed by Greta Garbo. And also the tragic death of Descartes, who had gone to Sweden to tutor the queen, but her castle was so cold that he contracted pneumonia. With luck, I would be there before the great philosopher's demise. I particularly wanted to take him to task over his offensive views that animals aren't intelligent. Speaking personally, I've met a lot of animals that are more intelligent than many people, Descartes included.

The draughty castle and the pneumonia certainly fitted with my experience of the swirling mist and the chilly air. I was glad I had been equipped with a long coat and gloves – Miss Blaine always said that although the missions were unpaid, my accommodation and necessities would be taken care of. And I registered that the person talking about 1650 was also speaking Venetian. Perhaps Stockholm was a popular destination for tourists from Venice in the seventeenth century.

"There's too few of us," came another male voice, also speaking Venetian.

"Don't be so negative." The first voice again. "You don't know what you're capable of until you try. We will do our best, and our best will surpass whatever we have dreamed of achieving."

I liked the sound of this. It was the sort of thing a Marcia Blaine teacher might say. I had no idea what they were talking about – perhaps they were organising Queen Christina's coronation, which I remembered had involved a six-mile procession of carriages, and fountains flowing with wine for days.

I decided to chance having a look at what was happening in the room. Very carefully, I pulled the curtain aside a tiny fraction so that I could peer in. I was completely taken aback by what I saw. My eyes still hadn't adjusted fully from the time travelling, but it was obvious that the room contained four big birds. They had beaks and bulging eyes. I reckoned they must be rehearsing some sort of pageant for the coronation. They were gathered round a table with plates of food on it, which explained the smell of herbs.

"Thank God," said one of the big birds, whose voice I hadn't heard before. "Reinforcements. Come and join us."

I scanned the large room but could see no sign of anybody else they might be talking to.

"This is no time to be shy," said the first speaker. "Get yourself in here."

Cautiously, I moved the curtain another millimetre, but couldn't see any other door a newcomer could have entered by.

"It's no good just standing around waggling your proboscis," the first speaker snapped. "There's work to be done."

To my horror, he walked straight towards the curtain behind which I was concealed, yanked it open, and grabbed me by the shoulder, pulling me in to join the group. Now that I was close to them, I could see that they weren't dressed up as big birds, but were wearing the bizarre PPE of doctors dealing with bubonic plague: a long goatskin overcoat covered in wax, gloves, a wide-brimmed hat to show they were doctors – and the extraordinary bird mask with its long curved beak and small glass portholes to see out of. This uniform made them all look identical. They were even all the same height. I could see that I was going to have a problem telling them apart.

A sudden thought struck me. I brought my gloved hand up towards my face, and encountered an impediment, presumably the proboscis he had referred to. I must be dressed the same way as them, which was a relief. There was nothing wrong with my eyesight, or my temperature control. The problem was the glass portholes and the fact that there was a mask over my face.

And now that I was close up to the doctors, I realised that the scent of herbs was coming from them, and that each one was different. The one who had seized me, who had the can-do attitude, was exuding oregano. I shook my head slightly and was conscious of a faint rattling in my beak. Aniseed balls. That was a nice touch, since aniseed balls had played a part in my very first mission, and I also like the smell.

"So, Doctor," said Dr Oregano, "where are you from?"

I smiled behind my mask, preparing to impress them with my

credentials "*Vegno da Edimburgo*," I said in my perfect Venetian, a phrase quite different from the Italian *vengo da Edimburgo*. "I'm from Edinburgh."

The reaction was absolutely not what I expected. Dr Oregano took a step backwards, spluttering in apparent horror. The others were sniggering.

"You went to a jumped-up village school that presumes to call itself a university?" Dr Oregano was despairing. "It's barely fifty years old. At least if you'd been to the University of Glasgow, it's been going for a couple of hundred years."

Now it was my turn to splutter in horror. I'm not used to hearing that anything in Glasgow is superior to what you find in Scotland's capital.

"And what does the University of Edinburgh know about medicine?" sniggered Dr Parsley.

I was about to say that Edinburgh had one of the most distinguished medical faculties in the world when I realised it didn't. The medical school wasn't founded until 1726. So I just spluttered a bit more.

"Useless," said Dr Oregano. "We need help here, not a liability."

Dr Parsley had unfastened his mask, and was helping himself to some of the snacks. Suddenly, he made a strange squeaking noise, his hands scrabbling at his throat, his face puce.

I didn't hesitate. I gripped him round the waist and jabbed my fist inwards and upwards. His mouth opened, and a fried sardine shot out. The others also had their mouths open, but nothing emerged, not even words.

"Just part of my medical training," I said. "It's called the Heimlich manoeuvre."

"A German technique? You studied in Heidelberg University's distinguished medical faculty?" said Dr Oregano.

"Not exactly," I hedged. I find it quite difficult to tell outright lies. "It was more of a distance-learning thing." That was true enough, Dr Henry Heimlich having first written about the technique in 1974.

Dr Oregano sniffed disdainfully. "At least you seem to know something," he said. "We can use you for the heavy lifting."

I had no idea what heavy lifting might be called for. And I was bemused as to why we were all dressed as plague doctors. It was about three hundred years since Sweden had had the plague, and another outbreak wasn't due until 1710. It was unlikely to be forward planning, so it was probably the same as advocates in the High Court in Edinburgh, still wearing wigs and gowns in the twenty-first century because that was what they had worn hundreds of years earlier and nobody had thought to update the dress code.

There was a sudden commotion downstairs, with people calling out, followed by a loud thud.

"Another one," said Dr Marjoram gloomily.

"You, Doctor." Dr Oregano waved his beak at the last member of the group, who hadn't yet spoken. "Go and deal with it and take Dr Distance-Learning with you."

I trotted obediently down the stairs after Dr Rosemary. There was a figure lying in the entrance hall where it had apparently been thrown. Dr Rosemary knelt beside it and examined it.

"Dead," he said perfunctorily. "Right, help me shift the body."

This wasn't the sort of heavy lifting I'd imagined.

"I don't understand," I said. "We're here to cure people. There's not much we can do with a body. And what's it doing here anyway?"

Dr Rosemary shrugged. "People bring them here because they're scared."

"Of ghosts?"

"Of the plague."

"Why are they scared of the plague?" I asked.

He sighed. "You really don't know much, do you, apart from that German party trick? The plague is a terrible disease that kills people horribly."

"I'm perfectly aware of what the plague is, thank you," I said. "But there isn't any around at the moment."

He sighed again. "If only that were true. We thought we had seen the last of it in 1631. But here we are, less than twenty years later, and it's re-erupted."

Stockholm had been in robust good health in 1631. I was going to have to try another option. The canals had made me wonder if I might also be in Bruges or Birmingham. But everyone was speaking Venetian here. Sometimes the obvious answer is the right one. I gambled, crossing my fingers and toes that I wasn't assuming, but simply making an educated guess.

"Yes, here we are," I agreed. "In Venice."

Dr Rosemary sighed for a third time, but didn't contradict me. It was good to know where I was at last, but it was also perplexing. The plague had definitely disappeared from Venice in 1631, never to return, at least according to the history books. But on my previous mission, when I had met Macbeth, King Duncan and some very weird sisters, I had discovered that the history books could get things seriously wrong.

Perhaps these missions were not merely to make the world a better place, but to set people straight on what had actually happened.

"But we've no time to chat like this," said Dr Rosemary. "We need to move the body into the storeroom."

"Why are we moving the body into the storeroom?"

A fourth sigh. "You really ask a great many questions. We move it because otherwise we would have to keep stepping over it to get out of the front door, and we move it into the storeroom because it's the coolest room, and it's on the ground floor. Taking it upstairs would involve considerable effort, and you really don't want to have decomposing corpses around you when you're eating. Come along."

I was less than happy about this. I always like to be as helpful as possible, and to muck in with whatever needs to be done, but I had never contemplated or aspired to shifting dead bodies.

And then it came to me. Dealing with the plague was my mission. When Miss Blaine appeared to faint, it had been a

12

ruse. She was testing me, to see how well I coped with a medical emergency. In the ice cream parlour, she had been insistent on my telling her what medical skills I had, and she must have been satisfied, or I wouldn't be here.

I can't pretend I wasn't disappointed to find myself in Venice in 1650, when there was nobody interesting around. No Titian, no Vivaldi, no Henry James. It was also disappointing that I had discovered where I was, when I was, and what my mission was within an hour of arrival. I usually look forward to more of a challenge. But since it was my medical expertise that was required, the sooner I got on with it, the better.

"Stop daydreaming," said Dr Rosemary. "You grab the body under the arms, and I'll take the feet."

I admit, I hesitated for a moment. Applying tourniquets and splinting broken bones was one thing. Moving dead bodies was quite another. And apart from anything else, the plague was extremely nasty. I was very glad I was up to date with my vaccinations.

TWO

My heavy-lifting skills had passed muster, and I was now one
of the boys. In fact, my heavy-lifting skills had been very much
better than those of Dr Rosemary. I found him positively feeble
in keeping his end up. I had no such difficulty, since I regularly
weight train. Building muscle mass when you're fifty-something is
crucial, boosted by getting enough protein in your diet.

I felt that might be where Dr Rosemary and his colleagues
were going wrong. We were all sitting round the table having
something to eat, and apart from the fried sardines, it was quite
carb-heavy. There was buckwheat pasta with an onion sauce, bean
soup with pasta in it, risotto with peas, and cornmeal biscotti. But
as the newbie, I thought it wise to wait for a while before giving
them a lecture on nutrition.

We had taken off our beaked masks in order to eat. There was
an awkward moment when Dr Marjoram said, "What a very
peculiar hairstyle you have."

I had been very pleased with my latest haircut, and actually
meant it when I said to the salonista, "Thank you, that's lovely,"
so I didn't appreciate his remark.

Dr Rosemary nudged him and whispered, "Ssh, that's probably
the fashion in Edinburgh. Since their medical development is so
primitive, you can't expect their barber-surgeons to be any good."

I appreciated this remark even less, but decided to let it pass
and studied my new companions. They were all much younger than
I expected. Even Dr Oregano, who seemed to be the leader, could
only have been around thirty. He was tall, thin, ascetic and intense.

Dr Parsley looked a bit of a daft laddie. Not playing at being

14

one, actually being one. Big and lumbering and probably not that coordinated. I couldn't see his medical school featuring him as star alumnus any time soon. I hoped Dr Oregano would keep an eye on him. He would be great at the heavy lifting, though.

Dr Rosemary was a very different proposition, and not just because of his ineptness at heavy lifting. He too had the look of a laddie, fresh-faced and slender, but definitely not a daft one. While I was assessing him, I had a suspicion he was assessing me.

Dr Marjoram was predominantly gloomy. He helped himself to some more risotto as though it was the best of a very bad lot.

"Which of you does the cooking?" I asked. I could perhaps choose my moment and quietly advise the individual responsible on the appropriate balance between protein, carbs and fat.

"We're doctors. We don't cook," said Dr Oregano sharply. "We have a woman who does."

"I didn't notice her. When does she come in?"

They exchanged glances as though I'd said something silly. I recognised the look since I've had occasion to use it myself on several occasions. But I was unused to having it directed at me.

"She doesn't come in," said Dr Rosemary. "Nobody comes in." I stopped myself saying that I had come in.

He nodded to the far side of the room, where beyond the large windows I could see a loggia, a covered gallery open to the elements, projecting out from the building to overlook the canal. "There's a staircase."

Of course there was. With all of the posh rooms in grand Venetian houses being on the first floor rather than the ground floor, you found snobs not wanting to come in the front door on the street, which they considered the tradesmen's entrance, preferring to come directly to the grand rooms from the canal.

"The woman gets the gondola to stop outside, then she comes up the staircase and leaves our food in the loggia."

"This woman, how old is she?" I asked.

Dr Parsley considered this. "I would say around sixty."

"I think she's nearer seventy," said Dr Marjoram.

"Let's just say she's not in the first flush of youth," I said. "And yet you have her clambering up stairs, weighed down by your food. Can't you pick it up from her when you're out on your rounds?"

They did the exchanging glances thing again.

"We don't go out on our rounds," said Dr Parsley, now fully recovered from choking on the fried sardine.

"We don't have to," said Dr Rosemary. "You saw. They bring the bodies to us."

"Also," said the gloomy Dr Marjoram, "if we go out, people scream when they see us in our masks because they associate us with the plague."

That explained the woman screaming and pointing when she saw me, and the whole crowd legging it.

"Idiots," said Dr Parsley. "Do they think we wear these beaks for fun? We're the ones who are protected."

"Are we?" Dr Marjoram sounded even more glum. "Our beaks could be useless for all we know."

This was something that was puzzling me. I knew that medics at this point believed in theriacs, compounds they reckoned protected against poisons and the plague. But if my nostrils were to be believed, there were no compounds around, just individual lots of herbs.

"I thought you were supposed to have lots of different things up your nose at the same time," I said. "Including cinnamon and fennel and myrrh and honey."

Dr Oregano looked at me pityingly. "We don't just do things the way we've always done them. We believe in progress. Each of us has chosen a particular herb, and we'll discover which is most efficacious against the plague by the order in which we succumb. I detect that you're using aniseed. That will be very useful for our researches."

"Researches," said Dr Marjoram gloomily. "That's one word for it. An unnecessary attempt to reinvent the wheel, if you ask me. We haven't the faintest idea what we're doing."

"Will you stop being so defeatist?" said Dr Parsley. "You can read, can't you? We have textbooks, which tell us everything there is to know about the practice of medicine."

"Apart from the Heimlich manoeuvre," I said under my breath, not loud enough to be heard, before joining in the conversation with, "Textbooks are very useful, but in a profession like yours, I mean ours, it's also essential to have practical training."

"Is it indeed?" Dr Marjoram was getting gloomier by the minute. "Then it's a shame that all the previous plague doctors died of the plague, taking their knowledge to the grave."

I was feeling quite gloomy as well. Dealing with a bacterial disease like the plague without antibiotics was pretty difficult. I had felt distinctly apprehensive when helping Dr Rosemary to shift the latest victim into the storeroom. Thankfully, the glass portholes in my mask meant that I couldn't see terribly clearly. I deliberately kept my eyes as unfocused as possible, although I could still see that the unfortunate individual was covered in hideous black and red spots. There were a number of other bodies on the floor that I had avoided looking at as well, so I wasn't sure how many there were.

I also wasn't sure what was going to happen to them. Venice was very different from Morningside in several respects, including the burying of people. I remembered reading about a twenty-first-century discovery of plague victims' skeletons on Venice's quarantine island, well away from the city centre. That led me to muse that the word "quarantine" itself came from Venice, protecting itself from the plague in the fourteenth century. If a ship arrived from somewhere dodgy, it wasn't allowed to dock, but had to sit at anchor for forty days, which in Italian is *quaranta giorni*. And the island they were lurking beside became somewhere to keep suspected plague victims.

"Have you got many people on the quarantine island?" I said. "Why are the bodies being brought here? Wouldn't it be simpler to leave them there?"

"You ask a great many questions," said Dr Parsley.

"I've already told him that," said Dr Rosemary.

"Asking questions is a means of gaining knowledge," I pointed out.

"And coming from Edinburgh, you have a great deal of knowledge to gain," said Dr Oregano, and I distinctly heard chortling from the others. "We've not had a chance to do anything about the quarantine island."

"The plague's taken hold in the city," said Dr Oregano. "The bodies aren't being transported here from the quarantine island; they're being brought to us directly from the alleyways."

"Alleyways?" I was aghast. "What are the bodies doing in alleyways?"

"Not a lot," said Dr Parsley and there was more sniggering.

"Why aren't they at home?" I demanded. "And why aren't you making house calls? It takes at least three days for someone to expire from the plague, if not a couple of weeks. You should all be out there, doing good, soothing fevered brows."

Dr Oregano gave me a pitying look. "Is that what they teach you in Edinburgh? Oh, no, I forgot – they can't teach you anything in Edinburgh because there isn't a medical faculty. These people were hale and hearty a few hours, if not minutes, before their demise."

He was talking complete nonsense. Or was he? If the medical histories had all got it wrong about the dates of the plague, they could well be wrong about its symptoms and effects. My first-aid skills, though good, definitely weren't up to treating plague victims. Perhaps Miss Blaine had sent me here not as a paramedic but to ascertain the true facts.

"And what are you going to do with the bodies?" I asked.

"We haven't decided yet," said Dr Marjoram gloomily. "At the moment, we're just collecting them."

"That doesn't sound very hygienic," I said.

"Very what?" he asked.

In another twenty years, research would show the existence of germs and bacteria, but if I tried to tell this lot about microorganisms, they'd probably have me carted off to an asylum.

"It doesn't sound very nice," I said.

"It's not," said Dr Parsley. "That's why we keep them in the storeroom with the door closed. How many is that now?"

"Six," said Dr Rosemary.

"And how long since the outbreak started?" I asked.

They all turned to Dr Oregano.

"Around two and a half days," he said. "I was the first to be called, and immediately diagnosed the plague." He gave me a complacent smile. "I trained in Padua."

The Edinburgh Medical School of its day.

"Are you all from Padua?" I asked.

"Oh dear me, no," said Dr Oregano with an indulgent laugh. "I'm the only one. The others haven't had my level of education."

I could see why he'd taken on the leadership role, but I could also see a lot of lip pursing and jaw tightening. There was very little need for him to brag about his education – Padua was good, but it wasn't the Marcia Blaine School for Girls.

"My practice is here in the city, and the senators called me immediately the first body was found," Dr Oregano said. "They were very upset to hear that the plague had returned, but I reassured them I would assemble the finest medical team possible to deal with it. I sent out a call and these are the gentlemen who answered."

He swept his hand round as if to introduce the first responders.

"I'm from Perugia," said Dr Parsley.

"I'm from Bologna," said Dr Rosemary.

"And I'm from Genoa," said Dr Marjoram.

"But they're all miles away," I objected. This was an era before high-powered Italian sports cars. "How did you get here so quickly?"

"These are the universities where we studied," said Dr Rosemary. "We all work here in the Veneto and came as soon as we heard."

Dr Parsley suddenly gave me a stare. "And how did *you* get

here so quickly, Dr Distance-Learning? Edinburgh's even further away than Perugia."

"I found myself in the area, and I wanted to help," I said. It was true enough.

"And you just happened to be wearing your plague protection outfit?"

"It's only sensible when travelling," I improvised. "As you've discovered, you never know where and when your next lot of plague is going to appear. Also," I added, inspired, "my luggage got washed overboard and I don't have a change of clothes."

"You'll find a nightshirt in your sleeping area," said Dr Oregano. "I organised places for twenty doctors, but so far it's just the five of us. Doctors seem very reluctant to contract fatal diseases these days. Of course, once we ascertain which herb ensures survival, that should encourage more volunteers."

"I bet it won't be marjoram," said Dr Marjoram gloomily.

I felt a bit gloomy as well, assuming we would all be in a dormitory together. But yet again, Miss Blaine's warning against assuming proved well founded. We all had our own rooms on the *piano nobile*. Mine was the last available: if any more doctors turned up, they would have to lodge on the floor above. Unless they came from Padua, in which case they would no doubt take precedence over me.

It was a large, pleasant room. The bed had an ornate sculpted wooden headboard, painted in pastel colours and outlined in gold. A substantial wooden chest sat by the wall. I opened it to find another full set of PPE, including the beaked mask, a box full of surgical instruments, which looked utterly revolting, and the promised nightshirt.

I went to the window and looked out on to the canal, unhampered by my beak. I found my first foggy view of La Serenissima had had little to do with steamed-up glass portholes. The famous Venetian mist was in, and I could scarcely make out the buildings on the other side. It was still very hazily picturesque, and I was sorry Miss Blaine didn't allow me to bring my phone to take a few pictures.

I wondered whether she had left anything in the room for me. These missions are unpaid, but I get board and lodgings, reasonable expenses and, very often, items crucial to my success. She scolded me when I thanked her for the compostable bags I found on my previous mission, saying she had better things to do than micromanage what I was up to. So I've concluded that her desire to make the world a better place has unleashed a benign force in the universe that sorts everything out.

I couldn't find anything apart from the items I'd already discovered in the wooden chest, so I decided to change into the nightshirt and go to bed. It was as I was undressing that I discovered I wasn't wearing my trusty DMs, but a pair of light leather sandals. I was quite shocked that I hadn't already noticed, but it showed how discombobulated I had been by the stifling mask and heavy robes, the screaming woman, and the task of shifting plague victims. Although the leather sandals were comfortable, I wasn't happy. My DMs are essential. They're comfortable as well, but also practical for both advancing and retreating.

I scoured the room and even sent up a silent plea to Miss Blaine, but no DMs were to be found. That was when I heard a faint noise. Someone was closing their door very, very quietly. So quietly that it was unlikely anyone had heard, apart from me: I do have very acute hearing. The lightest of footsteps moved along the corridor in front of my room, heading in the direction of the main reception area where we had foregathered.

Even more quietly than the sleepwalker, if sleepwalker he was, I opened my bedroom door and slipped out. The light leather sandals were perfect for sneaking around.

"Thank you," I whispered in the general direction of the universe. "Great shoes. I should have been more trusting."

I peeked round the door of the reception room just in time to make out a beaked figure in the loggia begin to disappear down the stairs to the canal. It was already dark, the figure wasn't carrying a torch or a lantern, and I couldn't tell whether it was ascetic Dr Oregano, lumbering Dr Parsley, young Dr Rosemary or gloomy Dr Marjoram. Because he was at a distance, there was no herbal scent to guide me.

I tiptoed across the room. My medical colleague, whoever it was, had left the doorway to the loggia open, and I sneaked into the covered walkway. The wind was chill, and the mist continued swirling. I regretted having come out in nothing but my nightshirt and flimsy sandals.

Reaching the end of the walkway, where I calculated it would be difficult to see me, I snatched a look over the low parapet. I could see someone holding a torch. But it wasn't one of my colleagues, it was a gondolier. In the torchlight I could see there was a gondola waiting at our building. And I could hear a distant sploshing sound, suggesting that someone had just stepped aboard. The gondolier doused his torch and more sploshing let me know that he was aboard as well. Another gondolier must already have been waiting for them as there was an immediate gentle rhythmical rippling, which gradually faded. So, three people in all.

This was most mysterious. Why was one of the doctors going out at dead of night, thinking himself unobserved by the household? And which one was it?

Shivering, I retreated from the loggia back to my room, determined to keep watch. But the time difference between twenty-first-century Morningside and seventeenth-century Venice had more of an effect than I thought, and while I was keeping watch, I fell asleep.

THREE

I stood at the edge of St Mark's Square, relaxing now that I knew I was in Venice, drinking in the view, a view that was utterly glorious despite being shrouded in mist. I was positively quivering with delight. What a scene. What a building. Incredible that architects could design something so perfect, so magnificent – and yet, how could they not, given the sacred purpose of the edifice, and the wonders within?

Reverently, my back to the rather gaudy façade of St Mark's Cathedral, I prepared to enter the magnificent Marciana Library, discreetly elegant in monochrome limestone. From my usual perspective in Morningside Library, I thought of it as ancient and venerable, one of the earliest surviving public libraries. But right now, it was the new kid on the St Mark's block, proclaimed the Official Library of the Republic of Venice in 1603. I slowly climbed the staircase up to the vestibule, the steps themselves an embodiment of the message in the decoration that the soul rises to wisdom through study. The library's founders could almost have been Blainers. They pronounced the name of the place in their own way, Mar-CHA-na, but to me, it would always look like Marcia's Library.

I walked through the vestibule to the reading room, large leatherbound books chained to the wooden benches where scholars could sit and carry out their research.

The librarian was seated on a stool at a lectern from which he could supervise the readers, although to my relief, nobody else was there. He gave me a brief glance.

"Medical library's down the road," he said.

Then he suddenly sat upright, looking at me properly.

"You're not a doctor, you're a librarian," he said. It wasn't accusatory, it wasn't surprise, it was a simple statement of fact.

"*Sì,*" I said. "*Vengo da Edimburgo.* I'm from Edinburgh."

Not a single titter.

"Ah yes," he said. "Edinburgh, city of literature. Where Walter Chepman and Androw Myllar set up the first printing press in Scotland in 1507, if I'm not mistaken."

"You're not mistaken," I said.

"And," he said, looking at me keenly, "you're a woman."

Considering I was in full plague doctor gear, and he couldn't even see my face, that was impressive. But of course one should never underestimate a librarian.

"That's not generally known," I said. "I'm here undercover."

"Under quite a lot of cover," he said. "Don't worry, your secret's safe with me. I presume there's a good reason for it. Not that there has to be, but I can't imagine you would be doing anything without a good reason."

"I'm on a mission," I said.

"As are we all," he said. "The curation of books is a weighty responsibility."

I was about to tell him that my mission had nothing to do with books, but I realised that wouldn't impress him. I gave a nod of my proboscis.

He got down from his stool and came over to me, his robes swishing. He was quite a slight figure, younger than me, and a lot less muscled. I wondered how he would manage to carry books, let alone bodies.

He held out his hand. "I'm Librarian Zen."

I almost said, "Like the detective?" when I remembered that the Zens were a noble Venetian family, including journalists, admirals, hydraulic engineers and doges. Also, the Aurelio Zen novels wouldn't be published for another 338 years.

I stepped forward to shake hands and the librarian swiftly moved to one side. He was a bit shorter than I was, and I realised that as I approached him, my proboscis had almost taken his eye out. I was impressed by his reflexes.

"Do you mind if I take my mask off?" I asked.

"It might be safer," he said.

Once I had managed to unfasten it and park it on a nearby bench, I finally got to shake hands with Librarian Zen.

"I'm Librarian McMonagle," I said. "Sorry, that's probably a bit difficult for you to say."

"Difficult? Scarcely. Mac as in macaroni, Mona as in Mona Lisa, and Gle as in glissando. Pleased to meet you, Librarian Macaroni Mona Lisa Glissando."

What a guy. He could tell I was a librarian despite my medical garb, he didn't mind me being female, and he could pronounce my name.

I looked around me in appreciation. "You've got a lot of books," I said.

Librarian Zen inclined his head in acknowledgement of the compliment. "We do. The key texts are in manuscript, but we've got an increasing number of printed books."

There was no mistaking the pride in his voice. I felt thoroughly ashamed of myself, blaming Miss Blaine for sending me to a time when nothing was happening and there was nobody interesting around. Who and what is more interesting than a librarian and a library?

"We've had printing presses here even earlier than Edinburgh," he said. "And they keep getting better and better. Have you heard about our octavos?"

"Have I heard about your octavos!" I breathed.

"If you don't know, I don't think I can help you," said the librarian, sounding disconcerted.

"It's an expression," I explained. "I mean of course I've heard of your octavos."

"Ah," he said. "Expressions are interesting. They vary very much from language to language."

"They do," I said, and we pondered this for a moment, nodding in agreement.

We were standing near enormous leatherbound volumes, embossed with brass decorations that lifted them up from the desks and stopped them getting damaged. But I knew that the octavos were something else entirely. Small, portable, about the size of a paperback, they were also a consummate example of the printer's art.

"Could I see one?" I asked tentatively.

"Of course," said the librarian. "Since they can't be chained to the desks, I keep them in a cupboard."

"I keep books in a cupboard as well!" I exclaimed. "But not for the same purpose as yours."

"Really?" he said. "What purpose could there be other than protecting books?"

"I keep them in a cupboard to protect readers. There are some books that are too dangerous for them to see."

"Ah," said the librarian. "the alchemical texts of Artephius, and suchlike. I understand."

"Exactly that principle, but nothing to do with alchemy," I said. "Let me explain. I have had the finest education in the world, at the Marcia Blaine School for Girls."

He nodded. "The Ursuline Sisters do wonderful work in educating girls," he said. "I take it that Marcia Blaine is the Mother General of the order in Edinburgh?"

I worried that Miss Blaine being mistaken for a nun was the sort of thing that might provoke her to stamp on my big toe. "She's imposed her own order," I said quickly. "An autonomous organisation."

"Admirable," he said, although I wasn't sure he fully appreciated that poverty, chastity and obedience might not be Miss Blaine's guiding principles.

"A thoroughly reprehensible woman by the name of Muriel Spark wrote a novel—"

"A novel?" he interrupted, and I realised that the novel had not yet developed as a recognised genre.

"It's a long story," I explained.

"That's all right," he said. "There are no readers in, I've got time to listen."

I started again. "Muriel Spark told terrible lies about my school in the guise of fiction. And not everybody who reads can tell the difference between what's true and what isn't."

"That's also the case for those who don't read," he said. "Sometimes more so."

I was trying to make a point, and I wasn't in the mood for a philosophical discussion. "She trashed the reputation of the teachers at the Marcia Blaine School for Girls. She invented a teacher who has an affair with one man while also being in love with another who's married."

The librarian swallowed hard. "That's the sort of thing you read about in Boccaccio," he said. "People in holy orders up to no good. I don't agree with it myself, but it certainly attracts a readership."

"Not in my library," I said crisply and noted his look of admiration. "But if I could trouble you for a glance at an octavo?"

I had to admit that his cupboard was a lot more spectacular than mine, which is simply shelving behind a door in one of the upstairs rooms. Librarian Zen had a freestanding wooden cabinet, intricately carved, about 120 cm high, four feet in old money. He took a key from the pouch tied round his waist and unlocked it. There, stacked on the inner shelves, were dozens of octavos, made up of sixteen-page sections. He picked up the top one and handed it to me.

I opened it with nervous fingers. And there they all were, every single printed letter of the alphabet, leaning apolitically to the right.

"Italics," I murmured, feeling another surge of guilt about my lack of gratitude in being sent to this time period. Italics, invented right here in Venice, because they took up less space than blackletter and Roman type and looked more like the handwriting you got in manuscripts.

"Thank you," said Librarian Zen. "Thank you for your

enthusiasm and appreciation. Sometimes I get quite blasé about what we have here. But I have to confess I'm very old-fashioned, and I prefer original manuscripts to these modern printed books. We have some very interesting work by Leonardo da Vinci."

I found myself looking at an extraordinary diagram. I knew all about Leonardo inventing the helicopter, but this was something else. It showed a two-wheeled vehicle with handlebars – not a bicycle, because there was very obviously an engine between the wheels, with not one but four cylinders. This was particularly fascinating, since all the descriptions of his helicopter design explained that the engine had not yet been invented, which was why take-off relied on four men running around a central shaft. And yet here was proof positive that he had actually invented a prototype engine.

"Isn't it beautiful?" murmured Librarian Zen. "I would love a machine like that. I would cherish it as though it were a living thing."

I had a lovely image of Zen maintaining his motorcycle.

"And here," he said, guiding me to another book. "This is another of my favourites."

The volume he put in my hands looked positively scabby, with a worn brown leather cover, but when I opened it, I found not only some very stylish calligraphy but also charming illustrations.

"A man sitting on a big banana!" I said.

"Not a banana," said Zen, sounding ever so slightly disapproving. "That would be ridiculous. It's a dolphin. This is the story of the Greek poet Arion."

Before I could say, "A dolphin? Really? It looks very like a banana" and "I know all about the Greek poet Arion," he was off, and I didn't like to interrupt.

"Arion was a gifted singer and was travelling back home after winning a musical competition in Sicily when he was captured by pirates. They were about to murder him for the bag of silver coins that was his prize, but he persuaded them to let him sing one last song. When he finished, he leaped overboard, preferring to drown rather than be cut to pieces. But a dolphin, attracted by the beauty of his singing, rescued him, letting him sit on its back and taking him home to Corinth."

"Marvellous," I said. "Aren't mammals wonderful?" I felt I should say more, after my gaffe about the banana. "I wish there were manuscripts in my library. All our books are printed."

"How very modern," he said, and again I sensed slight disapproval.

"I don't mean we don't have manuscripts in Edinburgh," I said. "We've got loads. But they're all in the National Library of Scotland. My library isn't even the Central Library, it's a local library for local people."

"You're provincial?" I thought I was going to plummet in his esteem, but he said, "Your work is the most important there is. Scholars can travel wherever they want. They can come here, they can go to Rome or Florence. But you, you bring learning and literacy to the common people in their own habitat."

His aim was to praise our library, I knew, but I wasn't sure what the denizens of Morningside would think of being referred to as "common people".

"I wonder, Librarian Macaroni Mona Lisa Glissando, whether I might ask you a great favour?" he said.

"Anything," I said expansively and then added, "within reason."

"I would hope everything we librarians do is within reason," he quipped, and we beamed at one another, our kinship strengthening still further.

"There's a meeting today that I would be interested in attending, if..." His voice tailed off.

"If you could find someone to look after the library for you?" I supplied. "I'd be delighted. It's a lovely building, and if I get bored, I can always read a book. What's the meeting?"

"The Academy of the Unknowns."

I was well impressed. A group of intellectuals who discussed all sorts of fascinating topics, the Venetian equivalent of the

Morningside Heritage Association.

"Off you go and don't worry about a thing," I reassured him. "I don't stand any nonsense from library users. There'll be no carving their names on the desks with me in charge."

"Thank you, Librarian Macaroni Mona Lisa Glissando," he said gratefully. "Oh, and we have a timing system for the most popular books. Readers can have them for an hour only. The hourglass is over there." He went on to point out an inkwell and a small wooden stamp. "Let's see. It's about 11am. In that case, stamp their right hand under their middle finger. Noon to 1 pm, under the right-hand ring finger."

"Yes, I understand," I said. "Then 1pm to 2pm, under the right-hand little finger – and after that, returning from the little finger of the left hand?"

"Exactly," he said with a nod of approval. "Thank you. It's reassuring to be able to leave the library in such good hands."

He went off and I installed myself behind the desk as temporary librarian of the Marciana. I kept a close eye on the readers, and a closer nose. Beyond the smell of aniseed, I could smell something else.

"No eating of fried sardines in the library," I boomed, and the miscreant quickly bundled up his snack and put it back in his pouch.

I was obliged to intervene on several other occasions. "No nodding off on top of the books in the library." "No singing under your breath in the library, especially not with a voice like that." "Don't even think of talking back, the librarian's ruling is final."

I duly stamped the hands of those wanting access to the most popular books, although some of them complained that I stamped too hard.

A while later, everyone in the library having unaccountably left even though it wasn't closing time, I heard squelching noises coming up the staircase. Puzzled, I shifted to face the doorway to see what manner of creature was approaching.

"Librarian Zen!" I exclaimed as he appeared, clutching his

robes round him. They were sopping. "You're all wet!"

"I've been in the canal," he said, as he dripped copiously on to the marble floor. "Excuse me a moment. I've got a spare set of robes to change into in my cubicle."

I hadn't realised that the fad for wild swimming had been around in the seventeenth century. I was particularly surprised by it, since this was an era between naked bathing and the invention of the bathing suit, and swimming in all your clothes seemed unnecessarily awkward.

He eventually returned in a fresh outfit.

"How was the meeting?" I asked.

"I didn't actually get to it," he said.

I've noticed that wild swimming turns into an obsession with many people. A lot of them swear by daily immersion.

"Do you go into the canal a lot?" I asked.

"No," he said, "this was the first time. I was just on my way to the meeting when I was set upon by footpads. Fools. They didn't realise that all my riches are here." He tapped his forehead.

"Not great rates of pay, then?" I said sympathetically. "The City of Edinburgh Council's not too bad an employer, but I can't say I'm rolling in money either."

"Rolling in money? That sounds extraordinarily uncomfortable. I can't imagine how one would do such a thing," he said.

"It's another expression, a direct translation from English," I explained.

"A particularly odd one," he said. I felt this was a bit much from the speaker of a language that said, "in the wolf's mouth" instead of "good luck".

I relinquished my seat at the lectern and the librarian perched on it. "Any problems while I was away?" he asked.

"Nothing I couldn't handle."

Librarian Zen nodded approvingly.

"But that's dreadful about the footpads," I said. "It sounds like a bit of hassle you could have well done without."

"Yes, it was frustrating to miss the meeting," he said. "But it's so chilly at the moment that I felt I needed to change out of my wet clothes as soon as possible to avoid catching a cold."

"Actually, that's a myth," I said. "The common cold is a viral disease – it's not caused by a bacterial infection. You get it through being close to someone who's already got a cold, or by coming into contact with contaminated surfaces."

He raised an eyebrow. "I thought you weren't a doctor?"

"I'm not. Merely an interested amateur who's managed to pick up a few facts along the way. That's what we do, isn't it, we librarians? We absorb information from all the wonderful sources of knowledge available to us."

"You're right," he said. "So I could have gone to the meeting anyway without risking catching a cold? It still wouldn't have been pleasant, sitting there in wet clothes."

I looked at him, perched on the stool. He might have a formidable intellect, but he was a slight, non-threatening figure. He had said "footpads", which suggested more than one assailant. How had he actually managed to get away? The doctors had got irritated with my asking questions, but that's not something that would ever irritate a librarian. We thrive on responding to readers' queries.

"How did you manage to get away from the footpads?" I asked. "How many of them were there? How did they set upon you? How did you fall into the canal?"

He settled himself more comfortably on the stool. "I can answer all of your questions, but it will probably make better sense if I answer them in a different order."

"It's your story. Tell it however seems best," I said, plonking myself down on the nearest bench and preparing to listen intently.

He closed his eyes as though conjuring up the scene, and said, "I had just got off the gondola and was heading to my meeting when three footpads suddenly loomed out of the mist and grabbed me."

Three individuals, not two. Probably men, although I could see no reason why women couldn't be footpads as well. Returning to my original question, I really couldn't imagine how he had managed to get away.

"They attempted to drown me," Zen went on. "They pushed me into the canal, two of them holding a leg each, and the third trying to keep my head under the water with some sort of wooden pole."

"That's dreadful," I said, picturing the scene and thinking that it would have been quite impossible for him to manage to get away. "I take it they'd frisked you first, and decided to drown you because they were cross you didn't have any money on you?"

"No, they just grabbed me and shoved me into the water," he said.

This was odd. "Then these were not common-or-garden footpads," I said. "These were assassins. Does anyone have a grudge against you?"

"Oh yes," he said. "Librarian de' Pazzi in the San Marco Library in Florence. The Florentines have some silly idea that they're our rivals, but we do our best to ignore them."

"We have a similar situation with a place in Scotland called Glasgow," I said.

"Extraordinary," said the librarian, shaking his head. "We have a lot of manuscripts that Librarian de' Pazzi thinks he should have. I told him not to act like salami."

I was just thinking that salami would be pretty terrible at acting, no doubt the reason why one has never played the lead in a Royal Shakespeare Company production. But then I remembered that this was another weird Italian expression, telling someone not to be an idiot. And this from someone who had quibbled about "rolling in money". I could see there would be tensions between the two of them, but it's unusual for librarians to attempt to murder one another.

"Has he ever been violent towards you?" I asked.

"No, but he shuns me at parties. It's quite hurtful," said Librarian Zen, looking quite hurt.

He was such a lovely man that I couldn't imagine anybody wanting to kill him. Which left only one possibility – the hit had been ordered by someone who hated librarians. A little selfishly, I was glad I was dressed as a doctor.

"Anyway," I said, "we'd got as far as these assassins grabbing you and shoving you in the water. Then what happened?"

"Fortunately," he said, "I have excellent core stability."

"As do I," I said, rather surprised.

"I don't doubt it," he said courteously. "So I seized the wooden pole, pulling the fellow into the water while simultaneously propelling myself back on to *terra firma*. A couple of elbow strikes were enough to persuade the two other assailants to let go of me, and they ran off."

I was in total awe. "That's fantastic – three of them trying to finish you off, and you got the better of them. When you started telling me what had happened, I had no idea how you'd managed to get away."

"When I went headfirst into the canal, I had no idea either," he admitted. "But the way of the warrior is not about overcoming an opponent, but overcoming yourself. Once I unified mind, technique and body, all was well."

He sounded very zen, which was only appropriate. I was hugely excited to discover an additional bond between us.

"I study martial arts as well," I said. "I go to a dojo in Edinburgh. How did you come to get involved?"

"I met a traveller from an antique land. He taught me the rudiments," said the librarian. I was more than startled to hear this. His first sentence was the opening line of "Ozymandias" by Percy Bysshe Shelley. It must be a common Italian phrase. Shelley had lived in Venice – he probably picked up the phrase then, and worked it into a poem. It had the right rhythm and everything. Very wisely, he never used "in the wolf's mouth" in any of his work.

But no, he'd written the poem the year before he moved to Italy. He could have heard the expression from his friend Byron, who already had a home in Venice. Shelley probably then decided to come to Venice as well because he thought he'd find other interesting phrases to improve his poetry. If only Miss Blaine had sent me here in the nineteenth century, I could have met Byron and Shelley.

I stopped myself dwelling on this, partly to avoid the sharp pain in my big toe, but also because if I'd gone to Venice later, I wouldn't have met Librarian Zen, who was still reminiscing about his traveller from an antique land.

"We owe a great debt to Marco Polo," he said. "Our trade routes with Asia Minor and the Far East bring us individuals as well as books and other artefacts. Exchanging knowledge is much more profitable, wouldn't you say?"

"I would," I said. "Do you fancy exchanging some martial arts knowledge?"

"Delighted," said Zen.

We went to a clear bit of floor, well away from the benches and books, and bowed to one another. I was resolving to go easy on him as he started running towards me. A moment later, he levitated, and I was the victim of a flying kick, myself flying across the library until I crashed into a portrait of Aristotle.

"Librarian Macaroni Mona Lisa Glissando, I hope I haven't hurt you," the librarian called anxiously. "I thought you would side-step me."

I lay there, winded, reflecting that I had just made a far worse mistake than assuming. I had underestimated a librarian. Of course the traveller from an antique land would have found him a quick learner. Librarians are quick learners at everything. He was small but he was wiry, and that kick packed a punch.

I hauled myself to my feet. "No harm done."

"Are you sure?" he asked. "The portrait of Aristotle is unharmed?"

"It's fine," I said rather testily. "Anyway, nice sparring with you, but I should get back to my billet." I retrieved my mask and fastened it back on. I was getting used to it. The smell of aniseed was rather nice, and I could see quite well out of the glass portholes as long as I squinted.

"I don't want to interfere with your mission, but if you're free, might you be able to look after the library again for a couple of hours on another occasion?" the librarian asked. "Having missed today's meeting of the Academy of the Unknowns without sending my apologies, I really feel I should go to the next one."

"I'll be glad to help if I can," I said, and I genuinely meant it. I couldn't make a firm commitment since I didn't know where the mission would take me, but I had forgiven him for being as worried about the portrait as he was about me. After all, he knew that a fellow librarian would be resilient, but portraits are fragile things.

"I do hope to see you," I said. I didn't know then that I definitely would see him, after I had made the most horrifying, blood-chilling discovery.

FOUR

On the way back from the Marciana Library, I decided to have a bit of a wander. Yes, I was on a mission, but I felt I should be allowed a little downtime. Now that my beaked mask was back on, I tried to stick to the narrowest, least-populated alleys to avoid upsetting people.

But I miscalculated in the fog, rounded a corner, and found myself at the Rialto market where crowds were busy shopping. The screams started. One, then two, then three.

"There it is again!" a woman shrieked.

I was about to take issue with her referring to me as it when I realised that nobody was looking and pointing at me. Instead, all their attention was on the Grand Canal. I peered in that direction and, through the fog, I could make out the curious sight of a golden angel, head bowed, wings outstretched. I was used to meeting all sorts of unusual people on my missions, but an angel was something new.

With an angel, you don't waste time on small talk. As I was trying to think of something profound, I saw that the golden angel seemed to come equipped with a jet-black background. It wasn't a genuine heavenly messenger at all, simply an ornate figurehead on the front of a gondola. An odd sort of gondola in that it was progressing down the canal very, very slowly. A very odd sort of gondola, much longer than the usual ones, with some sort of structure in the middle of it.

I peered through the swirls of mist, trying to make sense of what I was seeing. The structure was square, with a sort of awning, and like the gondola itself, was black with gold decorations. Four black hooded figures steered it slowly and silently down the canal. I remembered that at this point, the gondoliers' uniform had been black rather than stripey, but I hadn't known about the hoods. Another bit of information to take back.

"Death and doom!" shrieked the woman, a cry taken up by others in the crowd.

That clarified things. The woman must be a professional mourner. So I was looking at a funeral, and this was a funeral gondola, the Venetian equivalent of a hearse. These were designed to transport the deceased to their final resting place under the paving stones, an unhygienic practice that lasted until the nineteenth century when the nearby island of San Michele was designated Venice's cemetery. But this funeral gondola didn't appear to be transporting anyone deceased. There was no sign of a coffin on the raised central platform. The black curtains swished gently as the gondola continued its stately progress, and I could see that the dark interior was empty.

It was passing directly in front of me now, and through the fog I discerned a black banner with gold lettering. It took a while to piece the letters together, but eventually I worked it out: "Take a Cornetto Gondola and Die."

My heart sank. I had a pretty good idea what had happened. The phrase was heavily reminiscent of "See Naples and Die", made internationally famous by Goethe when he quoted it in *Italian Journey* about his eighteenth-century travels. It was already a well-known Neapolitan phrase at that time, and the black and gold banner clearly suggested it was in use in 1650. The Cornetto gondola company had noted the success of Naples' advertising slogan and had decided to adopt it. But while the original phrase implied that you could pass away peacefully after visiting the city, since it was the most beautiful thing you would ever see, the gondola was inadvertently sending out a very different message. It gave the distinct impression that if you travelled on a Cornetto gondola, that would be the end of you. I had my mission to get on with, logging an accurate history of the plague, and helping with the heavy lifting, but I would try to make time to get in touch with the Cornetto gondola company's marketing department and explain their mistake. I'd have to present them with an alternative, of course, since otherwise they would just get despondent. "The Best Gondolas are Cornettos." Sometimes the simplest messages are the best.

People were so disturbed by the sight of the gondola that I managed to get back to the doctors' residence without too much screaming about my beak. But Dr Oregano wasn't pleased with me.

"Where have you been?" he demanded.

"I've been for a walk," I said. "Walking is key to improving cardiovascular fitness, strengthening bones and muscle, and increasing energy levels."

"What's he talking about?" said Dr Parsley.

"I'm talking about maintaining good health," I said. "That's the problem with our system of allopathic medicine. It focuses too much on treating illness and not enough on prevention."

Dr Oregano turned to the others. "Gentlemen, here we are, graduates of Padua, Perugia, Bologna and Genoa, but what is our professional knowledge compared to that of someone from…" He paused for effect. "…Edinburgh?"

They found that very amusing. I didn't.

I was about to elaborate when Dr Oregano fixed me with a stare and said, "We've been waiting for you. The bodies are stacking up, and we need to make space for new ones. We're sending the first lot to the Lazzaretto Vecchio for burial. So get moving."

Not the island where incomers were quarantined, but the one next to it, specifically for plague victims.

Once again, I was paired up with Dr Rosemary. There's a reason a dead weight is so called, and it's tricky lifting one when the person carrying the other end is utterly feeble. The lumbering Dr Parsley would have been a much better co-worker, probably able to carry a body all by himself, but I realised it was a hierarchical thing. Dr Rosemary was the youngest and I was apparently the least well medically qualified, so between us, we had to move the plague victims from the storeroom to the canal entrance. Thankfully, they were all now wrapped in winding sheets, so I didn't have to worry about catching sight of those hideous black and red spots.

A gondola was waiting outside, another large funeral one, and we stacked the bodies on the central plinth, then got on ourselves. The three doctors who were too grand to do any actual work watched us from the loggia, Dr Marjoram giving a little wave as we slowly set off.

It was rather macabre being on a funeral gondola piloted by four silent hooded black-clad gondoliers, taking a pile of bodies to their final resting place. But it was really very exciting to be gliding down a Venetian canal. I sent a small "thank you" through the mist to Miss Blaine.

"I'm glad we're not on a Cornetto company gondola," I said to Dr Rosemary.

His beak swivelled towards me. "What?"

"The poor marketing," I said. "Not very professional."

"This *is* a Cornetto gondola," he said. "It's what was ordered."

But this wasn't what the doctors ordered.

"No, you're mistaken," I said, "this isn't a Cornetto gondola. You can tell because it doesn't have the corporate banner on it."

"What do you mean? What corporate banner?"

These doctors really weren't keeping up with current events.

"They've got a marketing slogan that doesn't work. Actually, if you have any contacts in the company, let me know, and I'll try to help them come up with something better. What do you think of 'The Best Gondolas Are Cornettos' – to the point, or a bit bland?"

"I don't understand a word of what you're saying." Dr Rosemary's voice was shaking, most likely with the cold since it was really quite chilly.

"The Cornetto company's funeral gondola. They've got a banner on it to attract business. 'Take a Cornetto Gondola and Die.'"

Dr Rosemary lurched sideways on his seat. "How will that

attract business? That will destroy business!"

"Exactly," I agreed. "You've worked that out right away. It's amazing how often advertisers get things wrong when all they need is a couple of focus groups with ordinary people. It's a shame the Cornetto company didn't think of that."

"This is nothing to do with the Cornettos," shouted Dr Rosemary.

I was surprised to hear that. I had no idea that it was possible to outsource advertising in the seventeenth century. I sent another quick "thank you" through the swirling fog. Carrying out these missions for Miss Blaine was allowing me some fascinating insights that we never heard about in our school history lessons.

The cold was really getting to Dr Rosemary, as he had curled up and was rocking backwards and forwards in an obvious attempt to get himself warm. The southern Europeans are very thin-blooded.

When we reached the Lazzaretto Vecchio, there was a solemn welcoming committee of black-robed figures who, like the other doctors, were too important to get involved in manual work. And the gondoliers had some sort of demarcation rules that meant they refused to get off the gondola. So, once again, Dr Rosemary and I were left to get on with it.

We had just unloaded the last of our melancholy cargo when a much smaller gondola arrived at speed carrying two men who looked like medical assistants.

"Nice timing, guys," I said sarcastically as they disembarked.

But they ignored me completely, dashing over to the waiting group, gesticulating and shouting, "He must be here!"

If they were looking for a particular deceased, that was unfortunate, since they would have to unwind all the winding sheets. But they, and now the welcoming committee, showed no interest in that either, heading instead through the mist towards the buildings that presumably housed the resident staff.

I raced after them. "What's going on?" I asked the nearest black-robed figure when I caught up with him.

"The guards have come to get him."

Not medical assistants, then.

"Come to get who?" I asked.

"An escapee from the quarantine island," he said. "Spotted swimming in our direction."

"Why would someone on the quarantine island swim to the plague island?" I asked.

"You ask a lot of questions," said the black-robed figure irritably.

"He does," agreed Dr Rosemary, catching up with us. "We've told him about it, but it hasn't stopped him."

"And I've explained that asking questions is a key means of understanding what's going on, which right now isn't at all clear," I said.

"It's perfectly clear," snapped Dr Rosemary. "Someone has escaped from the quarantine island before their quarantine is up. They've come here because they're swimming to Venice in stages. And we have to stop them reaching the city centre or heaven knows what sort of unpleasant diseases they might bring us."

I was going to say we were already quite well provided for on the unpleasant diseases front when there was sudden shouting. The two guards reappeared from behind a building, one limping, the other shivering. Between them they dragged a small squirming figure whose clothes were dripping wet. They were different clothes from the Venetian ones, a style of jacket and trousers typically worn by merchants during China's Qing dynasty.

"I might have known," said the irritable black-robed figure. "A traveller from an antique land. They just don't follow rules."

Not the same traveller who had taught martial arts to Librarian Zen, since that one had obviously come out of quarantine.

"We're arresting you on the orders of the doge," one of the guards was telling the small squirming captive.

"Arresting me for what? I haven't done anything," the captive protested.

"Yes, you have, you've broken quarantine, and risked bringing death and destruction to Venice."

"I'm perfectly healthy," said the captive. "And I don't want to go anywhere near Venice now. I'm fed up with the whole place, and I want to get as far away as I possibly can. I came here with a gift for your doge, the start of a great business opportunity for him, and then I found out about your mad forty-day rule. I'm not here for a holiday and if your doge won't see me, I'm taking my business elsewhere. So let go of me, and I'll get back to my ship and go somewhere more business-minded. I haven't got time for this."

The black-robed figure looked at him sternly. "I'm afraid it's not as simple as that. You may come from some lawless faraway country of which we know little, but you're in civilisation now. You've broken the law and the penalty for that is death." He nodded to the guards. "Take him away."

"Stop right where you are," I thundered in the voice I used as a prefect when a fourth-year tried to leave the lunch huts without stacking the plates. "That's outrageous. Fine him a couple of hundred ducats if you must, but you can't go around executing people who just want to go home."

"Call yourself a Venetian?" sneered the black-robed figure. "We've got one of the most enlightened governments in the civilised world and you dare to criticise it?"

"I may speak fluent Venetian, but I'm not from here," I said. "*Vegno da Edimburgo*. I'm from Edinburgh."

The guards' attention shifted to me, and at that moment, the prisoner, in a beautiful fluid movement, kicked backwards, and the limping guard fell, winded, to the ground. The other, shivering guard gamely tried to hang on to his captive-turned-attacker, and Dr Rosemary rushed forward, presumably to offer medical assistance. There was a confused scuffle before the traveller emerged unscathed, sprinted to the shore, leaped into the water and shot off at an impressive speed – never was the word "crawl" so inappropriate. These travellers from an antique land knew a thing or two.

"Quick, after him!" wheezed the limping guard.

The second barely moved. "No point," he said tersely. "Look at the speed of him. He'll be back on board before we get anywhere near him."

"We'll get a right bollocking if we go back without him," said the first guard.

"Not necessarily," said the second.

They looked at one another, then looked at the black-clad figures and gave a nod. Before I had time to register what was happening, I had been seized and pinioned with ropes provided by the black-clad figures. I was in utter shock. How could I have been so inattentive? I was profoundly grateful that Miss Blaine had told me she didn't micromanage these missions. I don't think I could have survived the embarrassment if she had been watching. It should only have taken me a couple of seconds to evade capture – but I hadn't seen it coming, and now it was too late. I'm pretty good at martial arts, but I'm not Harry Houdini.

"There," said the first guard with satisfaction, "now we've something to take back."

Dr Rosemary was belatedly getting to his feet, brushing dust off his goatskin overcoat.

"Tell them," I pleaded. "Tell them I'm necessary. Tell them I'm a doctor."

"But you're not," said Dr Rosemary, which was pretty much the most unhelpful thing he could have said. "You're a traveller from an antique land."

The guards brightened.

"Excellent," said the first. "We lose one, we gain one."

"Scotland may have been populated since the Paleolithic era, but it really doesn't come under the category of antique land," I said. "That's generally understood to refer to somewhere beyond Europe, and the Scots have always been good Europeans."

This had no effect.

"You're foreign, so you've broken quarantine, and risked bringing death and destruction to Venice," said the guard, just as he had to his previous captive.

"I'm not suffering from the plague. I've had my vaccinations," I assured him.

He merely stared, as it would be almost another fifty years before vaccinology was founded.

"Tell them," I said again to Dr Rosemary, a slight tone of desperation entering my voice. "Tell them I'm one of your colleagues, here to help combat the plague, not to spread it."

Dr Rosemary's beak moved slowly from right to left to centre.

"I can't do that," he said. "You haven't gone to medical school."

"I know the Heimlich manoeuvre and I'm better than you at heavy lifting," I reminded him.

I should probably have worded this in a more tactful way since he shook his beak more vigorously.

"One trick and a few muscles don't make you a doctor. I had to study to get where I am."

One of the black-clad figures gave me a shove. "Move it."

I was hauled roughly away by the guards, who clearly saw me as little more than a navvy. They manhandled me on to the waiting gondola. The gondolier, a tall gangly lad with a thin moustache, whose black outfit made him look equally thin, gave me a sympathetic look. We took off and after a few minutes the plague island disappeared in the mist, and it was as though we were cocooned in white candy floss.

"I really do know quite a bit about healthcare," I said.

"Shut up," growled the limping guard.

"There's no need for rudeness," I said. "My aim is to help. You, for example, are suffering from plantar fasciitis."

The other guard edged hastily away. "Is it catching?" he asked nervously.

"Don't listen to him," blustered the invalid. "There's nothing wrong with me."

"So you're happy with that ache in your heel, the stabbing pain when you put pressure on it, and the limp when you try to avoid standing on it?" I asked.

"He's right,"_exclaimed the other one. "I've noticed you've been walking weirdly for the past couple of weeks." He turned to me. "It's the plague, isn't it?"

"Not only is it not the plague, but it's treatable," I said. "Same with you, and the ague."

"What are you talking about?" he protested. "I'm in perfect health."

"That'll be why you're shivering all the time," I said.

"I'm shivering because it's cold with all this mist."

His partner studied him suspiciously. "But you're sweating. You should be in quarantine."

"You're both basically fine," I said. "When we reach our destination, I'll need some silk and a spoon, and you'll both feel better in no time."

Now I was the one being viewed with suspicion.

"Are you a necromancer?"

"No, because there's no such thing, although there are a lot of charlatans around," I said. "Just try what I suggest and see if you feel better."

"I've got a sore shoulder," said the tall gangly gondolier unexpectedly, taking one hand off the oar to point at the sore bit, which made the gondola lurch alarmingly.

"Mind what you're doing," snapped the plantar fasciitis guard. "Nobody wants to hear from you."

"Excuse me," I said, "I'm more than happy to hear from the gentleman. We're all equally important when it comes to medical care." My philosophy is that we're all equally important when it comes to anything. We are, in that Scots declaration of egalitarian sentiments, "a' Jock Tamson's bairns". The gondolier might not realise that he and I were effectively Tamson twins, but I knew it, and addressed him accordingly. "I'm afraid it's likely to be a work-related problem. There isn't a pill you can take to put muscle strain right, but once we dock, I'll teach you a few exercises that should help, as long as you do them regularly."

"I will," he promised, and I hoped he would. People can be very slipshod about therapy when they're not supervised.

We docked about ten minutes later, and I was helped on to dry land rather more gently than I had been hustled off it.

A large birdlike creature came rushing towards us, exclaiming in shock.

"What have you two idiots done now? This isn't a traveller from an antique land – look at what he's wearing. He's a medical man! Release him immediately!"

The plantar fasciitis guard started twisting his hands in a Uriah Heepish manner. "We caught the traveller just as you instructed, but he overcame us through necromancy and disappeared in a puff of smoke."

"That's not actually true," I said. "I've already told you, there's no such thing as necromancy. He basically used some rather good self-defence techniques on you and disappeared into the lagoon."

The gondolier nodded in confirmation, but Uriah Heep said to the island doctor, "Please don't worry, this person only looks like a doctor, but we have it on the best authority that he isn't one."

"He sounds like one," said the gondolier. "He's got cures for us all."

The island doctor fumbled frantically at the ropes around me to undo them. "I'm so sorry," he said. "I should never have sent these two out in pursuit of the escapee, but I didn't have anyone else. Please come inside and have a seat to recover from your ordeal."

He ushered me into a long low building that exuded peace and serenity, perhaps because it was completely empty. The two guards and the gondolier followed.

"We'll return you wherever you want, at our expense, of course, but perhaps you could tell us about these cures?" said the doctor. "I'm always anxious to learn."

I was anxious to get away, but I couldn't ignore a plea for knowledge, or an opportunity to help.

"This man," I said, indicating the first guard to the doctor, "is suffering from inflammation of his plantar fascia, the part of his foot that connects his heel bone to the base of his toes. It was easy to tell because of the way he kept his foot flat while walking with the prisoner, and wasn't able to raise his heel up. He also turned side on to get into the gondola to reduce the flexion-extension at the ankle."

"This is a revelation," said the doctor. "I could see the fellow was limping, but I certainly don't have your diagnostic powers. I suppose amputation is the only solution?"

The guard backed away nervously in a flat-footed manner.

"No need for anything like that," I said. "Do you have a piece of silk I could use?"

"Of course," said the doctor. "These travellers from antique lands leave all sorts lying around."

He handed me a length of silk and I quickly folded it down into a pad.

"This is an orthotic to cushion your heel," I told the guard, putting it into his shoe at the appropriate place. "It allows the calf muscle and the plantar fascia to operate in a slightly shortened state, thereby reducing the pull at the painful site of attachment."

The doctor was peering and nodding at the process.

"Remarkable!" he said. "You truly are at the forefront of medical discoveries."

"Although this chap has an old favourite, the ague," I said, indicating the second guard.

"Has he?" said the doctor without much interest. "I hadn't noticed."

I wasn't impressed that he didn't seem to consider the staff as potential patients, or to find the ague as exciting as the plague. I prepared to impress again.

"I can assure you that that's what he's got," I said. "What treatment would you suggest?"

He shrugged. "A bit of purging and blood-letting, obviously."

Now it was the other guard edging nervously away.

"Really?" I said. "Rather old-fashioned, I think. I prefer more modern methods. Powdered tree bark."

He looked at me blankly.

"Brought from Peru to Europe by Spanish priests," I said. "Marvellously effective." There was no point in telling him it was full of quinine, as that would be discovered only in the next century. "Could you get me some prosecco and a spoon?"

The guard cheered up enormously at this. I had such faith in the supplementary support I get on my missions that I hadn't even checked my pouch before pronouncing; and my faith was not misplaced. When I opened my pouch, it was full of Peruvian tree bark. I mixed some in with the prosecco and gave it to the guard to drink.

He drained it in a oner and declared, "I'm feeling better already."

"That's the placebo effect," I said, shaking the remaining contents of my pouch into a nearby bowl. "I prescribe taking it every four hours."

"Thank you very much," he said, snaffling the bottle.

There was a diffident cough behind us. The gondolier. "My arm?" he said.

I turned back to the doctor. "You'll have noticed that gondoliers work asymmetrically, which increases the risk of musculoskeletal problems. With this gentleman, the internal rotation at the shoulder has increased the attrition on the supraspinatus tendon. And this has caused friction on the tendon between the head of the humerus and the under-surface of the acromion process. I would say it's led to either supraspinatus tendonitis or a subacromial bursitis, or even both. What do you think?"

The doctor was nodding so much that he could have been put on the rear shelf of a Ford Fiesta. "Yes, either the … yes, the first thing you said, or indeed the second, but perhaps both."

"Exactly," I said. "I'm glad you agree. Always useful for the patient to get a second opinion."

I went over to the tall gangly gondolier. "You can temporarily relieve the discomfort by gently swinging your arm in a pendular fashion, like so. But you really need to do something more

49

preventative – when you're working, try to rotate more through your spine and hips. And stretch your pectoral muscle as often as you can by reaching backwards with your palm upwards."

"Yes, yes," the doctor said eagerly. "Most important to stretch the pectoral muscle. And to keep the palm upwards. I trust the gondolier will remember all that when he's taking you back. And I shall make a note of these valuable treatment plans. After all, there may not be much we can do about the plague, in the few days before they expire. We're not barbarians. Although…" I could almost feel him glaring under his mask at the guards, "… you wouldn't know it from the way you've been kidnapped. We'll get you home right away."

"Much appreciated," I said. "If you can arrange for me to be dropped off around St Mark's Square, that would be ideal."

"No problem," said the gondolier. "I'll add it to the account."

I was so anxious to leave that I almost forgot my mission, to bring back an accurate history of the plague.

"You mentioned that you tried to treat the plague victims' other problems," I said to the doctor.

"Indeed," he said enthusiastically. "I'll particularly be on the alert for plantar fasciitis, the ague and the sup … the sup—"

"The supraspinatus tendonitis or possibly subacromial bursitis," I provided. "Do you have many people in at the moment?"

"My comment about treating plague victims was theoretical," he said. "We don't have a single one. The outbreak's confined to the city centre, and they've all died before there's been time to bring them here. We haven't had any patients here since 1631, and I took over only a month ago."

"What about the traveller from the antique land? Didn't he have the plague?" I asked.

"I don't think so," said the doctor. "I didn't see any black or red pustules."

"Then what was he doing on the plague victims' island?"

"He just turned up," said the doctor. "He was supposed to be out there on his ship for forty days, but he got fed up waiting and jumped overboard. He thought he had swum to Venice – he was babbling about some business opportunity for the doge – but thankfully he never made it to the city centre. I explained he had to stay here for the rest of the quarantine period, but before I could call the guards, he jumped into the water again. These things have to be logged, so you can imagine how alarmed I was at the thought of losing an inmate before their period of quarantine was up. You'll know yourself what it's like when you take on a new job – you have to make sure everything's done properly."

"That's why we grabbed this bloke instead, to replace the other one. That keeps the numbers straight," grumped the previously limping guard.

"You can't replace a traveller from an antique land with a member of the medical profession," snapped the doctor in exasperation.

"But the other doctor said this one *was* a traveller from an antique land," protested the previously shivering guard.

"And I explained that while that was technically accurate, it's not the way the phrase is generally understood," I said. "After all, Venice dates from the year 421, but we don't refer to it as an antique land."

The doctor nodded approvingly. "Exactly so," he said. "May I ask where you're from?"

"*Vegno da Edimburgo*. I'm from Edinburgh."

The doctor sprang to his feet. "Imposter! How can you have the gall to pass yourself off as a medical man when you come from such an undistinguished town with absolutely no tradition of medicine?"

"I may not have a medical degree," I said, "but as you've seen, I've been able to help these gentlemen, and I have a wide range of other skills, including splinting broken bones, applying tourniquets—"

"Don't try to exonerate yourself," the doctor cut in. "You're nothing but a fraud, a disgrace to your beak. I can tell you right now that you will serve the whole quarantine period, starting from now, and I certainly won't be taking off the time already served by the traveller from an antique land."

I was going to say that wasn't fair when I recalled that no one ever said life was fair. I tried another tack. "But if I'm the replacement for the traveller, and I serve more time than is set out, that'll throw your records out of sync."

The doctor shrugged. "I don't care. There's always the excuse of administrative errors. Forty days, not a minute less."

"Unless you've got the plague," said the previously limping guard with relish. "In which case, you'll be here till you die and then you'll go to the plague island for burial."

"Does this mean I'm not being paid to take him back to St Mark's Square?" asked the tall gangly gondolier. "I can't hang around here doing nothing. I've got a living to earn."

"Sorry," I said. "It wasn't my decision. I would have been very grateful for a lift. Don't forget to do your exercises, and I'm sure you'll see an improvement."

"Stop giving medical advice when you're not qualified," grated the doctor.

"This is the trouble with the professionalisation of healthcare," I said. "It militates against people taking responsibility for their own well-being."

I was about to give the gondolier a few more words of encouragement when I realised he'd already left, and moments later there was the sound of the swish of an oar through water. He must really need a new fare.

"We could have a good interchange of information," I told the doctor. "I'd be very interested in your take on the plague, and I can teach you cardiopulmonary resuscitation, that's reviving someone who's collapsed with a heart attack."

"I have no interest in necromancy," retorted the doctor. He stalked off, beak in the air, giving me no chance to explain that CPR wasn't necromancy. Perhaps that was just as well, since telling him that it had first been demonstrated around 300 years later would certainly have had a whiff of magic about it.

The no-longer-limping guard gripped me by the arm. "Come along," he growled.

"Foot feeling better, I see. No, don't bother to thank me," I said, but he missed my ironic tone and took me at my word. I was deposited in what looked like a monk's cell, and a very single-celled cell it was. There was a narrow bed with a thin mattress and a manky blanket and that was it. Still, it had been quite a day and I was feeling pretty tired, so I lay down and wrapped the blanket round me.

I fell asleep almost immediately, but just before I did, it struck me that this was my second night in Venice. I was allowed a calendar week to complete a mission. Being stuck in quarantine for forty days wasn't compatible with those terms. I remembered the words of the traveller from the antique land: "I haven't got time for this."

FIVE

The school song is the most uplifting piece of music I know.

> *Whatever mission we go on,*
> *Where'er we chance to be,*
> *We Blainers sing our cheerful song,*
> *Which makes all troubles flee.*
> *So in this life, let's leave our trace,*
> *And may we never slow our pace,*
> *To make this world a better place,*
> *Cremor, cremor cremoris.*

Cremor cremoris, the crème de la crème. I had our reputation to live up to, which meant I had to get off the plague island and back to the city. After a good night's sleep, I had been let out by the guards and told to go for a walk. It turned out they were very keen on fresh air as a means of combating the plague, although they hadn't grasped the importance of keeping two metres' distance away from other people, and just got surly when I tried to explain it to them.

I was slightly miffed that they just let me go off by myself without attaching me to a chain or anything. I would have expected them to be more careful after the escape of the traveller from the antique land. It suggested they didn't think I had the *nous* to do what he had done, and swim to freedom. But in fact, because of the persistent fog, I couldn't see my way clear. I couldn't even see the sun to help me navigate. As the traveller had done, I risked ending up in completely the wrong place.

This was bad. Given that there were no plague victims here,

this wasn't where I should be. Not for the first time on a mission, I wondered what would happen if I couldn't get away before my mission deadline expired. Would I expire as well? Miss Blaine had never spelled out what the sanctions were for failure, but I suspected they were worse than a rap over the knuckles with a ruler or a pain in my big toe. There was only one thing to do: sing the school song again.

And then I heard a splashing in the distance. It was coming closer, at regularly spaced intervals, a gondolier's oar curving through the water. I might be able to bribe my way on board. Reasonable expenses would surely extend to a bribe if that was the only way to escape from my island prison, and if they didn't, I could pay Miss Blaine back. A bribe in 1650 would surely only be a couple of pence in the twenty-first century.

As I rummaged in my robes for a purse, the splashing sound came nearer. I deduced that the gondolier must be quite brawny, since the oar was being driven through the water with considerable force. I had thought I was getting the hang of looking through the glass portholes in my mask, but I was wrong, since what I could see approaching through the fog looked less like a gondola than a big banana. A banana that was bouncing towards me at speed.

And then it stopped at the water's edge and looked straight at me, smiling broadly. Not a gondola, not a banana, but a dolphin. I remembered the story about Arion, the Greek poet saved from drowning by a dolphin that was attracted by the beauty of his singing. Modesty forbids, but I *had* been singing the school song, and I often got the solo in the school choir.

The dolphin was resting now, and it gave a few whistles interspersed with clicks.

"I'm terribly sorry," I said. "I don't speak Dolphin."

Its smile changed from friendly to forgiving, and I realised that despite the obvious language barrier, it understood me. I have something of a gift for communicating with animals, and during my past missions have been on speaking terms with a dog, a cat, an owl and a wolf.

"I wonder if I could trouble you to take me to St Mark's Square," I said.

It looked at me in a quizzical way. I wasn't sure whether it didn't understand me, or if it was worried about helping me leave the plague island.

"I've not got the plague," I said. "I've had my vaccinations. I'm quite keen to get back to St Mark's Square. I'm on a mission with a deadline."

The dolphin jumped into the air, did a somersault, and came to rest in the water just beside me. I took that as a yes.

I was just in the process of saying, "Thank you very much, that's most kind of you" when there was a sudden bellow, "Step away from the dolphin!"

The two guards, definitely restored to full health, neither limping nor shivering, were racing towards me. If they caught me, that would be it. Despite their enthusiasm for fresh air, they'd put me back in my cell and lock the door for the next thirty-nine days. I didn't hesitate. I leaped aboard the dolphin, just above its dorsal fin, and clung on for dear life.

But even as we set off, the guards commandeered a passing gondola, yelling, "Follow that dolphin!"

The dolphin whistled and clicked. It was no good. Most of the creatures I'd been involved with on previous missions had actually spoken to me. In English.

"I don't understand," I said desperately as the gondola began to gain on us.

The dolphin gave what sounded very like a sigh, and whistled and clicked more slowly and more loudly.

"No, still not getting it," I apologised, feeling rather stupid, and wondering whether this was how people without a Blaine education felt the whole time.

The dolphin squeaked in a distinctly impatient manner, and once again whistled and clicked. This time, it clicked with me as well. Two hundred years before Samuel Morse would invent his Code, the dolphin was using sequences of short and long resonances to communicate with me in Venetian. It was child's play to work out the words now that I had grasped the system, and I felt thoroughly embarrassed that it had taken me so long.

The dolphin was saying, "Crazy to go to St Mark's Square if they heard you say that's where you want to go."

It had obviously understood what I was saying when I had spoken to it previously, but I couldn't talk in Venetian now, since that would risk being overheard by the guards. I would have to use Dolphin. Concentrating hard, I clicked and whistled agreement that this was no longer a good idea, and that I was happy to be dropped wherever seemed best.

The gondola was picking up speed, so I added a further suggestion.

"Evasive diction?" the dolphin queried.

"Sorry. I meant to say evasive action," I corrected. "I'm not completely fluent yet."

"You're doing very well," said the dolphin.

"Thank you," I said. "Maybe we could try a bit of the evasive action now-ish?"

"Okay," said the dolphin. "Hang on."

Hanging on to a dolphin is even more complicated than speaking its language, given the lack of a saddle and reins. But I channelled my inner limpet as the dolphin veered right before accelerating backwards, letting the gondola shoot past us into the mist. I was going to say something, but realised that the most important thing right now was to maintain radio silence, giving the guards no clue as to where we were. Except there was a very definite clue in the sound of our splashing. Above the noise we were making, I could hear the swish of the gondola turning to follow us. I was tempted to slip off the dolphin and swim quietly away, but since I wasn't equipped with sonar or echolocation, I would most likely drown from exhaustion before finding my way back to dry land.

The dolphin squeaked, clicked and whistled even more loudly, and at speed. I was busy translating my response, "Sorry, didn't quite catch that," when the sound of splashing increased tenfold. The dolphin hadn't been talking to me but to its mates, who were now surrounding us, leaping up into the air, then belly-flopping in order to prevent the guards from working out which particular splashes were caused by us. Faintly, I could hear the guards yelling in alarm and demanding to be returned to their island as quickly as possible.

"Brilliant strategy," I clicked. "Thank you, and please thank your friends for me as well."

"Not at all," the dolphin replied. "It's fun. I've never been involved in a high-speed escape before. And I'm sure they're all enjoying upsetting the gondolier. It's only fair – I can't tell you the number of times we get smacked on the nose by an oar."

I felt slightly guilty that an innocent gondolier was in difficulties just because my guards had flagged him down, but then I thought that if he and the rest of his profession were so careless as to hit dolphins on the nose, they deserved everything they got.

I still had a question for my rescuer. "I take it you were attracted by my singing?"

There was a lengthy whistle. "I certainly was," it said, and I allowed myself a brief smile of satisfaction.

"I really felt I had to do something before you sang any more," it went on. It was an unfortunate choice of words for what it clearly intended as a compliment. I understood it was simply trying to tell me how quickly it had rushed to hear me so as not to miss anything. Translating from Dolphin to Human was always going to be an inexact science.

I could begin to discern buildings through the mist. We were nearing the city.

"Just take me down some of the wee back canals and I'll find my way," I said.

The dolphin did some indignant clicking, interspersed with a few squeaks, which I interpreted as meaning that the narrowness of said canals was such that it increased the risk of being smacked on the nose by an oar.

"The lads will keep that other gondolier busy for ages – you needn't worry," it said. "I'll drop you at St Mark's Square, no problem."

It had been a trying sort of day, but my spirits rose as I saw the elegant Doric lines of the Marciana Library appear through the fog. The dolphin bounced to a halt and waited as I scrambled ashore.

"Thank you so much," I said. "It's been lovely whistling and clicking with you."

"Likewise," it said. "Take care." And it shot off down the Grand Canal, standing upright and propelled by its tail, no doubt to avoid getting smacked on the nose by any rogue oars.

I was close by the library, but even so, my beaked appearance provoked a fair bit of screaming before I was able to dodge into the hallowed halls and drip my way into the reading room. There were a few readers loafing about, supervised by Librarian Zen from his stool at the lectern. He scrutinised me with concern.

"Librarian Macaroni Mona Lisa Glissando!" he said, but in an undertone, so as not to disturb the readers. "You're all wet. An unfortunate encounter with footpads?"

"Thankfully not. I've just had a lift from a dolphin," I said as quietly as I could.

He nodded, unsurprised. "That would do it. But please, I have some spare robes you can change into, and hang yours up to dry. I'll show you where."

"Do you have time?" I asked as I followed him to his cubicle. "I don't want you to miss your Academy of the Unknowns meeting."

"I've still got a few minutes. And I greatly appreciate the effort you've made to come here to let me get away. I can't imagine the dolphin was your first choice of transport."

I hesitated, unsure whether to admit that I had escaped from quarantine. And then I thought, a librarian is, as it were, a second self. I quickly explained what had happened, concluding, "I don't have the plague – I've had all my vaccinations."

"Vaccinations," he mused. "I haven't heard that word before. I presume it has something to do with cows?"

He was exactly right, Edward Jenner having made up the word from *vacca*, the Italian for cow, when he developed the first vaccine from cowpox. As I went into the small cubicle to change into Librarian Zen's spare robes, I outlined the vaccination process for him.

He listened attentively with the occasional exclamation of enthusiasm.

"Your city of literature is even more advanced than I thought," he said as I emerged in dry clothes. "Librarian Macaroni Mona Lisa Glissando, I think you should come with me to the Academy of the Unknowns meeting. This is exactly the sort of thing they should be discussing."

"But I can't come with you," I protested. "I'm here to run the library while you're away at your meeting. It's not as though we can just close it."

"That's exactly what we can do," he said. "I'll eject the readers who are in at the moment, and then lock the place up. If access to the library is restricted, they will appreciate it all the more when they are allowed to come in."

"We take much the same view ourselves," I said. "We close at 5pm on Thursdays, Fridays and Saturdays, rather than staying open until 8pm."

Librarian Zen shooed the handful of readers downstairs to the front door, responding to their querulous enquiries about when the library would reopen with, "You'll just have to see, won't you?"

He took a sizeable key out of the pouch hanging from his belt, and we were free. Since I was no longer in my beaked medical outfit, nobody screamed when they saw me, which was refreshing.

"What should I say when I introduce myself?" I asked. "*Vengo da Edimburgo* or *vegno da Edimburgo*? Italian or Venetian?"

"Librarian!" His tone was unexpectedly sharp. "You will not introduce yourself, nor will you be introduced. It is the Academy of the Unknowns. Nobody knows who anybody else is."

"Really?" I said.

"No, of course not really," he said as we made our way across St Mark's Square. "We only have 140,000 inhabitants in the city, and since the academy members ignore anyone who isn't an intellectual, it's easy to work out who's who."

I was going to ask if he would tell me who they were, but he seemed so keen on keeping up the pretence of their being unknown that I decided not to.

"Did the dolphin tell you about its distinguished ancestor?" he asked, quite clearly changing the subject.

Miss Blaine had warned me never to assume. But Librarian Zen was under no similar constraint, and I was really very touched that he just assumed I had been able to communicate with the dolphin. I was also very glad he didn't know how long it had taken me to learn the language, which I'm sure was just because of my anxiety about being pursued by the quarantine guards. Under other circumstances, it would have been the matter of a moment. Dolphin turned out to be a language with quite a simple, unsophisticated syntax.

"No, we were too busy escaping to have such a relaxed conversation," I said. "Who's its distinguished ancestor?"

"I'm not sure how many greats there were in front of 'grandfather'," said the librarian. "I lost count of the number of clicks."

It was comforting to know that not even Librarian Zen was completely fluent in Dolphin.

"But he's very famous in our Venetian republic because he had his portrait painted," he continued.

"With Arion on his back? Looking like a banana?" I asked.

"Looking nothing like a banana," said Zen, a touch tetchily. "He posed alongside an anchor."

I gasped. "Not – not for Aldus Manutius? The genius who pioneered italics?"

The librarian gave me an approving smile. "The very same. Aldus wanted a logo for his publishing house, but couldn't decide

61

what to have. He was so preoccupied by the matter that he didn't look where he was going, and walked straight into a canal. He was rescued by a passing dolphin, a creature of such grace and nobility that he realised at once that this was exactly the emblem he wanted for the Aldine Press. To begin with, he suggested an upright image of the dolphin, but the cetacean propelled itself through the water so quickly that the artist's illustration was too blurry. They tried again with the dolphin lying down, but Aldus said..." the librarian gave a heavy sigh, "...that it looked too much like a banana."

I bit my lip in order to prevent myself saying, "Told you so."

"And then the dolphin suggested that it might lean against an anchor, which Aldus realised was the perfect solution."

From what I remembered of the logo, the dolphin wasn't so much leaning as doing a pretty good impersonation of a pole dancer. I wondered whether my dolphin's ancestor was in fact a gender-fluid forebear.

"You'll enjoy the Academy of the Unknowns," Zen said, to head off any further discussion of dolphins and bananas. "It specialises in sophisticated and erudite debate that you, as a librarian, are perfectly qualified to engage in."

And also as a former pupil of the Marcia Blaine School for Girls, where I gained the finest education in the world, I thought.

"We discuss topics such as ethics and aesthetics, religion, literature and the other creative arts."

It definitely sounded my sort of place.

"We currently have a particular interest in music, notably opera," he went on.

"I attracted the dolphin with the beauty of my singing," I murmured modestly. "If you would like me to give a small recital, I'd be very happy to oblige."

"Splendid," enthused the librarian. "I look forward to it. Ah, here we are."

He pushed open a door and I could hear a babble of voices. I could hardly contain my excitement at the prospect of meeting

Venice's leading intellectuals. There were long-sleeved cassocks in a fetching deep violet colour hanging from coat hooks, and Librarian Zen took down a couple for us to put on, accessorised with two beret-like caps. I followed him into a room where a dozen or so gentlemen were sitting on heavy, carved wooden chairs. They were all wearing plain cassocks, nothing like the fancy lace-decorated outfits and the knee breeches worn by the populace outside. I realised this was to avoid any distinguishing marks that would reveal their true identities. And it also meant that nothing would detract from the quality of their scholarly discussions. Quivering with excitement, I got close enough to hear what they were saying.

"And I've found a marvellous little place that does a lovely ristretto," one intellectual was saying.

"I've no idea how you drink that stuff," another intellectual said. "I'd be up all night. Give me a cappuccino any time."

"You can't have a cappuccino any time," said a third intellectual. "It's a breakfast drink. It would be unthinkable to have one after 11am."

"How dreadfully conventional," drawled a fourth intellectual. "I hoped we were all free spirits here, iconoclastic, irreverent."

"I'm as heterodox as the next man," retorted the third intellectual. "But some things, like the sun going round the earth and not drinking cappuccino after 11am, are immutable laws of nature."

Venice, I remembered, was a key supplier of coffee at this point, and opened the first coffee house in Europe in 1645. But I was very disappointed by the level of discussion, which I felt fell far short of being intellectual.

I cleared my throat. "I think you'll find Galileo supported Copernican heliocentrism, observing that the earth actually goes round the sun."

This would provoke a proper intellectual argument. Poor old Galileo had recently died after years under house arrest because of his scientific views, which had been condemned as heretical by the Roman Inquisition. If these intellectuals really were iconoclastic, irreverent and heterodox, this was precisely the sort of issue they should be debating.

They all turned and looked at me. Under other circumstances, I would have expected them to ask who I was and where I came from, but of course that was completely inappropriate in the Academy of Unknowns.

"I think *you'll* find," said the first intellectual, "that Galileo came from the Duchy of Florence."

And with that, they all turned back to continue their conversation.

"So," said an intellectual who hadn't yet spoken, "where exactly is this place that does a lovely ristretto?"

"Not far," said the ristretto fan. "Just by the Campo Santa Maria Formosa."

I tried to make allowances. I could imagine a situation where I might comment that so-and-so was from Glasgow, and then of course there would be no more to be said. But the academicians were scarcely showing themselves to be golden-mouthed orators if they preferred discussing coffee to scientific theories.

"By the way," the intellectual went on, "what about these sightings of the gondola of doom?"

There was an excited outburst from the others.

"I saw it on the way here," said the second intellectual, shuddering. "It really gave me a turn, looming out of the mist like that. I couldn't take my eyes off it. I just stood there, watching, until it disappeared."

"Horrible, the way it just creeps up on you when you're least expecting it," said the first intellectual. "One thing's for sure, I'm going nowhere near a Cornetto gondola ever again."

"Let me stop you right there," I said. "I'm afraid you're guilty of a misunderstanding."

He stiffened. "Let me stop *you* right there," he retorted. "Members of this august academy misunderstand nothing. Our understanding is beyond dispute."

I thought it ill-behoved him to try to take the scholarly high ground, when a first-year Blainer would have run rings round him in a debate. But I was a visitor, and I had to be circumspect.

"The fault is not yours," I said with a reassuring smile. "You're the victim of a misguided marketing strategy, based on the famous phrase 'See Naples and die'."

He frowned. "Why would anybody want to see Naples? You'd have to go south for that."

"And why would you want to see Naples if that meant you died?" said another. "You'd make sure you gave the place a wide berth."

They definitely didn't have the sophistication of a twenty-first-century audience. Advertisers in this era must be having a hard time of it.

"You have to start from the premise that these words are not intended to be taken literally," I said.

The third intellectual frowned. "But literally is the only way to take words."

Now it was my turn to shudder. This was exactly what I feared when it came to *The Prime of Miss Jean Brodie*. If I couldn't trust intellectuals to understand the concept of fiction, what hope was there for the general public?

"No it's not," I said sharply, only slightly cheered by the thought that I was actually stimulating debate rather than leaving them to waffle about coffee houses. "Words can be used playfully. misleadingly or contradictorily. You can't simply take them at face value. And that's precisely what has gone wrong here. Cornetto Gondolas have embarked on an advertising campaign to boost their customer base, but the clumsy wording has put people off instead."

"It's certainly put me off," said the fourth intellectual. "I've taken my last Cornetto gondola. I'm too young to die."

I closed my eyes tight and focused for a few seconds. Then I returned to the fray. "You're not following what I said, and I've actually been very clear. The slogan is not intended to suggest that if you take a Cornetto gondola, you'll die."

"It's nothing to do with the slogan," said the third intellectual. "It's a matter of fact. If you take a Cornetto gondola, you die."

"No you don't," I said.

"Yes you do," he said.

This level of debate wasn't going to win any prizes. "Define your terms," I said.

He thought for a moment, then said, "If you take a Cornetto gondola, you get the plague and you die."

There was an outbreak of nodding from the others.

"A moment ago you told me that the only way to take words is literally, but now you're just making things up," I said severely. "That's an example of being contradictory."

"No he's not, he's being literal," said the first intellectual. "Everyone who's died of the plague had just been on a Cornetto gondola."

"What do you mean?" I asked.

"I mean what I say," he said.

I found myself beginning to feel very like Alice at the Mad Hatter's tea party. This was the worst debate I'd ever been involved in. Out of the corner of my eye, I saw the fourth intellectual sidle up to Librarian Zen, and I distinctly heard him mutter, "No offence, but your guest isn't very bright."

The librarian said loudly, "One of the most interesting discussions we've had recently has been on that fascinating musical development, opera. I wonder whether anyone would care to advance the topic?"

I immediately realised that this was his way of paving the way for me to sing for the company. That would impress them. Definitely not a Neapolitan folksong, though. I was weighing up the respective merits of a Monteverdi madrigal or a Scottish ballad when the intellectual I'd tried to support over the cappuccino drinking said timidly, "I've actually had an idea for an operetta."

"Wonderful," said Zen. "Do tell us about it."

I felt he could have told the cappuccino drinker to wait his turn until after my performance, but the man was touchingly keen to reveal his project.

"It's about gondoliers," he ventured.

"Not Cornetto ones, I hope," came a voice from the back, which provoked some silly giggling.

"It's about gondoliers," he repeated. "I've called them Marco and Giuseppe. There's a back story featuring Don Alhambra del Bolero, the Grand Inquisitor of Spain, who takes the infant son and heir of the King of Barataria to Venice to be brought up by a gondolier who has a son of the same age. But the gondolier drinks too much—"

"Too much what? Cappuccino after 11am?" came another voice from the back, provoking more silly giggling.

"The gondolier drinks too much prosecco," the cappuccino drinker clarified. "And he becomes confused about which child is which—"

"Hang on," I interrupted. "This is the plot of *The Gondoliers*."

"I know," he said. "That's what I'm telling you about, the plot of my operetta about gondoliers."

"Not very bright at all," I heard the fourth intellectual mutter to Librarian Zen.

There was no point in my mentioning Gilbert and Sullivan, since nobody would have heard of them, but I was shocked by the implications of what I'd just heard. It sounded very much as though the Victorian partnership was guilty of plagiarism, nicking a story that had been created by a Venetian intellectual a couple of centuries earlier. The partnership broke up shortly after the operetta was produced, with Gilbert forbidding Richard D'Oyly Carte to perform his librettos again. He actually said to Sullivan: "In point of fact, after the withdrawal of *The Gondoliers*, our united work will be heard in public no more."

All of the reports of the row claim it was about money, but what if that wasn't true? Perhaps my mission to set the record straight on the plague also included setting the record straight on light opera. If nothing else, there might be information of interest to EDGAS, the Edinburgh Gilbert & Sullivan Society.

And then I realised this was nothing but a superfluous diversion. This was now my third day in Venice and, as yet, I had no sensible information to report on the plague. Instead, I had been enjoying dolphin rides and relaxing with so-called intellectuals. I really had to get a move on.

Odd, though, that it was Gilbert, the librettist, who had cut up rough, rather than Sullivan, the composer. Was it Sullivan who had told Gilbert what to write, and then when Gilbert discovered it wasn't an original idea, he decided they could no longer work together?

"Your operetta," I said to the cappuccino drinker, "does it go anything like this?" At least now I had an opportunity to burst into song.

> We're called gondolieri,
> But that's a vagary,
> It's quite honorary
> The trade that we ply.

The cappuccino drinker looked quite animated. "No, but I like that a lot. It's very catchy." He closed his eyes and hummed the tune I had sung as though fixing it in his memory.

I had done a wrong thing. I should have kept my mouth shut. Now I had given him the gondolier tune, he would write it, leaving it to be nicked by Sullivan in the future. Without my intervention, those notes wouldn't now have existed in that order. Had I been a crew member of the starship *Enterprise*, I would have been court-martialled for breaching the Prime Directive. I wondered whether Miss Blaine had a similar stricture, that nothing should interfere with the natural development of another civilisation, and there should be no introduction of advanced knowledge before that civilisation is ready for it.

And then I thought that surely any civilisation deserving of the word should be open to receiving advanced knowledge at any point. And if Sir Arthur Sullivan was a plagiarist, that was on him, not me. I can't be held responsible for the behaviour of unprincipled middle-aged composers.

I was about to sing "Take A Pair of Sparkling Eyes" as further inspiration for the cappuccino drinker when the third intellectual said, "The theme of your opera, gondoliers, strikes me as rather jejune."

There were audible gasps from the others. I thought they were shocked by the rudeness of the comment, and then I realised these were actually gasps of excitement. The academicians moved to form a square round the offensive intellectual and the cappuccino drinker as though they were in a boxing ring. The cappuccino drinker stood stock still, awkwardly facing his aggressor.

"Forgive me, Academician, but I don't think you yet have enough information to allow you to form that opinion," remonstrated Librarian Zen, who, like me, wasn't part of the group surrounding the pair. "The theme of gondoliers is merely a starting point. It tells you nothing about what the composer, the librettist, the artist will make of it."

"I've got all the information I need," drawled the offensive intellectual. "I know the person whose theme it is, and his only claim to fame is that he wears a funny hat."

The gasp this time came from the cappuccino drinker. "I'm not wearing a funny hat," he protested, breathing hard.

"Maybe not right now," said the offensive intellectual. "But once you get home, you'll pop it on right away, won't you?"

The cappuccino drinker didn't reply, but just stood there in the middle of the square that had formed, sweat beginning to break out on his brow.

"Academician!" Librarian Zen addressed the offensive intellectual. "May I remind you that we are all completely unknown to one another, and thus you can have no idea whether any of us do or do not wear a funny hat at home."

"Just a guess on my part about the hat," said the offensive intellectual. "But going purely on the basis of our earlier conversation, if someone is so unsophisticated and naïve as to drink cappuccino after 11am, it stands to reason that anything they produce will be jejune."

"Academician!" Librarian Zen remonstrated again, but whatever he planned to say after that was lost as the cappuccino drinker slumped to the ground and lay still. There were groans of disappointment all around as the others realised the prospect of a fight had disappeared.

The intellectual closest to him gave a sudden cry of shock.

"He's dead!"

"Nonsense," said the offensive intellectual uneasily. "He's just fainted."

"He has not just fainted," said the shocked intellectual. "He is no more. Had he a perch, he would have fallen off it."

A glance told me that the cappuccino drinker had gone into cardiac arrest, his face bluish due to lack of circulation. But all was not yet lost.

"Let me through," I said. "I can treat him."

"But he's dead," said the shocked intellectual. "Nothing can be done."

"I can do something," I said. "That is, if you get out of the way."

"Are you a necromancer?" he whispered.

"Call yourselves intellectuals?" I said, and they all nodded vigorously.

"The question was intended ironically," I explained. "How many of you believe in necromancy?"

A few tentative hands went up, then more, until about two-thirds were admitting to it. I was relieved to see Librarian Zen wasn't one of them.

"Necromancy isn't real," I said. "Cardiopulmonary resuscitation is. This man is in cardiac arrest, which means that his heart has stopped beating and is no longer pumping blood round the body. CPR mimics the action of the heart to keep the blood flowing. Every second is vital, so, I ask again, please will you stand back and let me perform the necessary procedure?"

The academicians turned to look at the person who had brought me, Librarian Zen.

He nodded. "Trust him, he's a doctor," he said.

They let me through, and I knelt down beside the motionless cappuccino drinker. I put the heel of my right hand on his breastbone, my left hand on top of my right hand, and pushed downwards with my whole body weight before releasing the compression. Not only was I saving a life, but this was a perfect opportunity for more singing, since the ideal rhythm for CPR, 100 to 120 compressions a minute, is the Bee Gees' "Stayin' Alive".

"Uh, uh, uh, uh," I sang, timing my hand movements to match the words.

This caused some consternation behind me.

"What's that unearthly sound?" I heard someone say.

"He's chanting a chant, a magic spell," said someone else.

"I thought he said he wasn't a necromancer?"

"He would, wouldn't he?"

I had no time to take issue with this, since I had to keep up the compressions if there was to be a chance of saving the cappuccino drinker. Despite their reservations, the academicians crowded anxiously round me to watch, occasionally shooting reproachful looks at the offensive intellectual. When they had thought there was going to be a verbal tussle, they were all for it and, I suspected, were backing the offensive intellectual to win. But as rational beings, if a little short on debating skills, they had no truck with any form of physical violence, and clearly knew who to blame for the cappuccino drinker's collapse.

The offensive intellectual was the most anxious of all, hopping from foot to foot, since presumably his anonymity applied only within the academy's premises. He was potentially facing a charge of culpable homicide if the patient expired, which they all thought he had done already.

But I was confident that my CPR skills would succeed. The patient was relatively young, and had seemed fine apart from his diffidence. This was just a blip. As I sang another chorus of

"Stayin' Alive", the academicians unconsciously swaying along in time, the patient's eyelids fluttered open, and he took in a great gulp of air. A second later, there was a huge exhalation of relief from the rest of the company.

"Where am I?" the patient faltered.

"On the floor," I said and then, in case further clarification was needed, "at a meeting of the Academy of the Unknowns."

He clamped his eyes shut as though the light was too strong for them. "Ah yes," he murmured. "My operetta was said to have a jejune theme."

The offensive intellectual cleared his throat loudly. "Not at all. Or rather, I think I must have got the wrong word. My French isn't really up to scratch."

There was a disapproving tutting from the others. Language skills were probably a prerequisite for membership.

"Actually," the offensive intellectual continued with a careless wave of the hand, "I'm not entirely sure what jejune means."

"It means tedious, superficial, uninteresting," I supplied helpfully.

"Goodness! That's definitely the wrong word. No, what I meant to say was that your operetta sounded full of joie de vivre. I always get those two mixed up."

"You said his only claim to fame was that he had a funny hat," another academician said accusingly.

"Did I?" The pretending-not-to-be-offensive intellectual sounded astonished. "Again, I've obviously got it terribly wrong. I couldn't possibly know whether our distinguished colleague has a funny hat, but the point I was attempting to make was, that if he did have such a thing, it would be funny in the sense of lifting the spirits of all who saw it."

"And," said yet another academician, "you had a go at him for drinking cappuccino after 11am."

"Cappuccino," said the patient weakly. "That would be nice."

There was a chorus of agreement. "It would, wouldn't it?" "It sounds exactly what you need – what we all need, in fact." "Where

72

was that coffee house we were talking about earlier? Let's go right now and have a cappuccino."

The offensive intellectual, now very obviously shunned by the rest of them, bit his lip, a sulky expression on his face. With any luck, they would revoke his membership.

The patient, who was recovering fast, wanted to get up on hearing the unexpected enthusiasm for cappuccino. Librarian Zen came over to help me lift him to a standing position, and as he did so, said quietly to the patient, "You may not be aware of it, but our visitor has just saved your life."

The patient looked at me with interest. "I'm very grateful to you. May I ask who you are?"

Librarian Zen pursed his lips. Apparently this was a club with rules that were unbreakable even following a near-death experience.

"Let's just say I'm someone who's happy to help," I said. "And I'm happier to say, because you were treated so quickly, you'll make a full recovery. Take it easy with the cappuccinos, though. If you drink more than six cups a day, you increase the risk of cardiac arrest by over twenty-two per cent. Have you had any already today?"

"Five," he muttered sheepishly.

I clapped him on the back. "Then you're fine to have another one. Off you go and enjoy yourself."

"You're not coming too?" asked Librarian Zen.

"I'm more of a tea drinker," I said. "And I really need to get on with my mission."

"I understand," he said, handing over a key to me. "You need to go to the library to change. I'm sure your clothes will have dried out by now. You'll probably have gone by the time I get there, so don't let any readers in. They try to eat fried sardines if they're unsupervised. Just drop the key behind one of the pillars at the front."

"Thanks," I said. "And thank you for letting me get on with the CPR by telling the academicians to trust me."

He dropped his voice so that he couldn't be overheard. "I know I said, 'Trust him, he's a doctor', but of course what I meant was, 'Trust her, she's a librarian.'"

Thankfully, when I got to the library, the readers had got tired of waiting and gone home. I went to unlock the imposing front door. I noticed scratches all round the lock, fresh scratches, recently made. But I had no idea how recently. When I had come to the library before, the door was open, and when Librarian Zen locked the door as we left for the Academy of the Unknowns, he was between me and the keyhole. It was entirely possible that at some point, he had had a wee prosecco too many, and had made the scratches as he tried unsuccessfully to insert the key. This was disappointing behaviour from a librarian, but it wasn't my library, so I tried not to be judgemental.

I climbed the stairs up to the reading room and the cubicle where my PPE was drying out, and I had a sudden extraordinary sense of foreboding. Something was wrong, badly wrong. I had no idea what. I tried to get a clearer sense by focusing on possible areas of concern: Morningside Library, the school, Miss Blaine, Librarian Zen. None of these specifically led to an increase in my unease, and yet my unease was increasing. Something was wrong in the Marciana Library. I went quickly to the cubicle to change into my doctor's outfit, which was slightly damp around the hem, but otherwise fine, and then stood, trying to absorb more information.

I felt drawn to the reading room, drawn and simultaneously repelled, as though I was being led to something I didn't want to find. Reluctantly, I walked over the marble floors, my feeling of discomfort intensifying with every step.

I found myself in front of the cupboard, the intricately carved wooden cabinet in which Librarian Zen kept the italicised octavos. I was positively tingling with agitation. I didn't understand. I had never had a similar feeling of distress in front of my own cupboard, even though it contained innumerable editions of that defamatory book about my beloved school. And I hadn't felt like this when the librarian had shown me the cupboard earlier. What book could he possibly have put inside the cupboard to create such a terrifying atmosphere? I hesitated, but I knew I had to do something. The library was becoming more polluted by the second.

The big key for the front door had a smaller key attached to it, which must be the one for the cupboard. But this keyhole too had fresh scratches round it, scoring the wooden frame. My unease increased. This didn't look like carelessness on the librarian's part. This looked like the handiwork of someone else entirely. What dreadful thing had they done? For a moment, I seriously contemplated turning tail and letting Librarian Zen deal with it. But I knew that if he was in Morningside Library and felt something so badly amiss, he would take immediate action. I would be letting him down if I left now.

Steeling myself, I approached the cupboard with the key. It took all my courage to put the key in the keyhole and turn it. Swallowing hard, I opened the cupboard door.

I could never have imagined such horror. I've seen some dreadful things on my missions. But never anything like this. Never hideous, pitiless mutilation.

SIX

I stumbled back to the doctors' residence, scarcely aware of the screams from passers-by when they spotted my beaked mask. That was because, inside my mask, I wanted to scream myself. They were worrying about something that might never happen, but I had seen real horror, right in front of me. I always try to give people the benefit of the doubt, but there was no doubt in this case. This was sheer wickedness. An hour before, I couldn't have conceived of such barbarity; now I was clutching the evidence under my goatskin overcoat.

I had wondered how I could possibly break the news to Librarian Zen that such a terrible crime had been committed, with the dreadful evidence discarded in his own institution. And then it came to me that to conceal the tragedy from him was not only the simplest thing to do but also the kindest. I would bear the weight, literally and metaphorically, by myself.

I reached the street entrance of the residence and silently made my way to my bedroom, where I changed out of my PPE and then carefully concealed the poor mutilated thing under my bed. Some people would find my actions absurd or even repellent since there was nothing that could be done for it, but I felt the remains should be with someone who cared. I sent a brief and uncharacteristically forceful message across the ether to Miss Blaine, that I made no apology for this diversion. In all conscience, hideous sight though it was, I couldn't have left it in the cupboard. I felt the touch of a light soothing breeze: Miss Blaine understood my decision.

I felt sickened by what I had seen, but it was a long time since I had eaten, and I had to keep my strength up for my mission. I went to join the doctors, who were sitting maskless round the dinner table, plates of food and glasses of prosecco in front of them. They gaped at me.

"You're supposed to be in quarantine," Dr Rosemary stuttered.

Since the dreadful discovery in the library, I had completely forgotten about my incarceration on the plague island, and the helpful dolphin who had facilitated my escape.

"No, it's all right, I'm exempt," I bluffed, helping myself to pasta in an anchovy sauce, and sitting down beside them. "It was all an administrative mix-up. I'm afraid that doctor on the island really isn't on top of things. He's new, only been there a month. I believe..." I lowered my voice, "...that he trained at the University of Naples."

"Naples!" exclaimed Dr Oregano in disgust.

"See Naples and die because all the medics there are completely useless," said Dr Parsley.

"Just as well you're exempt," said Dr Marjoram gloomily. "If you'd just escaped from the island, you'd be facing execution."

"I can't believe they arrested you in the first place," said Dr Rosemary.

You didn't exactly help, I thought, but didn't say. They were so obsessed with this ludicrous hierarchy of medical schools. It was an advantage to me when it came to the University of Naples, a frustration when it came to the University of Edinburgh.

"We should lodge an official complaint," Dr Rosemary went on.

I definitely didn't want to be drawn to the plague island's attention, especially not if it might lead to my being executed.

"Don't worry about it," I said hastily. "We've all got enough to do without that. How's the research into the efficacy of the different herbs in your beaks?"

"They all seem to be plague-proof," said Dr Parsley. "As you can see, none of us is dead."

"Yet," added Dr Marjoram gloomily.

"Apart from you, Dr Distance-Learning, I'm actually the only one who's had anything to do with the plague victims," said Dr

Rosemary, sounding slightly annoyed.

"How's it going with the bodies?" I asked.

"Still piling up," said Dr Oregano, which made Dr Parsley snigger. "I must admit I'm glad to see you back, Dr Distance-Learning. You're needed for the heavy lifting into the funeral gondola."

That was awkward. I definitely didn't want to go anywhere near the plague island again. "Actually, I think we should leave that for a while," I said. "Four days should do it."

Four days, after which I would be safely back in Morningside Library, having successfully completed my mission.

"Why is that?" demanded Dr Parsley.

"Because they were saying on the island that they've got a bit of a backlog with burying the bodies, and they asked us to hold off for a while until they'd caught up."

Dr Rosemary said suspiciously, "I didn't hear them say that."

"It was while you were helping the guards apprehend the traveller from an antique land," I told him. "I had a bit of a chat then with the island staff."

He looked inclined to argue, so I thought it best to distract him.

"I overheard an interesting conversation on my way here," I said. "Someone was saying that everyone who's died of the plague has just been on a Cornetto gondola."

"That's absurd!" Dr Rosemary burst out. "A lie! Impossible!"

My bid to distract him was remarkably effective. It was an unexpectedly strong reaction. And it sounded as though it was going to be extremely helpful to my mission, accurately recording the history of the plague.

"Yes, I thought it was a bit of a sweeping statement," I said. "I take it your evidence is to the contrary."

Dr Oregano was looking at him closely. "You've been gathering evidence, Doctor? I'd be interested to hear it."

"So would I," said Dr Parsley.

"Evidence," sighed Dr Marjoram. "What evidence do we need, other than that they're dead?"

"We need evidence of where it's coming from and how it's spreading in order to take defensive action," I explained. "And if it's true that there's a link between the plague and the Cornetto gondolas, then we need to stop people going anywhere near those gondolas."

Dr Parsley nodded sagely. "A prudent strategy. We should inform the doge."

"Don't be ridiculous!" cried Dr Rosemary. "This has nothing to do with Cornetto gondolas!"

"Your evidence, Doctor?" repeated Dr Oregano. "Where are the victims coming from?"

Dr Rosemary's jaw jutted. He almost looked like a sulky teenager in front of the head teacher. "I don't know," he muttered. "People just throw them into the hallway. But it's preposterous to suggest that there's some link with gondolas."

"Just Cornetto gondolas," Dr Parsley reminded him. "If you ask me, what's preposterous is your refusal to accept that it's a possibility. If you have no evidence to the contrary, how can you refute it?"

Dr Rosemary stood up abruptly, sending his chair clattering on the tiled floor. "I'm not listening to any more of this nonsense," he declared, storming out of the room.

Dr Oregano and Dr Parsley exchanged glances.

"I think that tells us all we need to know about the quality of training at the University of Bologna," said Dr Oregano.

"Exactly," said Dr Parsley. "I'm glad I chose to go to Perugia. Shall I draft a message to the doge, advising him to confiscate all of the Cornetto gondolas on the grounds of public safety?"

Dr Oregano lifted his filigree glass goblet, which had undoubtedly been made on the neighbouring island of Murano. He took a long, thoughtful swig of prosecco before saying, "Not yet. The doge has been very good to us, providing the money for us to fight this terrible disease. If it turned out we were mistaken about the gondolas, he wouldn't be happy."

"And when the doge isn't happy, the people who made him

unhappy end up even less happy," said Dr Marjoram gloomily. "We'd never work again."

I haven't seen much evidence of you working so far, I thought to myself.

"What we need," said Dr Oregano, "is that which our young colleague has signally failed to supply."

"Sense?" asked Dr Parsley.

"Evidence," said Dr Oregano. "We require information on where these bodies are coming from."

"That would indeed seem a wise approach," said Dr Parsley.

"Sorry," I said, "the doge has been paying you to be plague doctors, and it's taken you how long to come up with this brilliant idea of trying to find out where the plague's coming from? Quite apart from anything else, I suggested that very thing five minutes ago."

"How dare you talk to us like that?" snapped Dr Parsley. "You're not even a proper doctor."

"Hush," said Dr Oregano. "Dr Distance-Learning has his uses. And since he insists this is his idea, who better to gather the information we require?" He turned to me. "You will take up your station in the hallway, and when a body is delivered, you will enquire where it was found and under what circumstances."

I was about to take issue with this peremptory order when it struck me that this was exactly the data I needed to accomplish my mission. But I didn't want them to think they could order me around as they pleased.

"Fortunately, I'm not work-shy like the rest of you," I said. "But I've had a trying time, being unlawfully detained on the plague island until the idiot from Naples realised his mistake." I thought this would demonstrate that there were others below me in the food chain. "I'm off to get a good night's sleep, and I'll begin this new project in the morning."

Before they could argue, I stood up and headed for my bedroom. In fact, I was ready to start work right away. My plan was to hold myself in readiness, preparing to spring into action the minute I heard anyone at the front door.

But the moment I got into my room, I felt a sudden tingling, my autonomic system reminding me of the poor mutilated thing under my bed. I got down on the floor and tenderly retrieved it from its hiding place. I sat cradling it on my lap, looking down at the lacerated pages. It must have been a beautiful book before it was so viciously sliced in two across its middle. It had been bound in exquisite red silk, which was now frayed beyond rescue, its long scarlet threads trailing dolefully. The slashed pages weren't printed, but covered in traditional Chinese calligraphy. My Mandarin is quite good, but I couldn't bring myself to try to read such a hideously incomplete volume, with only the top half of each page available. I gently stroked the cover. Attacking an innocent book – what sort of a person could do such a thing?

I suddenly heard a faint noise in the corridor outside, just as I had on my first night. Quiet footsteps, deliberately quiet. I hastily concealed the poor half-book under the bed again, and carefully opened my door. A figure was disappearing into the reception room. Even more quietly, I followed.

The figure silently crossed to the loggia and headed downstairs. I followed briskly. They could no longer see me, and my footfall would be inaudible. I peeked over the low parapet. The figure, wearing a beaked mask, reappeared on the edge of the canal, and approached a gondola that was waiting outside our building. I could see, but not hear, the gondolier greet the figure, and I leaned further over the parapet, hoping that my super-acute hearing would pick up something of the conversation.

And then I felt myself plummeting. Something – someone – had shoved me from behind, and I had toppled over the parapet. I was assailed by a number of simultaneous thoughts. The first was that I must have twisted slightly in a bid to stop myself falling, since I had spotted that my assailant had a beak. My second was berating myself for failing to notice someone creeping up on me. My third was that the person I was following and the person following me were both doctors. My fourth was, which ones? My fifth was the worry that I was about to be splattered all over Venetian paving stones. My sixth was wondering whether my Morningside Library colleagues would miss me when I never returned after lunch. My seventh was wondering how cross Miss Blaine would be about my failure to complete the mission. My eighth was to admire once more the ability I've always had to think a large number of thoughts in a tiny space of time.

These thoughts all disappeared a moment later as I found myself plunging into water. This led to a whole new series of thoughts. How fortunate it was that the loggia extended far enough out from the building to prevent my being splattered all over the Venetian paving stones. How fortunate it was that I had just missed being impaled on the gondola's iron prow-head. How fortunate that this was one of Venice's deeper canals. How fortunate it was that I wasn't wearing DMs, which would have dragged me down to the bottom of the deep canal, where I might very well have drowned before I managed to unlace them. How cold the water was. How unattractive I found the idea of wild swimming.

I corkscrewed my way back to the surface where, spluttering and choking, I made it to the Venetian paving stones and managed to haul myself on to dry land. I sat there, shivering, and saw that two things were notable by their absence. The gondola was heading off at speed. And the doctor who had been talking to the gondolier had disappeared completely.

"Dr Distance-Learning!"

The call from Dr Oregano came from above me, and when I looked up, I saw my four colleagues standing on the loggia, waving at me. None of them had a beak. But all of them were wearing their long goatskin overcoats.

"What happened?" called Dr Parsley.

"Are you all right?" called Dr Rosemary.

"It's a wonder you're not drowned," called Dr Marjoram.

Dripping, I made my way back up the steps, where Dr Oregano was waiting with a length of thin cotton. He displayed it as though it were a Dior original.

"You won't know what this is," he said. "It's called a towel. I got it on a trip to the Ottoman Empire. It absorbs water and you can dry yourself with it."

He looked so proud of his holiday souvenir that I forbore to mention that I had several much more effective-looking towels at home.

"Remarkable," I said. "What will they think of next? I could also do with a change of clothes."

"Not a problem," said Dr Marjoram gloomily. "We've got lots of spare outfits in the rooms ready for all the doctors who never came. I'll get a set for you."

I was feeling pretty chilly after my soaking, and what I really wanted was a wee cup of tea. I didn't realise I'd spoken the wish aloud until Dr Oregano said, "Tea? The woman who does has gone off for the night, but I'm sure our young colleague here could make some."

"How dare you!" flared Dr Rosemary. "Lumbering me with domestic duties just because I'm…" He suddenly faltered, and I waited for him to say, "…from the University of Bologna." Instead, he concluded lamely, "…so young."

"The tea, Doctor," said Dr Oregano curtly, and the young man went off without further protest. Medicine is a very hierarchical profession. Dr Oregano had no doubt had to make the tea often enough when he was a junior doctor, and wasn't going to make life any easier for the next generation.

By the time I had towelled myself down, changed into dry clothes, and rejoined the doctors, the tea had been brewed.

"Any chance of some milk?" I asked, and Dr Oregano gave me a disbelieving stare.

"Dr Distance-Learning, do you know nothing about the basics of medicine? Milk so late in the day plays havoc with the digestive system."

That explained the criticism of drinking cappuccinos after 11am. I accepted the milkless tea.

"You still haven't explained what you were doing in the

canal," said Dr Marjoram.

I looked round at them all. I had been pushed from behind. By someone who had been in the house. Someone with a beak. A reasonable conclusion was that one of these four doctors had just tried to murder me. But which one? And why? Dr Oregano was very scathing about my coming from Edinburgh, but surely that wasn't a reason to kill me? Especially not given my expertise with the heavy lifting. And he had just appointed me plague statistician. I couldn't say any of them was my new best friend, but I thought I got on reasonably well with them all.

There was nothing to be gleaned from the way they were dressed. They were all wearing their overcoats, but these obviously doubled as dressing gowns, and it would be natural for them to put them on when coming out on to the open loggia. My attacker could simply have stashed his mask somewhere – as could the doctor I had seen approaching the gondola. What was that all about?

I gave them an innocent smile. "I was admiring the view from the parapet, and I overbalanced."

One of them knew that wasn't true. But they were all looking at me with a mixture of concern and contempt. It would take quite an effort to topple off the parapet. They possibly thought I'd been surreptitiously knocking back the prosecco.

"My own stupidity, really," I said, and nobody contradicted me. My smile got even more innocent. "I was so impressed that you came to look for me so quickly. I'm very grateful to whichever of you raised the alarm."

"I didn't hear an alarm," said Dr Marjoram. "I just heard a loud splash, as though something very heavy had fallen in the water, so I came out to look. I was the last to get there."

"I think you were there first," said Dr Parsley to Dr Oregano. "You must have very quick reflexes."

"I do," said Dr Oregano. "And my bedroom is next door to the reception room. But I wasn't first. Our young friend must have even quicker reflexes."

Dr Rosemary went pink. "I had trouble sleeping. I came to see if any of the pasta in anchovy sauce was left."

"Anchovy sauce would scarcely help you sleep," said Dr Oregano caustically.

"Yes, of course, silly of me. But it meant I was very close to the loggia when I heard the splash."

"The loud splash," said Dr Marjoram.

"Very loud," agreed Dr Parsley.

I felt there was no need to dwell on the loudness. But I was extremely interested in Dr Rosemary's response. His unease was palpable, though there was scarcely anything reprehensible about having a spell of insomnia. And he was giving a bit too much detail about his proximity to the loggia, the sort of detail one would give when one was making the whole thing up. I was surprised to find that Dr Rosemary was the one who had attacked me. His feebleness at carrying bodies suggested he would have been incapable of upending me, but I suppose I was already leaning over the parapet, giving him a degree of momentum.

I beamed at him guilelessly. "I hope you can get to sleep now. Thank you for the tea. That was exactly what I needed."

He muttered something without making eye contact, the sure sign of a would-be murderer.

"You'd better get to sleep soon as well," Dr Oregano said to me. "You've got a big day tomorrow."

I assumed he was talking about my new job of logging where the bodies were coming from. I went to my bedroom, lugged the wooden chest across the room to block the door and stop anyone trying to murder me during the night, and slept well despite having had quite a quantity of anchovy sauce.

The next morning underlined the danger of assuming.

"You seem to have some rudimentary understanding of our craft," Dr Oregano said. "And you're proving quite useful at the more basic tasks. I think it's time you had a little practical training."

"Such as the Heimlich manoeuvre? Oh, I forgot. I can do that, but you can't," I thought but didn't say.

"I've decided that our young colleague will teach you dissection," he went on.

I was horror-stricken. We did do some dissection in biology at school, but it was an ox eye, and the ox wasn't actually there at the time.

"Impossible," I demurred, trying not to let my revulsion show in my face. Real would-be doctors would expect to be taught a bit of dissection. "I'm just starting my new job of logging where the plague victims come from. I need to get comfortable with that first, so can we leave the dissection for another three or four days?" By which time I would be safely back in Edinburgh.

"Nonsense," said Dr Oregano. "No time like the present. You'll get trained in the room on the ground floor, and you can easily pop out if people turn up with more bodies."

This didn't fit in with my plans at all. Quite apart from not wanting to witness a dissection at any time, I had decided that I needed to sneak out to visit Librarian Zen. When I found the horror that was the sliced book, I hadn't waited to show it to him. I had no idea how long he would be, and I was so distraught that I couldn't face any delay. All I wanted to do was get the poor book away from the place where it had been locked up. I also wondered whether I should spare the librarian the trauma of finding out about the book, and keep the whole terrible episode to myself. But on reflection, I realised he must be told. If something so appalling happened in Morningside Library, I would want to be fully informed. But now Dr Oregano was putting my visit to the Marciana Library at risk.

"I'm really no good at multi-tasking," I said. "I mean, it's not like I'm a woman."

"Women can multi-task because what they do is of no importance," said Dr Oregano sententiously.

I was seriously tempted to give him a smack, but contented myself with saying, "What about the woman who does? Is cooking your meals of no importance?"

"Good point," said Dr Rosemary unexpectedly, and I was heartened to think that there have always been supportive men around. And then I remembered that Dr Rosemary had tried to murder me. That was a very good reason not to be alone in a room with him, especially if he had surgical instruments to hand.

"And I'm sure your young colleague has better things to do than to try to train me," I said. "I'm very ham-fisted."

"That's the importance of training," said Dr Rosemary with alarming enthusiasm. "It teaches you to do the things you're not naturally good at, until you find you are. I'm more than happy to pass on the expertise I've got. And otherwise, we'll just be sitting downstairs waiting for more bodies, so it will help to pass the time."

And might help me to pass away, I thought.

"That's settled, then," said Dr Oregano. "Off you go. Got your surgical instruments?"

Dr Rosemary patted his coat. "Always. I carry them with me."

"In my room," I muttered.

"Then go and fetch them," said Dr Oregano, shooing me off.

I contemplated clambering out of the window to escape, but my room was like the loggia; it protruded over the narrow street, and I would just fall into the canal again. The others would be alerted by what they kept insisting on describing as a "very loud splash". And it would take me away from my mission to document the truth about the plague.

I squawked at a sudden pain in my big toe, as though someone had trodden on it very hard. It was particularly sore given that I was wearing light leather sandals rather than my customary DMs. This normally indicated displeasure on the part of Miss Blaine. I wondered what I had done wrong, and then it came to me. There was no need to avoid the training; all I had to do was be careful. The real danger was when somebody was trying to murder you and you didn't know. Here, forewarned was forearmed, and I would even have my own set of surgical instruments to retaliate with.

"Sorry, Miss Blaine," I whispered. "I wasn't thinking."

It may have been my imagination that I heard a whisper in return: *Indeed you were not, girl.*

I opened the box of instruments to have a proper look. All of them could inflict serious damage, even though they were intended for therapeutic purposes. There was a thing that looked like a car's starting handle, which would be used for trepanning, drilling into the skull. A hacksaw for amputations. A pair of pliers for extracting teeth. A bladed device that wouldn't have looked out of place on Edward Scissorhands – I recognised it as a bistoury, a surgical knife with finger rings like a knuckle duster.

Reassured that I could now parry any murderous assault, I picked up the box and headed out to join Dr Rosemary. We put on our beaked masks and went downstairs. Just as we reached the ground floor, the front door opened. A couple of burly Venetians dumped a body wrapped in a sheet in the hallway and prepared to leave.

"Just a minute," I said. "Is this a plague victim?"

"Yes," said the burlier of the two. "That's why we brought him here. Orders of the doge. He doesn't like infected bodies cluttering up the streets."

"So he was found in the street?" I asked.

"Obviously," said the less burly of the two.

"Why obviously?" I asked.

"Why all the questions?" said the burlier one.

"I'm afraid there are loads more," I said. "We're having to fill in forms now, the usual tick-box exercise. Orders of the doge."

I wondered whether Dr Rosemary would contradict me, but he kept quiet.

"The doge!" said the burlier one disgustedly. "Sits there in his fancy palace, nothing to do except give orders. He only comes out once a year for his marriage ceremony."

The less burly one sniggered. "Can't wait to see it. What a prat. Remember last year? Pathetic."

I was going to pursue this – I had never heard of a polygamous doge, and this sounded like another fascinating fact for me to bring back to the twenty-first century. But my mission's focus was the plague, and I had enough questions to ask about that.

"So could we go back to what you said earlier? Why did you say the body was obviously found in the street?" I asked.

"Because they always are," said the less burly one.

"It's quite a lengthy form," I said. "Could you expand a little on why you said, 'They always are'?"

The burly one sighed. "Honestly, that doge. Anyway, every single plague victim has been discovered in the street, shortly after disembarking from a gondola."

"And not just any old gondola," the less burly one put in. "A Cornetto gondola. You be sure to write that on the forms. The sooner the doge closes that company down, the better. Although customers are voting with their feet, and avoiding Cornetto gondolas anyway."

"Avoiding them like the plague," said the burly one and they both laughed.

The next person to speak was Dr Rosemary. "Have you collected every plague victim yourselves?"

"Of course not," said the burly one.

"Then how can you possibly say that every single plague victim has been discovered in the street shortly after disembarking from a gondola, specifically a Cornetto gondola?"

"Because that's what everyone's saying," said the less burly one.

"I see," said Dr Rosemary. "Because that's what everyone's saying. What you mean is that there are unsubstantiated rumours going around that it would be utterly remiss to take as fact."

"Don't forget the gondola of doom," said the less burly one. "It warns you that you'll die if you go on a Cornetto gondola."

"That's actually a marketing strategy that's gone terribly wrong," I said. "It shows why all this form-filling is valuable. We record facts, not idle gossip."

"Idle gossip, is it?" said the burly one. "Well, record this. The deceased, who died of the plague, was discovered in the street, shortly after disembarking from a gondola. A Cornetto gondola."

And with that, they both walked out, slamming the front door behind them.

"The information you're collating, it's not really for the doge, is it?" said Dr Rosemary in a small voice.

"No, purely in-house," I said. "I just mentioned the doge to make it sound more official."

"Because he's an idiot. He really could close down the – the Cornetto business," Dr Rosemary said.

"And so he should if a causal link is proved between their gondolas and the plague," I said. "That's not idiotic, that's sensible."

"But how can it be proved?" Dr Rosemary's voice was getting higher with agitation. "How can you get the plague from a Cornetto gondola?"

He made it sound like a rhetorical question, but I felt it could be answered, nonetheless. I tried to remember what I knew about the spread of the plague. "Fleas," I said. "Rats with fleas."

"There is not a single rat on those gondolas! They're immaculate," he insisted.

I couldn't help feeling enthused. A plague that had nothing to do with flea-ridden rats, and seemed to incubate in minutes rather than days. I was going to be bringing a whole new perspective to the pandemic, overturning the beliefs of centuries.

"Right," said Dr Rosemary with a sigh, going over to the newly arrived body, "let's get on with your dissection training. Take the other end."

I was much less enthused about this. As usual, I ended up doing most of the donkey work, manoeuvring the body into the storeroom and on to a table. Also, I didn't want to see a dissection, I definitely didn't want to participate in one, and I had serious reservations about being alone in a room with someone who wanted to murder me.

I opened my box of medical instruments and took out the surgical knife/knuckle duster, which I reckoned was the most versatile object for defending myself.

"Actually, you don't need that," said Dr Rosemary. "For the first lesson, it's best that you just watch and learn."

He needn't think I was going to fall for that, leaving myself unprotected.

"Thanks, but I'll hang on it, even if I don't use it," I said. "It makes me feel more involved."

He unwrapped the body, and beyond the aniseed in my beak, and the rosemary in my companion's, I could smell a new scent, something unexpected and yet oddly familiar. I just couldn't place it, and it also left me with a strange feeling that there was something I had missed earlier. The feeling was particularly strange, since I'm not used to missing things. The most likely explanation was that I hadn't missed anything at all, and this was simply the result of having to concentrate on not getting murdered.

"Okay," said Dr Rosemary, retrieving his saw and knife. "Let's get started. First of all, do you see these red and black spots? Definitely a plague victim. Absolutely textbook. Now I'll just open him up…"

I suddenly thought of a Rembrandt painting, *The Anatomy Lesson of Dr Nicolaes Tulp*, commissioned just a few years earlier. Dr Tulp is explaining the musculature of the arm to a group of medics, with the visual aid of a real, skinned arm belonging to the cadaver in front of him. Some of the medics are carefully looking elsewhere. If even professionals didn't fancy seeing a dissection, I felt I could be excused.

The great thing about my beak was that the glass portholes made things a bit indistinct, so even if I inadvertently caught sight of what Dr Rosemary was up to, it wouldn't be too bad. But I made sure I was looking elsewhere, simply keeping his hands in my peripheral vision in case he suddenly attacked me.

"There. Do you see?" Dr Rosemary kept saying, and I kept replying, "Ah" and "Mm" and "How interesting" while keeping a tight grip on my own surgical knife and preparing to strike back at any moment.

But Dr Rosemary was completely intent on his task. There was a ghastly sloshing sound and he said, "Good heavens!"

He sounded so astonished that I didn't think "Ah" or "Mm" were suitable, so I went for "How interesting."

"Interesting?" he said. "It's extraordinary."

"Totally extraordinary," I echoed.

"This casts a different light on it," he said.

"It certainly does," I said.

"But I don't understand what's happened," he said.

"It's a mystery all right," I said.

He was standing there in apparent bewilderment, his hands at his sides, one still holding the surgical blade. A perfect way of luring me forward to see what he was talking about, at which point he could easily fillet me. I wasn't born yesterday, so I turned my whole attention to that knife.

"No!" I normally keep my reactions under firm control, but I couldn't suppress the exclamation.

There was a gleam of something red on the knife, between the blade and the haft. Not blood. Threads. Red silk threads. Dr Rosemary was holding the knife that had been used to mutilate the book.

SEVEN

I was practically running in my anxiety to get to the Marciana Library, ignoring the screams of the passers-by.

I sprinted up the stairs two at a time and burst into the reading room.

"Librarian Macaroni Mona Lisa Glissando! Whatever's the matter?" said Librarian Zen. And then his expression became grim. "Oh," he said. "Oh dear."

Like any librarian worth their salt, he could sense bibliological vandalism from afar.

He clapped his hands loudly and called, "The reading room is now closed. Please make your way to the exit."

Startled, the readers looked up, saw me in my mask, screamed, and scuttled away.

Now that we were alone, I took my mask off, my expression as grim as my colleague's.

"Tell me," he said.

Words were inadequate. I produced the poor half-book. And then I prepared to deal with Librarian Zen fainting. The chains on the books were too short to allow me to bring them over to him to elevate his legs, but given his slight build, I calculated that I could bring him over to the books.

I should have known that Librarian Zen was made of sterner stuff. He swayed slightly, but he stayed standing. He held out his hand, and I gave him the book.

With a choking sob, he caressed the ragged pages.

"It was here, wasn't it?" he said. "In the library? I sensed something very bad had happened when I got back from the coffee house yesterday."

"I couldn't just leave it. I had to take it with me so that I could look after it," I said.

"Of course," he said with immediate understanding.

"It was in with the octavos," I said. "After we left for the Academy meeting, somebody broke into the library, then broke into the cupboard and dumped it there."

His expression darkened. "Who would do such a terrible thing?"

I knew exactly who had done it. And given the horror of the crime, I had been very careful not to assume.

"These are your surgical instruments?" I had asked Dr Rosemary, trying to keep my voice steady.

"Of course," he said.

It was important to carry out due diligence, and not to assume.

"They belong to you? You didn't just pick them up?" I indicated my own knife. "I found this in the chest in my room, as part of my plague kit."

"Yes, we prepared everything in case doctors joined us who didn't have the requisite equipment. But so far, you're the only one. I acquired my set as a graduate of the University of Bologna. I never go anywhere without them."

"Do you let people borrow them?"

"Of course not." He sounded appalled. "They might get damaged. They never leave my side."

I knew then that I had to get to the library as quickly as possible. Without another word, I ran upstairs to my room, where I grabbed the poor book and secreted it in the pocket of my goatskin overcoat.

When I emerged, Dr Rosemary was already in the reception room, saying to the others, "He just rushed away."

"Not able to cope with a little dissection," grumbled Dr Oregano. "And I thought we could make a doctor of him. Still, what can you expect from someone from Edinburgh?"

I let the gratuitous slur go. "Air," I mumbled. "I need fresh air." I didn't care if they thought I was a wuss; I needed to see the librarian.

And now that I was here with the librarian, I was able to say, "I know exactly who did it."

"They admitted it?"

"Of course not," I said. "How could anyone admit to being so depraved? But I have irrefutable evidence."

"And do you know why they would carry out such a horrifying attack?" said Librarian Zen, sinking on to a bench. "Surely there must be some mental disturbance?"

"Not at all," I said. "The guilty party is a professional man with his marbles intact." The librarian flinched slightly at this latest example of the informality of my expressions. "The only possible conclusion is that he acted out of sheer wickedness. I might add that he also tried to murder me."

"There must be a serious mental disturbance if the man attacks not only books but also librarians," he insisted.

"The perpetrator doesn't know I'm a librarian. He thinks I'm a doctor because of the way I'm dressed," I said. "He also thinks I'm a man."

"Still more proof that other professions cannot compare with librarianship," said my colleague, and yet again we shared a companionable moment of agreement.

"Librarian Zen," I said in a bid to cheer him up, "bad things happen in any library. We once had a borrower who returned a book and we found she'd been using a kipper as a bookmark."

"That's very bad," said the librarian. "But not the same level at all. Mutilating a book is evil."

"You're right," I said. "So what should we do about the perpetrator?"

Librarian Zen shook his head. "I'm afraid I'm incapable of advising you. I find this crime so abhorrent that I can't think in terms of justice but only of retribution. I would have the villain suffer the same fate as the book."

"Bit harsh," I said. "But I certainly think he should be given a substantial fine and banned from keeping books for the rest of his life."

"You're more compassionate than I," said Librarian Zen, giving the half-book a consoling pat. "What a tragedy that we don't have the other half. I'm certain our printworkers would have the requisite skill to reconstruct it. This cover, such exquisite silk. Obviously brought here by a traveller from an antique land." He opened it, and gasped. "What incomparable Chinese calligraphy! My Mandarin is a little rusty, but—"

"Don't," I said warningly. "Close it before you upset yourself further."

I saw his eyes skim down the page and then with a heavy groan, he shut the book. "You're right, Librarian Macaroni Mona Lisa Glissando. It's heart-breaking to get halfway down a column and then be able to read no further."

For a moment, I considered asking him what he had managed to read, but that would only cause him more distress, since he didn't know what came next.

"What should we do with the poor thing?" I asked.

He gave me as much of a smile as he could muster. "I think you should keep it. You obviously care about it very much, and I think it will be happiest with you."

"I'd be honoured," I said. There was one thing that was necessary if I was going to look after it properly. I retrieved my pouch and looked inside.

Thank you, Miss Blaine, I said silently as I took out what lay inside. Lightweight and multi-purpose. *This is perfect*. I thought again of the compostable bags I had used on the previous mission. And now here was one still lying unused in my pouch, ready for this moment.

The librarian looked at it with keen interest. "What is that?"

"The important thing is what it's not," I said. "It's not plastic. It's recyclable, compostable and waterproof. I'm going to put the book in it, and it's going to be completely safe, even if I fall in the canal again. Not that I'm planning to, but you can never be too careful."

"Indeed not," he agreed. "And what a marvellous innovation. I didn't recognise all the words you used, apart from the one about it being proof against water. If I didn't know that necromancy was non-existent, I would suspect you of it. I presume this is an invention of your Edinburgh printers, Chepman and Myllar?"

"A bit later than them," I said truthfully, carefully wrapping the book and stashing it in the pocket of my goatskin coat.

"We must keep a lookout for the other half," he said.

"We must," I said. We both knew it was a completely forlorn hope, but it was important to try to raise one another's spirits. "I have to get on with my mission now, but I hope I'll see you before I leave."

"I do hope so," he said. "Please come in and say goodbye if you have time."

"I certainly will," I promised. I had no idea then that the next time I saw him would be in a very different place from the library.

I put my mask back on and went out into St Mark's Square, men and women scattering like pigeons when they saw me. I paused to admire the two vast pink and grey granite columns. Atop the first, a sculpture of St Theodore doing battle with a crocodile, which is probably where they got the idea for the James Bond stunt. I hoped this meant that St Theodore had got rid of the crocodiles in the surrounding waters, just as St Patrick had got rid of snakes in Ireland, since I didn't like the idea of innocent dolphins getting nipped. Atop the second column, the lion of St Mark. There's an automatic kinship between Scots and Venetians because of lions. Venice has a winged lion as its emblem, gold on a red background, and we have a lion rampant, red on a gold background, both looking nobly ferocious. I wondered whether there was a family of lions who made themselves available for heraldic portraiture. It would be nice if the two were cousins.

Beyond the two great columns was a beautifully ornate building, a superb example of Venetian Gothic. Not only an architectural delight, but also an etymological one. In Italian, it's the Palazzo Ducale. However, we're not talking about a duke, we're talking about the Venetian version, a doge. But should it be the Doge's Palace, singular, or the Doges' Palace, plural?

I was pondering this as I admired the delicate arcades and the open-work tracery, when suddenly I had an idea. I certainly didn't agree with Librarian Zen's view that Dr Rosemary should be sliced in half. But equally, I thought it was quite wrong that the doctor should be able to get away with his appalling crime.

I went through the palace courtyard and into the nearest set of offices, which were open to the general public. I braced myself for the usual screaming, but the scribes were consummate jobsworths, most of them not even looking up from their desks at the intrusion, and those who did simply staring at me sullenly.

"Hello," I said to the nearest one. "Could I trouble you for a quill and paper?"

"Help yourself," he grunted, shoving the items across his desk to me.

"And maybe some ink?" I suggested.

He gave an exaggerated sigh. "What did your last slave die of?"

"Bubonic plague," I said.

"Everyone's a comedian," he said to no one in particular, leaving me to reach over for the ink.

I wrote my note, returned the writing materials and thanked him politely, which elicited another grunt. And then I went to find the letterbox, a particular kind of letterbox, called "the lion's mouth". Seeing the lion column in St Mark's Square and then the Doge's Palace had been a happy coincidence, giving me the brainwave for how to deal with Dr Rosemary. I looked around. And there, on the wall, was an image carved into the stone, with a hole where the mouth was. A handy place where you could post anonymous denunciations. Strictly speaking, it was for denouncing people who were guilty of fraud or tax evasion, and I wasn't sure that my letter would be taken seriously if I mentioned that the crime was a bisected book. It might be a matter of deep anguish to myself and Librarian Zen, but civilians don't have the same sensibilities. So I was both trenchant and vague in my unsigned letter: "There's a plague doctor with rosemary in his beak who is a thoroughly bad lot."

I gave the book in my pocket a reassuring pat. I hoped it wouldn't be too disappointed not to be avenged explicitly. I was certainly cheered by the prospect that my denunciation would lead to Dr Rosemary getting a firm reprimand and being warned about his behaviour in future.

My duty done, I felt quite limp. Discovering the truth about the poor book was traumatic, and I was sure Miss Blaine would allow me some downtime. I remembered the academicians talking about a good coffee shop near the Campo Santa Maria Formosa. It took me a while to get there as when I asked passers-by for directions, most of them screamed and ran away, but enough of them pointed it out in a bid to make me go away. The café was in the shadow of a large curvaceous church.

Fortunately, the waiter put profits over plague, and was quite happy to let me come and sit down, despite my plague gear, especially as he could charge more than if I stood.

It was before 11am, so I ordered a cappuccino, but I couldn't help adding, "What I'd really like is a tea."

"Then have a tea," said the waiter.

"You have tea?" I asked in amazement.

"You don't get out much, do you?" he said. "We've had tea here for decades."

I kept forgetting that Venice was a major international trading centre, which is why the traveller from an antique land had turned up with a business opportunity for the doge. And I was so happy to get a tea that I ordered a pastry to go with it.

But when they arrived, something was missing.

"Could I have some milk to go with the tea?" I asked.

"You really don't get out much, do you?" he said. "You don't put milk in tea."

Reluctantly, I decided that when in Venice, do as you're told, and the waiter left with a disdainful sniff.

Black tea drunk and relatively refreshed, I went back to the doctors' residence, ready to continue my meticulous logging of plague victims. I hoped Dr Rosemary had taken careful notes in my absence.

But as I approached the house, I became aware of a stramash. I could see two guards, their uniforms showing them to be the doge's men rather than the quarantine island ones I had escaped from earlier. Dr Oregano, arms akimbo, was shouting at them, "If you can't tell the difference between rosemary and oregano, you're in the wrong job!"

Dr Parsley was loudly highlighting the difference between rosemary and parsley. And Dr Marjoram was saying gloomily, "No, it's not thyme, it's marjoram. Everybody makes that mistake. Marjoram's woody, citrusy and floral. Thyme's much more leathery. But it's quite a subtle distinction for the average person."

In the doorway, the two guards were wrestling with Dr Rosemary, who was putting up quite a fight, scratching, spitting, kicking and pulling their hair.

"Decorum, Doctor!" snapped Dr Oregano. "Brawling in the street like a hooligan. I'm glad to say you'd never catch a graduate of the University of Padua behaving like that."

Eventually Dr Rosemary was subdued and dragged off down the street. I felt a little guilty, until I reminded myself of the atrocity he had committed.

"What's happening?" I asked the other doctors, since I thought that was probably what someone who knew nothing about the situation would ask.

"He's been denounced for smelling of rosemary and being a thoroughly bad lot," said Dr Oregano. "We might have known, with him being a graduate of Bologna. He's being taken off to prison before sentence is pronounced by the doge."

"Oh dear," I said. "I suppose that will mean a substantial fine."

"Is that what happens in Edinburgh?" sneered Dr Parsley. "We do things properly here. He'll be executed."

"Executed?" I felt quite faint. "Seriously?"

"Oh yes," said Dr Marjoram gloomily. "It's always serious when someone gets executed."

"But there has to be a trial," I said. "You can't go around just executing people."

"Of course you can, if they've been denounced. Why would you bother with the extra time and expense of a trial?" said Dr Oregano.

"Back in a minute," I said, and raced after the guards.

"Stop!" I yelled as I got closer. "Stop!"

They stopped, looked at me with suspicion and sniffed deeply.

"It's okay," said one of the guards to the other. "Not rosemary. Aniseed."

"That would have been awful if we'd found two plague doctors smelling of rosemary," said the other. "We wouldn't have known which one was a thoroughly bad lot."

"We'd have had to arrest them both," said the first one.

"We'd have had to call in reinforcements," said the second. "We can scarcely manage this one."

Dr Rosemary was thrashing around wildly like a fish out of water, and the pair of them increased their grip on him.

"I demand that you let this man go immediately," I said in my most commanding prefect's voice. "He is a distinguished doctor, a graduate of one of our oldest seats of learning."

"That's as may be," said the first guard. "But now he's under arrest. He's been denunciated."

"Denounced," I corrected. "And it's all a mistake."

"No mistake," said the second one. "We were sent out to arrest a plague doctor with rosemary in his beak. It was a bit tricky to start with because all these herbs smell a bit samey, but fortunately the other medics put us right. Clever of you to use aniseed, means you don't get confused with anyone else."

"Dr Distance-Learning!" gulped Dr Rosemary. "Help me! I don't want to die!"

"I'm trying," I said. "Look, gentlemen…" politeness costs nothing, and can often help to smooth the way, "…it would be wise to let the doctor go. I can assure you that he's done nothing wrong." I crossed my fingers behind my back.

"Yes he has," said the first guard. "There's been a den…" he hesitated, and looked at me. I looked back, giving nothing away, "…a denouncement," he concluded.

I felt there was no point in continuing the vocabulary lesson. "I know," I said. "And the denouncement was incorrect."

"How do you know?" demanded the guard.

"Because I was the one who made it," I said.

Dr Rosemary gasped.

The guard looked at me suspiciously. "You're just saying that."

"I know," I said. "I just said it."

"Prove that you're the person who made it, then," said the second guard. "Ha! You can't! It was anonymous."

"I can prove it easily," I said. "What I wrote was as follows – 'There's a plague doctor with rosemary in his beak who is a thoroughly bad lot.'"

"You overheard us saying all that. You're just repeating it," scoffed the first guard.

I was getting exasperated by their stupidity. "I'm telling you that I'm the person who wrote it. But it was a mistake. I withdraw it unreservedly. So will you let my colleague go?"

"Nice try," sneered the second guard. "Now get lost and stop obstructing us in the execution of our duty."

I gave an involuntary shudder at the word "execution".

They turned and began dragging Dr Rosemary away. He twisted round to make eye contact with me and blurted out, "Thank you, Dr Distance-Learning, thank you from the bottom of my heart for trying to save me. I really appreciate that you were prepared to perjure yourself on my behalf."

That made me feel really bad. I walked back slowly to the doctors' residence, wondering what to do. I was pretty sure that Miss Blaine would take a dim view of my getting someone executed, even given the severe provocation of the mutilated book.

The doctors were all tucking into dried fish pâté with yellow polenta when I got in. I couldn't face eating anything, especially not dried fish pâté with yellow polenta. I didn't even bother taking my mask off, but just flopped down on the nearest chair.

"You've been a long time," grumbled Dr Oregano. "Here we are, one doctor down, and we can't cope with your emotional instability as well, rushing off because you can't deal with a dissection, and then wasting time running after our young colleague. What was that all about, anyway?"

I couldn't believe the callousness, especially not from someone who was supposed to be in a caring profession.

"I was trying to rescue your young colleague," I told him. "None of the rest of you seemed to be doing anything, apart from insisting that you didn't have rosemary in your beaks."

Dr Parsley was indignant. "The fellows tried to lay hands on me. I couldn't believe the incompetence. Identifying the scent of various herbs should surely be part of their basic training. I'm thinking of making an official complaint."

It was like heaping burning coals on my head. Dr Rosemary's impending fate was thanks to my making an official complaint.

"We can't just leave him to die," I said. "Especially not because some lunatic libelled him in an anonymous note."

"Nothing to do with us," said Dr Marjoram. "We didn't write it."

I was feeling worse by the minute.

"Surely there's something we can do?" I said. "Go to the doge and give a character reference?"

"Impossible," said Dr Oregano. "We barely know one another. These gentlemen only joined me a few days ago after the first plague victim was found, so we're hardly in a position to go around giving character references for one another."

"We know he graduated from the University of Bologna," I said desperately. "Surely that's worth something?"

"Not a lot," said Dr Oregano. "It's scarcely Padua."

"And do we really know he graduated from there?" put in Dr Parsley. "That's what he told us, but we all rushed here to deal with a medical emergency – it's not as though he went through a proper interview process."

"He was very good at dissecting," I said.

Dr Oregano curled his lip. "And how could you possibly judge that, Dr Distance-Learning?"

I was going to tell him I'd once helped to dissect an ox eye, but I realised he wouldn't be terribly impressed.

"If you're not going to do anything, I will," I said. "I'll go to the doge myself and plead for clemency."

They all burst out laughing.

"What?" I demanded.

"You're foreign," said Doctor Marjoram. "Foreigners can't see the doge unless they're accompanied."

This was news to me, but I supposed that he wasn't just making it up.

"Then accompany me," I urged.

He shrugged. "The accusations might be true. I can't risk damaging my professional standing by getting involved."

Just then came the sound of the front door being shoved open. More bodies; that was all I needed. Yes, getting information about their provenance was my mission, but right now my priority was saving Dr Rosemary. I defied Miss Blaine to tread on my toe, and it remained unharmed.

But instead of the thud of a body hitting the tiled floor, I heard two sets of heavy footsteps thudding up the stairs. The two guards I had last seen dragging away Dr Rosemary burst into the reception room.

They stopped and sniffed deeply.

"There," said the first, pointing at me. "That's him. Aniseed beak."

Suddenly there were two swords pointing at me. Under other circumstances, I might have admired the weaponry – these were traditional Venetian schiavonas with double-edged blades and beautifully designed iron basket-hilts. But right now I had to move. I have excellent martial arts skills, but unarmed combat against two serious bits of sharpened metalwork can be an uncertain business. I jumped to my feet and backed away from them, calculating how far I was from the loggia and a leap to freedom in the canal.

But before I had taken more than a couple of steps, I found myself grabbed from behind. By three pairs of hands.

"Let me go," I protested.

"No. You must have done something," said Dr Oregano. "What's he done?"

"Broken quarantine," said the first guard, approaching with his sword at the ready. "When we got to the prison with the last one, we were telling everyone about the daft doctor ponging of aniseed who was trying to pretend he'd written the anonymous denouncement. 'Aniseed,' says Pierantonio, he's the one in charge of all the paperwork, 'there's a death warrant out for a fellow ponging of aniseed who escaped from the quarantine island.' So this is us back for him."

Dr Oregano's fingers were digging into my shoulders. "You said," he hissed, "that it was an administrative mix-up."

I was about to use the well-known phrase "economical with the truth", when I remembered it was based on Edmund Burke's discussion of truth as a virtue, and decided that perhaps I hadn't been very virtuous.

"I was simply revising the official version," I told Dr Oregano. "Now, would you please let me go so that I can get out of here?"

"Breaking quarantine's a very serious offence," said Dr Parsley.

"You may not have noticed, but we're actually fighting an outbreak of the plague here," said Dr Marjoram gloomily. "It doesn't help to have people breaking quarantine."

No point in telling them I'd had my vaccinations. The guards were approaching with their swords. It was time to cut and run, especially if that meant I could avoid getting cut. I've gone through excellent training in breakaway techniques, and I took a big inward breath, preparatory to putting it into operation.

It seemed that Dr Oregano's much-vaunted training at the University of Padua had been pretty good as well. He noticed the inhalation, and just as I was about to disengage myself from the doctors' grip, he whacked me over the head with his ceramic dinner plate.

I was stunned, literally and metaphorically. And that was how I found myself being dragged over the Bridge of Sighs to the prison. Still dazed, I peered out of the limestone latticing of the windows as we crossed, taking in my last view of the outside world.

A cell door was opened, and I was thrown into the darkness, landing on something softer than the floor. It turned out to be Dr Rosemary.

"Dr Distance-Learning!" he exclaimed. "It is you, isn't it? I can smell the aniseed. I'm sorry to see you've ended up here too. Is it because of your brave attempt to have me freed by pretending to have written the denunciation?"

"No," I said, "I've been arrested for something else."

"Another false accusation," he said in disgust. "Since obviously someone as kind and generous as you can't be guilty of anything. I'll never forget how you tried to help me."

This was quite embarrassing. "Think nothing of it," I said, and meant it.

"Have you had a trial?" he asked.

"There hasn't been any word of that," I said. "My impression is that it's a fixed penalty."

"And what's the penalty?" he asked.

"Death," I said.

He sighed. "Same as me, then. That's probably why we've been put in together. Still, I suppose we're lucky to be in one of the fancy new state-of-the-art cells."

I personally didn't think much of the cell, which might be spacious but was also dark, damp and malodorous, with no sign of an en-suite. There was a small square grating in the wall, but daylight was fading. I hated to think what the old cells must have been like.

And then Dr Rosemary burst into tears. I was slightly taken aback, because doctors are usually in firm control of their emotions. In the dimness, I caught sight of something light-coloured. Dr

Rosemary had taken a handkerchief out of his pocket, fine white linen with a Venetian needle lace trim. He dabbed his eyes and blew his nose loudly.

"I'm not crying for myself," he snuffled. "I'm upset for the family."

For a moment I thought we might be talking about the Mafia until I remembered this was the wrong time and the wrong place.

"The family?" I asked.

"I'm a Cornetto," he confided.

"Part of the gondola company?" I asked. "But you're a doctor, not a gondolier."

"I couldn't … that is to say, I didn't really want to. The asymmetric working puts tremendous strain on the musculoskeletal system. My brother suffers terribly from attrition on the supraspinatus tendon. I've tried to give him exercises, but of course he doesn't listen to me."

He snuffled some more. "And now it's too late. I'm about to die, and he doesn't know the proper exercises, and he'll get completely lop-sided."

"Your brother, is he quite tall and gangly, with a thin moustache?" I asked.

"That's him," Dr Rosemary said.

"Then you needn't worry," I said. "I met him a couple of days ago when he was complaining about a sore shoulder, and I gave him some exercises. Not just swinging his arm, but preventative stuff, spine and hip rotation and stretching the pectoral muscle. I got the impression he'll be quite disciplined about doing them."

I could see that Dr Rosemary didn't have the build to be a gondolier, not being as tall and gangly as his brother. Despite what he had said about not wanting to be a gondolier, I guessed he had actually been rejected as unsuitable.

He leaned over and shook my hand. "Thank you, Dr Distance-Learning," he said, a catch in his voice. "That's good to know. But maybe I'm worrying unnecessarily. Maybe he won't continue as a gondolier."

"Really?" I said. "I thought that gondoliering was a vocation, with the licences passing down from father to son."

Dr Rosemary dabbed at his eyes again. "That's right. The Cornettos have been gondoliers for centuries. We have our own company – uncles, nephews, cousins. But you heard yourself the dreadful things people are saying – that if you go on a Cornetto gondola, you die of the plague."

"This seems to be a very unusual, virulent form of the plague," I said. "It's really odd how quickly it incubates. Is there anything different you've been doing with your gondolas, any change in the soft furnishings, or a new kind of paint? Your brother hasn't been visiting any antique lands, has he? It's easy to pick up bugs without realising."

"How can you ask me these things?" He sounded on the verge of tears again. "We have absolute respect for tradition, and do everything the way it's always been done."

I knew that wasn't true. The first gondolas, dating from the eleventh century, were smaller and wider, and could be any colour. But in 1562, a law was passed, predating Henry Ford, saying you could paint your gondola any colour you liked, so long as it was black. However, Dr Rosemary was so upset that I decided not to point this out.

"Don't you see," he moaned, "this is a plot against us, trying to destroy our business."

That sounded a bit paranoid.

"Who would want to do that?" I asked in a reasonable sort of tone, so that he would realise his suspicions weren't justified.

"A rival company!" he burst out. "There are too many gondolas and too few passengers."

This was extremely alarming. The rival company must be utterly Machiavellian to contaminate the Cornetto gondolas with fast-acting plague. I still didn't understand what it was and how it worked.

"Is there a gondola company called Machiavelli?" I asked.

"Certainly not," said Dr Rosemary, making his disdain clear. "The Machiavellis come from Florence. They know nothing about gondolas."

"So any idea who it might be?"

In the gloom, his proboscis moved slowly from side to side. "No idea. I suppose some people would say the Canalettos are our rivals, because they're a long-established family firm like us, but it's friendly competition, nothing more. It's a terrible thing to think that another company could try to harm us in this way, because gondoliers are brothers."

This was the first I had heard of any other gondola company. I knew the name only from the painter Canaletto, whose surname was really Canal. Maybe his nickname had come from the rival gondola company since he painted quite a lot of gondolas. He wouldn't be born for about another fifty years – did that suggest that the Canalettos had driven the Cornettos out of business by that time? But Dr Rosemary seemed to be backing off from his own theory of a plot by rivals, arguing that gondoliers were brothers. That gave me a moment of uneasiness, remembering the cappuccino drinker's idea of an opera about brother gondoliers at the Academy of the Unknowns, when I might inadvertently have given him the inspiration for Gilbert and Sullivan, in a dreadful backwards and forwards time loop.

But Dr Rosemary was still talking. "It's a terrible thing to think, but it's the only possible conclusion, that a competitor is out to ruin us. But what can we do, when we don't know who they are or how they're doing it? All we know is that nobody will take our gondolas any more. My poor brother thought he had a lucrative fare the other day from the plague island to St Mark's Square, but it got cancelled. He hasn't had a customer since."

Now I had a new reason to feel bad. I was sent on these missions in order to do good, and so far I'd managed to get someone condemned to death, lost their gondolier brother much-needed income, meddled in the history of light opera, and was going to be put to death myself before I had a chance to complete my mission. I could imagine Miss Blaine being very cross with me. In fact, I was surprised she hadn't trodden on either of my big toes. And then I wondered whether instead of being surprised, I should be alarmed. What if I was doing so badly that she had already washed her hands of me? That would be catastrophic now that I was facing execution. I had assumed – the perils of assuming! – that she would rescue me if I got as far as the scaffold, spiriting me back to Edinburgh. But if she felt she couldn't rely on me for future missions, she might not bother herself.

Miss Blaine, I transmitted through the ether, *I'm very sorry this one hasn't worked out, but I think I did pretty well on the previous ones. And I'm needed in Morningside Library to suppress copies of Mrs Spark's book.*

No reply. Perhaps she was busy and would pick it up later. There was no point in worrying about it right now. I turned my attention back to Dr Rosemary.

"I tried to do something to help," he was saying. "Do you remember when we went to the plague island and the guards arrested the traveller from an antique land?"

That, arguably, was when all my problems had started. "Do I remember?" I said heavily.

"You should do," he said. "It was when we took the bodies on the funeral gondola."

I find there can be a lot of linguistic confusion when time travelling, especially with foreigners.

"Yes, now I remember," I said even more heavily.

"The traveller said he had come with a gift for the doge, a great business opportunity. It was a book."

"Really?" I said. That was interesting. Books are always interesting. "What kind of a book?"

"I don't know," he said. That made it less interesting. "But when he started fighting with the guards, he dropped it, and I picked it up."

I remembered how Dr Rosemary had rushed forward. I had assumed he was going to give first aid to the guard who had ended up on the ground.

"If you picked it up, how come you don't know what kind of a

110

book it is?" I asked.

"Because it's in an antique language," said Dr Rosemary. "I couldn't read it. All I know is that it's a business opportunity."

I felt a sudden tingling, and brushed my hand over my pocket where the half-book nestled in its compostable bag.

"This book," I said, trying to keep my voice steady, "what does it look like?"

"Exquisite," he said. "It's covered in red silk and even though I can't read what's inside, I can see it's beautiful."

"And what," I said, my tone dangerously expressionless, "have you done with the book?"

"The really crucial thing is to keep it safe," he said. "If these rivals put the Cornettos out of business, the family will have to turn its hand to something else, and the book will be key to that. I couldn't risk our enemies finding it and capitalising on the business opportunity, whatever it is."

The tingling at my side was getting more intense. "So how exactly have you kept it safe?" I asked.

"That's the clever bit," he said. "I cut it in half."

Five little words. And not a hint of shame or embarrassment. Quite the opposite: he thought he had been clever. I found it difficult to comprehend that someone could be so degenerate. If we had been back in my own time, I would have reported him to the General Medical Council.

My mouth was dry, but I managed to croak, "Why would you do that?"

"To stop our enemies discovering the business opportunity, of course. Even if they find one of the halves, they won't be able to do anything with it." He lowered his voice confidentially and said, "I broke into the Marciana Library, and hid half of the book in a cupboard. There's no safer place for a book than a library."

I bit back the retort that libraries preferred books that were intact. But while I couldn't begin to condone what he had done, I was beginning to understand the motivation, and see that it wasn't just mindless vandalism. Dr Rosemary had been thinking of his beleaguered family, who would presumably face destitution with everyone avoiding their plague-ridden gondolas. And he had clearly seen the library as a place of sanctuary for the half-book. Librarian Zen had said if we had the other half, the skilled Venetian printers would be able to reconstruct it. And he would then be able to read the Chinese calligraphy and discover what the business opportunity was.

Very slightly less tense, I asked, "And where's the other half?"

"I threw it in the canal," he said.

"You WHAT?" I exploded. "You ignorant barbarian! I'm not surprised the others look down on you because you went to the University of Bologna if your tutors didn't make it clear that one never throws books in a canal. One never cuts books in half, if it comes to that, although I can just about appreciate that you thought you were helping your family."

"I'm sorry," he said in a small voice. "I was so desperate not to lose the business opportunity."

"Which is exactly what you've done by throwing half the book in the canal," I snapped. "Putting a book in water is the worst thing you can do to it."

"Wouldn't setting fire to it be worse?" he whispered.

"Don't bandy words with me about ways of destroying books," I warned him. "You've done a terrible thing. I can't bear to think of that poor half-book disintegrating in a cold canal. Which canal did you throw it in, anyway?"

"I can't remember," he faltered. "Somewhere between the doctors' residence and the library. When I was sure I wasn't being watched, I just chucked it in. I was desperate to make sure nobody else got it."

"And now you've made sure nobody will get it," I said. All I had been thinking about was the book, but now something else struck me. "And while we're at it, why did you try to murder me?"

"I didn't try to murder you." He sounded surprised, presumably having thought that I would never work it out.

"It was a joke, was it, shoving me over the loggia parapet?" I said. "Or are you just obsessed with throwing things into canals?"

"I have no idea what you're talking about," he said.

"Look, given that we're both about to die…" (I very much hoped I wasn't, but there was no need to tell him that.) "…shouldn't you clear your conscience and admit it? It's not as though anything worse is going to happen to you?"

"Why would I want to murder you?" he asked.

"How would I know?" I said. "That's why I'm asking you. All I know is that I was pushed, and the other doctors said you were the first on the loggia. You had some ludicrous story about not being able to sleep and looking for pasta in anchovy sauce."

"All right, I lied," he said.

"There, doesn't it feel good to admit it?" I said.

"I suppose so. Even as I mentioned the pasta in anchovy sauce, I thought it sounded implausible."

"Never mind the pasta," I said. "Why did you push me in the canal?"

"But I didn't," he said. "The only thing I lied about was the insomnia and the pasta. I went down to the canal to talk to my brother and find out whether business had picked up. He said it was even worse – he's really upset about that funeral gondola that keeps popping up out of the mist and telling people that if they take a Cornetto gondola, they'll die."

I had to accept that it was a bit of seventeenth-century trolling rather than a flawed marketing campaign by the Cornetto family. But it hadn't been an unreasonable conclusion. The world of advertising is littered with catastrophic mistakes.

"When I heard you fall in, I ran back up to the loggia so that no one knew I'd been out, and my brother rowed away as quickly as possible so that nobody saw the Cornetto gondola."

It was Dr Rosemary I had seen talking to the gondolier – I had been leaning out to try to overhear their conversation.

"Then who was the person in the mask who pushed me over the parapet?" I asked.

"That should be easy to answer," he said. "Did he smell of

oregano, parsley or marjoram?"

And that was when I realised what had been bothering me. There had been no smell of herbs from my attacker's beak. And there had been no smell of herbs that first night when I caught someone sneaking down the corridor.

"It wasn't any of them," I said. "It was someone wearing a mask with nothing in it. There must be a rogue doctor skulking in the residence."

"I don't think so," said Dr Rosemary slowly. "We would have noticed something. No food has gone missing. There are plenty of spare plague outfits lying around. Somebody's swapped his herb-filled mask for an empty one, so that he can't be identified."

"And then tried to murder me. But which one, and why?"

"Impossible to say. They're all equally useless, if you ask me. They just sit around eating and drinking and getting paid. I'm the only one who ever does any work. You've helped a bit, I suppose."

He seemed to have forgotten my key role in the heavy lifting. Apart from that, all he had done was a little light dissecting.

That made me think of something else. During the dissection, we had had a very odd conversation when he seemed to have found something unexpected, but I never had the chance to ask him more, becoming distracted by the discovery that he was the book mutilator.

"You said something was extraordinary when you were showing me how to perform a dissection," I said. "I must have blinked momentarily, because I didn't quite see what you were talking about."

"It was indeed extraordinary," he said eagerly. "But you must have seen it, I was talking about the lungs."

I couldn't admit that I had been carefully squinting to avoid seeing anything unpleasant, which most certainly included the lungs.

"Ah, yes, the lungs," I said. "Remind me what was the most extraordinary thing about them?"

"The water, of course," he said.

"Of course," I said. "Sorry, as you know I'm quite new to the dissection business, but I'm anxious to learn. Could you say a bit more about the extraordinary thing of the water?"

There was a pause before he said, "You really didn't follow that? I'm not sure that medicine is the right career for you."

I was about to say that I saw it more as a hobby than a career when I reconsidered. Medicine was Dr Rosemary's career. If someone told me they saw librarianship as a hobby, I would give them pretty short shrift.

"Perhaps you're right," I said as humbly as I could. "But I'd still be very interested to hear what you thought was extraordinary."

"I've just told you. The water in the lungs," he said.

"And that's extraordinary because?"

"Because it means the deceased didn't succumb to the plague but died from drowning."

"They died from drowning?" I repeated.

"From drowning, yes."

"Not from the plague?"

"No, not from the plague."

I wanted to be sure I'd got this absolutely right. "What you're saying is that they died from drowning and not from the plague?"

"That's exactly what I'm saying," he said.

This certainly was extraordinary. And it was going to obstruct my job of reporting on the plague.

"We need to put a notice on the door," I said. "The idea is that people bring us plague victims. It's just going to confuse things if they start bringing us all-purpose dead bodies."

This time it wasn't a silence but a very exasperated sigh. On balance, I preferred the silence.

"Dr Distance-Learning, were you paying any attention at all during the tutorial? I said, did I not, that the deceased was most definitely a plague victim because of the red and black spots, which you surely couldn't have failed to notice. I remember noting that it was a textbook case. Your memory, however, seems remarkably unreliable."

I had always thought of Dr Rosemary as young and junior, but right now he seemed to be morphing into one of the more acerbic Marcia Blaine teachers. I felt thoroughly admonished.

"I thought you were trying to murder me," I mumbled. "I was concentrating on what you were doing with that knife."

"Except, apparently, when I was carrying out the lung dissection," he said acidly. "So I can assure you that the good citizens were doing their duty by bringing us a plague victim. It just so happened that he drowned before the plague carried him off. The poor man must have fallen into a canal."

The whole thing was extremely peculiar. There was something going on that I hadn't worked out yet. As Dr Rosemary had made abundantly clear, I wasn't a medic, but everything I'd read about the plague suggested that you weren't at all well, with some quite nasty symptoms including fever, vomiting and coughing up blood. The sorts of things that would make you want to stay at home in bed rather than wandering about falling into canals. I needed to log this variant in precise detail, and discover how it was being transmitted.

It was quite frustrating being stuck here in prison under sentence of death with unanswered questions. Ideally, I would be able to escape, but the only person who ever succeeded in breaking out of this prison was Casanova. First of all, that wouldn't happen for another hundred years, and second, he scratched his way out with a sharpened metal bar. There was a grating over the window of our cell that was aesthetically pleasing, as if the metalwork was woven, but it was actually inserted into the walls as they were built – no chance of wrenching it out. I didn't have a sharpened metal bar, merely a proboscis, which would just get squashed if I tried to scratch my way out with it. But I had to applaud Casanova's unique success. This one escapee, licentious though his life had been, ended his days as a librarian, and was therefore not to be underestimated.

And then I remembered Dr Rosemary saying he always carried his surgical instruments with him. The trepanning drill. The hacksaw. The pliers. The knife/knuckle duster. We were saved. He might be a bit unhappy about them getting blunted and bent, but with both of us at work, we'd break through the metalwork in minutes.

"Quick," I said. "We can use your surgical tools to get out of here."

"But I haven't got them any more," he said. "The guards took them off me."

"Oh," I said.

Since I could no longer see a means of escape, there was only one thing to do.

"Let's face it, this has been a pretty rubbish day for both of us so far," I said to Dr Rosemary. "I think we should go and have a power nap."

"What?" he burst out. "What's the point of resting now when in next to no time we'll be going to our eternal rest?"

"Sleep is hugely beneficial," I said. "It supports the immune system, lowers your blood pressure and clears out all the detritus of the day."

Dr Rosemary's proboscis waved madly, indicating a degree of agitation. "I have no idea how you can sleep," he said.

"Like this," I said, curling up on the floor and beginning to count backwards from one thousand. I rarely get to eight hundred and this was no exception.

I awoke after what felt like only five minutes later. Dr Rosemary was slumped against the wall, and what I initially took for snoring under his mask turned out to be muffled sobbing.

I had awakened from a very soothing dream about rescuing misplaced books in Morningside Library – borrowers can be remarkably careless when they're browsing. And that made me think of Librarian Zen. It had been wonderful to meet a colleague, especially one who was so perceptive and professional and could pronounce my name. Strange to think that he was just on the other side of St Mark's Square, going tranquilly about his business, making sure that books and readers were aligned, and that nobody was eating fried sardines.

He had asked me to come in and say goodbye if I had time. When I didn't return, he would simply think I had been too busy. I was still counting on Miss Blaine to rescue me before I was actually executed, but perhaps I would have to wait until I was on the scaffold. And that could well be between the two columns, the ones featuring the lion and St Theodore and the crocodile, just outside the library. I couldn't imagine that Librarian Zen was the kind of man to attend public executions, but he might spot me as he was heading home for his tea. That would be upsetting for both of us.

I wished there was some way of contacting him. If he knew of my predicament, I felt sure he would be able to intervene in some way, possibly producing a book with an ancient by-law prohibiting the execution of librarians. I concentrated hard, almost as hard as when I tried to communicate with Miss Blaine. *Librarian Zen, I'm in prison and I'd like to get out. Any help you can give me would be very gratefully received.*

I was obviously concentrating very hard, since it was as though I could sense him close by, as though I could hear footsteps approaching.

There was the sound of a key turning in the lock, and the cell door was flung open. I blinked as light flooded in from the torches in the narrow stone corridor. Three figures stood silhouetted there, two of them the guards who had arrested me, the third quietly authoritative in his long robes. Librarian Zen, come to get me released.

"Yes, I can smell the aniseed – that's our man," he told guards before I had time to greet him. "I wish to make an anonymous denunciation. He's guilty of necromancy, for which the penalty is death."

EIGHT

The guard nearest me rested his sword on the ground and sucked in his breath loudly. "That's you in real trouble, chum. Not one but two capital offences. Certainly wouldn't want to be in your shoes."

Frankly, I wanted to be in my DMs, and back in Morningside. I was utterly flabbergasted. I expected Librarian Zen to liberate me, not denounce me But was it really my colleague, or someone impersonating him? My anxiety to be saved might have made me imagine that this was him when in fact it was someone completely different. I peered at the trio, my eyes adjusting to the brightness from the corridor. The middle figure definitely looked exactly like Librarian Zen. And sounded like him, although his tone was harsh and unfriendly, quite unlike his usual courtesy.

Perhaps it was Zen's evil twin. But no, that sort of thing happened only in fiction. It was my colleague, behaving in an entirely uncollegiate manner.

"Let's make absolutely certain," he said. "After all, it might be someone else smelling of aniseed. It would be a terrible thing to anonymously denounce an innocent man."

He signalled to the guards, and the next thing they were pulling me into the corridor and wrenching off my beaked mask. I could totally have taken them both on, but I was so dumbfounded by Librarian Zen's peculiar behaviour that I just stood there.

He briefly studied my denuded face. "Yes, I can confirm that's him. I attended a meeting at which he was present. Tragically, one of the company suddenly dropped dead."

"The plague?" ventured one of the guards, backing away.

"No, he went blue rather than black and red," said the librarian.

"Cyanosis," I said. "Because his heart had stopped beating."

"Do you hear? He admits it," said Zen. "The poor fellow's heart had stopped beating. He was lying there dead when the necromancer began chanting a magic spell, and suddenly the corpse was reanimated. It began talking and walking."

The two guards shuddered.

"It wasn't a magic spell," I said. "It was a song by a popular beat combo that gave me the correct rhythm for chest compression, thus restarting his heart."

"Thus restarting his heart," Librarian Zen repeated. "The heart that had been stopped by death. The necromancer condemns himself out of his own mouth."

"I explained it all at the time," I said. I couldn't believe that the librarian was being so obtuse when he had always seemed so open-minded. He had been the one to persuade the Unknowns to let me treat the cappuccino drinker. "It wasn't necromancy, it was cardiopulmonary resuscitation."

"Enough of your vile language of the occult," said Librarian Zen. "Guards, kindly record my anonymous denunciation."

"You're not anonymous," I objected. "You're standing right there."

"But I'm not appending my name to the denunciation, which makes it anonymous," he said.

"Nevertheless," I said bitterly, using one of the Founder's favourite words, "I know who you are." I hoped my words and tone would force him to realise just what a dreadful thing he was doing in denouncing a fellow librarian.

"And I know who you are," he said. "I was passing by when I saw you crossing the Bridge of Sighs. I recognised you by the mask and I could sense the aniseed. I realised it was my civic duty to denounce you."

His own tone stayed the same, hostile and accusing, but the words were something else. The intricate stone latticing on the windows of the bridge made it impossible to see in: the idea was to give the prisoners a last look at the outside world. If he was able to sense me at that distance, then it was a librarian thing, and how could that ever be bad?

I decided to test it. "You could have saved yourself a journey," I said. "I've already been condemned to death for breaking quarantine, so you've achieved absolutely nothing by denouncing me."

"I know all about you breaking quarantine," he said. "I found that out the moment I started making enquiries about you."

He could have denounced me at any point after our visit to the Academy of the Unknowns, but hadn't. His sudden appearance here was after he had been making enquiries about me. That was surely a positive.

"But the necromancer's got a point," complained one of the guards. "He's going to be executed anyway, and now you're getting us involved in a whole lot more bureaucracy with this anonymous denunciation. It would be better for all concerned if you just dropped the whole thing."

"You're right," said Librarian Zen. "It would be better for all concerned, including the prisoner."

"What?" said the other guard in concern. "Better for the prisoner? What do you mean?"

"I'm sure you two gentlemen know the law much better than I," said Librarian Zen respectfully. "But of course your work is so onerous with all these scoundrels around that you may have overlooked the fine detail for a second."

The guards looked at one another in alarm.

"What have we overlooked?" the first one asked.

"No idea," said the second. "But we don't want to be overlooking things. It can lead to bother. Usually for us."

Librarian Zen discreetly cleared his throat. "Perhaps I could help? This reprobate is here for the crime of breaking quarantine, and will therefore be executed. Quite right too. But necromancy is an even more serious crime. For that, he will need to be brought before the doge, who will determine what penalty he faces. And I imagine that His Serenity will decide that hanging's too good for him. He'll probably invent something involving boiling oil." He gave an apologetic laugh. "But forgive me – I realise I'm taking up your time, gentlemen, and you'll just want to get on with executing the prisoner without further delay. I'm sure His Serenity will be more than understanding about the pressures of your work when he finds he's missed the opportunity of dealing with an exponent of the dark arts."

The guards moved slightly away in order to speak confidentially, but fortunately I'm blessed with exceptional hearing.

"We need to get this exponent of the dark arts over to the doge right away," the first whispered.

"You're not kidding," the second whispered back. "Just as well the librarian chap turned up to warn us, otherwise we might have been the ones in the boiling oil."

While their attention was elsewhere, Librarian Zen gave me a conspiratorial wink. I felt thoroughly guilty for ever having doubted him. Perhaps there are rogue librarians, but I've certainly never met one.

"Right, you," said the first guard, jamming my mask back on my head, and hauling me out of the cell, while the second one waved his sword in a threatening manner, "we're taking you to see His Serenity."

"Not so fast," I said. "You can't do that. The doge can't see me. I'm foreign. *Vegno da Edimburgo*. I'm from Edinburgh."

Confounded, the guards turned to Librarian Zen.

"Don't listen to him," he said. "He's just trying to avoid the boiling-oil scenario. As a foreigner, he can't see His Serenity on his own; he has to be accompanied by a Venetian."

"That's all right, then," said the second guard, his expression clearing. "We're accompanying him."

"I'm afraid that doesn't count," said Librarian Zen. "You're staff. It has to be someone external."

"You, then," said the first guard. "You're here anyway, and I'm sure it won't take that long."

"I'd love to, but unfortunately that won't work either. I'm not allowed to do it because I'm the person who made the anonymous denunciation," said the librarian.

"But you've made it anonymously," said the second guard.

"His Serenity won't know."

"Sadly, the necromancer knows, and he won't hesitate to use that information to prevent His Serenity from dealing with him," said the librarian.

"That's very true," I said. "I won't hesitate to use that information to prevent His Serenity from dealing with me."

The two guards pondered this for a while. Then one said brightly, "We could cut his tongue out."

"Ingenious," said Librarian Zen, and I had a moment of panic before he added, "but alas, he has to be able to answer a few questions to enable His Serenity to decide whether boiling oil is the best option."

The two guards did some more pondering before one darted into the cell and pulled Dr Rosemary to his feet. "You, are you Venetian?" he demanded.

"I may have graduated from the University of Bologna, but I would hope everyone can tell I'm a true Venetian," Dr Rosemary said slightly huffily.

The guards looked at him with suspicion. "If you're a true Venetian, why didn't you go to the University of Venice?" asked the first.

"I know the answer to that—" I began, but Librarian Zen interrupted with, "Yes, yes, we all know the answer. Moving away from the comforts of home is an important part of the maturing process for young students."

"Exactly," said Dr Rosemary. "I missed La Serenissima every moment of every day, but it was character-building."

That wasn't at all what I had been going to say. I had been going to inform the guards that Venice didn't actually have a university at this point, and wouldn't for a very long time, proving that Edinburgh was a vastly superior city. On reflection, that might not have done me a lot of favours. Zen would know as well as I did about Venice's university-free status. He had interrupted me because he was trying to keep the guards onside, and my pointing out their ignorance wouldn't have helped. But it must still have gone against all of his librarianly instincts: we like to ensure that people have the facts. I felt very touched that Zen was prepared to compromise his professionalism in order to help me. I hoped I would do the same for him, but if there was a situation where someone needed to be corrected, I wasn't sure that I would be able to stop myself.

"All right," said the first guard to Dr Rosemary. "You go with the necromancer, but don't speak unless you're spoken to."

"I won't," he promised.

We set off back the way I had come, Librarian Zen leading the way, then the first guard, then Dr Rosemary, then me, and finally the second guard, whose sword was menacingly close to a number of my vital organs. We crossed the Bridge of Sighs, and the sight of the misty outdoors was one of the loveliest things I had seen, even though I couldn't see much. We followed the librarian down narrow corridors, through drab halls and up a dingy staircase. We were heading up to the state apartments but definitely not by the route distinguished visitors would take.

Eventually the librarian halted in front of a modest wooden door.

"I'll leave you here, gentlemen, so that you can explain all about the necromancy to His Serenity. Have a good day, and I hope you don't have to spend too much time boiling the oil."

"Must you go?" gabbled the first guard. "It's just that I've never had one of these necromancy cases before."

"I wouldn't dream of encroaching on your authority," said Librarian Zen. "I'm sure even if you're not very comfortable with the subject, your colleague will be more than capable of outlining the basics."

"That's just it," said the second guard, stepping forward. "I've never had one of these cases either. It shows how good we've been at stopping necromancy." He glared at me. "And why we have to stamp it out as soon as it tries to reappear."

"I have a tiny amount of expertise in this area," said Librarian Zen. "Forgive me for being so impertinent, but might you allow me to go in to see His Serenity simply to pave the way for you?"

"On you go," said the first guard.

"Pave as much as you like," said the second.

"That's very generous," said Zen. He tapped on the door, waited for a moment, then went in, closing the door behind him. The two guards shuffled close to one another, both keeping their swords pointing at me.

"Don't try any of that necromancy malarkey," the first guard warned. "We'll run you through at the first sign of it."

"Really? I could turn your swords into ploughshares just like that." I snapped my fingers and the guards jumped backwards, quivering. As I spoke it occurred to me that ploughshares, if they were what I thought they were, would still make pretty lethal weapons; but thankfully the guards seemed unwilling to argue the point.

"Don't take it out on us," protested the second. "That's not fair. We're just doing our job. Your gripe's with the lawmakers."

"That's true," said Dr Rosemary unexpectedly. "But I've had to deal with patients suffering from necromancy, and unfortunately it's a very blunt instrument. You find that more or less everyone who's upset the necromancer is affected."

"What happens to them?" asked the first guard through dry lips.

"It's too ghastly to share with civilians," said Dr Rosemary. "It's the sort of thing that doctors share horror stories about at parties."

"Is that the time?" said the first guard, nudging the second. "I think we're needed back down there to sort out the thing."

"You're right," said the second. "We daren't be late to get back down there to sort out the thing."

They were just about to move when Librarian Zen emerged, closing the door behind him.

I heard a faint groan beside me. "Another minute and we could have escaped," breathed Dr Rosemary.

"Don't worry," I murmured. "It's going to be all right."

"How?" he whispered.

"I don't know," I whispered back. "Just trust me."

"Why should I? You're not a doctor."

The guards backed further away.

"Are you doing necromancy?" asked the first.

"No, just having a private conversation," I said.

Librarian Zen turned on us. "Be quiet, prisoners," he snapped. "Nobody wants to hear from you." He bowed to the guards. "Gentlemen, I've outlined the matter to His Serenity. He commends you for your diligence and bravery in apprehending these two dangerous criminals. He'll deal with the matter from now on."

Relief etched on their faces, the guards nodded to Zen and fled.

I beamed at my colleague. This was proof, not that any was needed, that we were singing from the same hymn sheet. We had both gone for identical strategies, getting rid of the guards. While I had opted for frightening them, Zen had found a more subtle, elegant method. He had gone into an empty room, pretended he had had an audience with His Serenity, and let the guards remove themselves. He obviously knew his way round the Doge's Palace and would lead us to a handy exit where we could make our escape. We would have to abandon our beaked masks somewhere, to avoid being identified by the scent of aniseed and rosemary. I still had my plague research to carry out, and increasingly less time to do it in, but there was plenty of spare PPE in the doctors' residence. This reminded me that someone in the doctors' residence had tried to murder me. I would have to be careful. But that, of course, is something that's second nature when I'm on a mission.

Librarian Zen didn't return my smile. "I've arranged for you to have an audience with the doge," he said. "Be careful."

And with that, he opened the door again. This wasn't at all what I'd expected, but I'm nothing if not adaptable, so I went in.

The wooden door was modest, but the room beyond it was anything but. Opulent wasn't the word. It was like walking into a wedding cake. The walls and ceiling were white, carved into the most elaborate curving shapes and designs, including picture frames round what I was sure were original old masters.

It was as I stood there taking in my surroundings that I was smacked right in the face.

NINE

The blow knocked my mask askew, and I could no longer see out of the glass portholes. I was aware that something heavy was weighing down my proboscis, and then suddenly the pressure was released as it rolled off and thudded on to the floor.

"I told you to be careful," came Librarian Zen's voice near my left ear.

There was another voice in the distance, and I had the oddest feeling that I had heard it somewhere before.

"I'm most terribly sorry," it said. "I didn't realise you would come in so soon, and I was just getting in a bit more practice."

"That's okay," I said feebly. "Excuse me a minute while I adjust my mask."

"Please feel free to take it off," said the voice. I had definitely heard it before. "I imagine it gets quite hot under there."

The mask had managed to get jammed with the impact of whatever had smacked me in the face, and it took me a few attempts before I managed to yank the thing off my head.

A man stood further down the room, surveying me anxiously. He was wearing long robes topped by what looked like an ermine-trimmed cloak, and on his head was a funny hat. It was round at the front, but the back stuck up like a blancmange that had set when the wind was in the wrong direction.

I was so fascinated by the hat that it was a moment before I recognised the person under it. The cappuccino drinker, the academician I had resuscitated after he'd suffered a cardiac arrest. I had no idea what he was doing here in what Librarian Zen had indicated were the doge's apartments.

And then the librarian said, "Most Serene Prince, perhaps you remember this gentleman?"

"Indeed I do," said the cappuccino drinker with enthusiasm. "If it weren't for him – well, leaving aside the personal distress, it would have involved an expensive new round of elections. I'm most grateful to you, Doctor."

The librarian had called him "Most Serene Prince", and he himself had talked about new elections. Astonishing though it seemed, the shy cappuccino drinker must be the doge, the highest authority in the city of Venice.

Everything the doge did was surrounded by enormous pomp and ceremony, and I wasn't sure whether I should prostrate myself on the ground before him. I don't normally hold with that sort of thing, but since the dogeship was an elected position rather than one gained by an accident of birth, I would be showing respect not to the individual but to one of the world's most remarkable places.

I was just bending forward when the doge scurried up to me and grasped my hand.

"I hope you don't mind me breaking protocol like this," he said. "I know I'm not supposed to know you, since we met in the Academy of the Unknowns, but you saving my life – that really was quite special."

No longer hampered by the mask, I could see Dr Rosemary out of the corner of my eye, and he was looking well impressed.

"Not at all, Your Electedness," I said. "As I told you at the time, I was happy to help. I'm glad to see your colour's good and you're moving well. It looks to me as though you've made a full recovery. Just take it easy with all those cappuccinos."

"I will," he said with the earnestness people show to doctors when they've absolutely no intention of following instructions. I was going to challenge him, but there probably wasn't any point. It was quite possible something else would get him first – the plague, for example.

"And," he said, "just as you were happy to help me, I'm happy to help you. The librarian tells me you're in a bit of difficulty."

"I'm under sentence of death twice, if that's what you mean," I said. "First for escaping from the plague island, and second for practising necromancy. But Librarian Zen tells me that you have to decide the exact penalty for the necromancy."

"Yes," said the doge, "he told me that as well. I had no idea. I must say, we're very lucky to have a librarian around, who has all that wealth of knowledge from books that nobody else has read. He's always coming up with interesting bits of information that we've never heard of."

I switched my peripheral vision to Librarian Zen, who was staring up at the carved stucco ceiling, his lips pursed as though he was about to start whistling. I began to wonder whether he had made the whole thing up about the doge and necromancy.

"Why don't we all have a seat and discuss it?" the librarian suggested, and we settled ourselves in a cosy group.

"And who is this other gentleman?" the doge asked genially of Dr Rosemary.

"A medical friend, also under sentence of death," I said.

"Oh dear," said the doge. "Another necromancy case?"

"Much more minor," I said. "I brought him along since I'm not allowed to talk to you alone, on account of being a foreigner."

The doge was visibly startled. "A foreigner? But you speak Venetian perfectly."

"I know," I said, as modestly as I could manage. "I've had the finest education in the world."

"Alas, not in the University of Venice," he sighed. "But that day will come, and soon."

I was going to say *Not that soon*, but thought I'd better not in case I was breaking the Prime Directive again.

"And where did you receive this fine education?" the doge asked.

"The Marcia Blaine School for Gi—" I began and found Librarian Zen talking over me, saying, " —School for Gifted Students." I had told the librarian about my schooling, and while he mistakenly thought that Miss Blaine was an Ursuline nun, he correctly understood that I had gone to a girls' school, which would certainly cause confusion in the conversation with the doge.

"It sounds a fine educational establishment," said the doge. "But while I'm delighted to make the acquaintance of your medical colleague, and I'm sorry to hear that he's under sentence of death, if you had to bring a Venetian with you, why didn't you simply bring our good librarian?"

I hesitated, reluctant to say that I was facing the death penalty for necromancy because it was Librarian Zen who had denounced me.

"There's a little-known law prohibiting my profession from taking on that role," said the librarian.

"Thank goodness you knew that," said the doge.

I was becoming more convinced by the moment that Librarian Zen was just making things up.

"Why was such a law enacted?" the doge asked.

"It was one of your predecessors who insisted on it, Most Serene Prince, after meeting a foreigner accompanied by a librarian. Although the librarian was merely there as a witness, and took no part in the conversation, the doge at the time found him intellectually intimidating, and banned librarians from then on."

Even if Zen had made up the occasional fact, this story definitely had the ring of truth.

"Librarian, you're a marvel," said the doge. "To have all this information at your fingertips – I must admit that at times, I feel a little like my predecessor in your presence."

"Not enough to ban me, I hope, Your Serenity," said the librarian.

"Never," declared the doge. "I value your wisdom too much. Now, shall we continue with the matter at hand, this charge of necromancy."

Librarian Zen stood up, his robes swirling around him as though he was an advocate in the High Court. "The matter concerns you, Most Serene Prince."

"Is this you beginning your intellectually intimidating games, Librarian?" enquired the doge. "Do you mean it concerns me because I have to deal with necromancy cases, or it concerns me in the sense that I'm worried about it?"

"I mean it concerns you as the doctor is accused of using necromancy to save your life," said the librarian. "They're saying that he raised you from the dead."

The doge tugged nervously at the white linen earflaps under his funny hat. "Am *I* being accused of anything?" he asked.

"Nothing at all, Your Serenity," said the librarian soothingly. "Apart from being dead."

"Which you're not," I said, just in case the doge needed to be reassured. He seemed quite a nervous individual. "And you weren't ever dead. You simply looked a bit dead because your circulation stopped, and you weren't breathing. But thanks to my excellent education, I was able to get everything started again, and no harm was done."

"As doctors, we have to promise to do no harm," Dr Rosemary piped up. "It's part of the Hippocratic Oath."

I wondered if he was about to out me as a non-doctor who had never actually signed up to the Hippocratic Oath, but he lapsed back into silence. I really felt the pair of us had struck up a bond in prison. If I managed to get reprieved, I determined to do my best to get Dr Rosemary reprieved as well. Especially as it was me who'd got him condemned to death in the first place.

"So you're saying there was no necromancy?" asked the doge.

"Absolutely none," I said. "Just good old-fashioned doctoring. Well, good very modern doctoring. Whoever's denounced me for necromancy has done it either from misunderstanding or malevolence."

The doge tugged even harder on his earflaps. "Then we must immediately find the person who denounced you, and sentence them to death," he said.

"Unfortunately," said Librarian Zen, "it was an anonymous denunciation, so there's no means of ever finding out who made it."

131

"Utterly preposterous," said the doge. "People running around making unwarranted accusations and dragging me into it while they're at it. It shouldn't be allowed."

Librarian Zen cleared his throat. "Then don't allow it."

"Sorry?" said the doge.

"Change the law," said the librarian.

The doge tugged at his earflaps so hard that he was in danger of wrenching them off. "I don't think I want to get involved in anything like that," he said uneasily.

"It would be very popular," said Librarian Zen, giving me a significant glance.

I picked up on it straight away. "Very popular indeed," I said. "Right now, the only people who benefit are those doing the denouncing. Honest citizens go about their business under a perpetual cloud, never knowing when they might be anonymously denounced. They'd be eternally grateful to whoever dispersed that cloud."

"Can I say something?" It was Dr Rosemary again. "I'm under sentence of death because someone, we'll never know who, denounced me for being a thoroughly bad lot, and for smelling of rosemary."

I winced at hearing my words quoted back at me. I hadn't actually had any problem with him smelling of rosemary: that was simply a means of identifying him. It had all been because of the mutilated book. But while cutting books in half was definitely to be discouraged, I now recognised that Dr Rosemary wasn't the monster I had taken him for.

He got to his feet, and clamped a hand on my shoulder. I hadn't wanted him to out me as a non-doctor; I definitely didn't want him to out me as an anonymous denouncer.

"This man," he said, his voice cracking, "this man actually tried to pretend to be the person who had denounced me so that the accusation could be retracted. What does that say about our republic, that this good man was forced to consider perjuring himself in order to protect me from a coward who didn't dare confront me in person?"

Librarian Zen was nodding in agreement. I wondered whether the doge might knight me, or whatever they did to honour acts of outstanding generosity. That would be a bit embarrassing, but I wouldn't really have an option other than to accept.

However, the doge didn't seem to be entirely focused on my humanitarianism. He was gazing into the distance and said, very wistfully, "Popular, you say?"

"Very popular indeed," I repeated.

"And the person responsible for passing such a law, they would be popular too?" he asked.

"Without a doubt," said Librarian Zen.

"It would be nice to be popular," the doge murmured.

He seemed a nice bloke, if a little timid. "I'm sure you're quite popular already," I said.

He shook his head. "Oh no. Everyone thinks I'm an idiot."

"I don't think you're an idiot," said Librarian Zen firmly.

"I've met you only a couple of times, but I don't think you're an idiot," I said.

I gave Dr Rosemary a quick nod of the head to indicate that he should join in the confidence boosting.

"I've heard lots of people say you're a total idiot," he began and as the doge's shoulders drooped, I felt he could have chosen his words more carefully. "I've known you for only a very short time, but you don't seem to be a total idiot."

"Thank you, you're very kind," said the doge with a watery smile. "So that's two people in the city who don't think I'm an idiot, and one who thinks I don't seem to be. As opposed to one hundred and thirty-nine thousand, nine hundred and ninety-seven who think I am."

It was useful to get information on the current population of the city, which would enable me to refine my statistics about the plague deaths. But I also had to correct the doge's arithmetic.

"I think you've forgotten that I'm a foreigner," I said. "Probably because I speak Venetian so fluently. So that means there are

133

actually one hundred and thirty-nine thousand, nine hundred and ninety-eight people who think you're an idiot."

Librarian Zen gave me a hard stare, the sort that wouldn't have disgraced Paddington. Again, I was staggered by his ability not to correct someone who had made a mistake. It must be really distressing for him.

"Oh," said the doge in a small voice. "Thank you for pointing that out."

I hoped the librarian was paying attention. The doge was happy to be put right.

"You are not an idiot, Most Serene Prince," said Librarian Zen firmly. "The worst that can be said of you is that you may be mildly dyspraxic."

The doge's face crumpled. "I'm dreading it," he said. "I told them right from the start, I'll be no good at it, but they just didn't listen – or probably just didn't care."

He sounded almost as gloomy as Dr Marjoram.

"You don't sound terribly happy in your work," I said. "Why did you stand for election in the first place?"

"I'm pretty sure I didn't," said the doge. "That's not how it works. In fact, nobody really understands how it works. It's a very complicated process. All I know is that when they tell you you're doge, you're not allowed to refuse."

"What would happen if you did?" I asked with interest.

"Something involving boiling oil, I dare say." He seemed to rouse himself slightly. "It's not all bad. The food's good, and my rooms are comfy. I think the hat suits me."

We all agreed heartily that the hat suited him very much indeed.

"But there are downsides. I get paid very little, and I'm forbidden to have any business interests, but I still have to pay taxes, so it's just as well I'm pretty rich to start with. And I'm not allowed to go out except in a ceremonial procession."

"You do sneak out sometimes, though," Librarian Zen reminded him. "You met the good doctor in the Academy of the Unknowns."

"But that's the only place I can go," said the doge. "The clue's in the name. Nobody knows who I am."

I was pretty sure everyone knew who he was. Especially the offensive intellectual in the Academy who had claimed the doge's only claim to fame was wearing a funny hat. But I said nothing, as I didn't want Librarian Zen glaring at me again.

"But I'm getting more and more nervous about the marriage ceremony after last year's disaster," the doge said.

I remembered how a couple of Venetians who had brought a body to the doctors' residence had talked about the doge only coming out once a year for his marriage ceremony. I felt I really needed to know more about it. Did it just mean that he and his wife renewed their vows annually, or did he actually jettison a wife and get a new one, like Bluebeard? If the latter, I didn't see how I could approve of it, and I would have to suggest that this was another law he needed to change.

"There's no need to be nervous, Most Serene Prince," said Librarian Zen encouragingly. "You've still got a few more months to practise."

I didn't like the sound of that, which definitely suggested a new wife rather than the old one. This was without doubt an issue I should tackle, since, as a good feminist, I'm always keen to promote equality.

"I was doing some practice before you came back in." The doge looked the picture of misery. "You saw how well that went. I hit the good doctor straight in the face."

This was bewildering. I looked back towards the door we had come in, not having registered at the time what had hit me. There on the floor was a large wooden ring.

"Sorry," I said. "I'm not following. Your marriage ceremony involves a game of quoits?"

"I don't know this word," said the doge. "What's quoits?"

"Throwing a ring," I said.

"Exactly," he said.

I was back to feeling as though I was at the Mad Hatter's tea party. This conversation was making absolutely no sense. I could understand why almost everyone thought the doge was an idiot.

"You still don't seem to be following," Dr Rosemary said to me in a tone that implied I was the idiot.

"The good doctor isn't from our city," said Librarian Zen. "Perhaps they don't have the same kind of marriage ceremony in Edinburgh."

"We most certainly don't," I said. "Throwing things at one another – you're thinking of a Glasgow wedding."

"It's not a case of throwing things at one another," said Librarian Zen. "It's not so much a marriage as a mystical union."

"Oh yes," I said sceptically. "I've heard about that sort of thing." It sounded suspiciously like the Marquess of Bath, who, despite having one legal wife, managed to acquire seventy-four "wifelets".

"But we call it the Marriage of the Sea, and His Serenity throws a symbolic ring into the Gulf of Venice."

"Ah," I said.

"It's a most moving ceremony," said Dr Rosemary. "His Serenity sails out on his gilded galley, the Bucintoro, dressed in gold and ermine, and pronounces the ritual words of marriage at the point of throwing the wedding ring into the sea."

The doge gave a terrible groan.

"Are you all right?" I asked. "Have you eaten something that's got stuck? I can do the Heimlich manoeuvre."

He held up a hand indicating that he didn't require any medical intervention. He was in emotional rather than physical pain.

"I was there last year," said Librarian Zen in a determinedly cheerful voice. "It really wasn't that bad."

"No," agreed Dr Rosemary. "I'm sure nobody noticed."

"You both noticed," the doge whimpered.

I seemed to be missing a key piece of information. "Noticed what?" I asked.

"It was nothing," said Librarian Zen.

"A tiny glitch," said Dr Rosemary.

The doge turned plaintive eyes on me. "It was a complete disaster," he said. "I tried to throw the ring into the sea, but I had the ritual words to concentrate on as well. It's complicated doing two things at once."

"Not for women," I said crisply.

"It must be so much easier being a woman," said the doge, and Dr Rosemary's proboscis moved in such a way as to suggest that he was tossing his head in disagreement. I was enormously heartened by this understanding of women's situation, and even more guilt-ridden that I had denounced him.

"So it all went wrong, and I threw the ring into the galley instead. It fell through a crack in the planks, and it took days to dismantle everything and find it." The doge's voice shook. "They say I throw like a girl."

I couldn't help it; I gave a snort of outrage. And almost simultaneously, Dr Rosemary gave a snort of outrage inside his mask. He really was one of the good guys, calling out sexist remarks made by other men.

I got up and went over to retrieve the wooden ring. "Let me show you how a girl throws," I said.

"But you're not a girl," objected the doge.

"I can still show you how one throws," I said through gritted teeth.

"The good doctor is using his expertise in anatomy," said Librarian Zen.

"And in throwing," I said under my breath.

There was a carving of a reclining figure halfway up the wall. With a quick rotation, I threw the ring overhand, and it clattered over the figure's head to end up as a necklace.

The doge gasped. "I wish I could throw like a girl!" he said. He went over to the reclining figure and removed the ring from round its neck, looking at it pensively. "I'm dreading the ceremony. Last year, I heard people saying it would bring bad luck, and when we suddenly had this outbreak of plague, people said that was the bad luck. At least they did until I passed a law declaring that anyone caught saying it would be executed."

"Speaking of being executed," I said, "as you can probably tell from our outfits, the pair of us are part of the medical team fighting the plague. In fact, we've just embarked on a statistical survey that should give us solid information on how the plague's spreading and, by extension, how to stop it. But if I could just remind you, we're both under sentence of death. I've been anonymously accused of being a necromancer for getting your heart restarted before you actually died, and there's another small matter carrying the death penalty as well. And my colleague has also been denounced anonymously for being a thoroughly bad lot, even though there's not a shred of evidence to substantiate this. Obviously we're firm believers in the rule of law, but if we get executed, we won't be able to help get rid of the plague."

"And I was going to offer to give you lessons on throwing like a girl, since I know all about anatomy as well," said Dr Rosemary. "But I'm afraid I wouldn't be able to do that if I was dead."

"I don't want to detract from the arguments being put forward by the good doctors," said Librarian Zen. "However, it seems to me that the most important point is the one I myself made earlier, that changing the law would be popular."

The doge had brightened considerably, particularly after Dr Rosemary said he could give him throwing lessons.

"I'll do it!" he said. "I'll change the law right away so that anonymous denunciations are no longer valid. Obviously we wouldn't want to stop denunciations completely, but people will have to give their name and address. And I think, Doctor, you said there was another matter?"

"Something of nothing," I said, "apart from the fact that I'm facing execution for it." I was about to explain all about the traveller from the antique land, and how I'd been arrested in exchange for him, and how I'd escaped from the quarantine island, when I remembered that the book Dr Rosemary had severed, half of which was in my pocket, and the other half somewhere in a canal, had been intended for the doge. It was as well not to go into too much detail. "It was an administrative mix-up," I said.

"I apologise on behalf of the administration," the doge said. "Consider it annulled."

"That's very kind," I said. "Just to make sure that everything goes smoothly from now on, I wonder if you could also pass an edict saying nobody's to try to arrest any plague doctors whose beaks smell of either rosemary or aniseed."

"Consider it passed," said the doge, who now seemed to be quite enthused by the idea of getting involved in legislation.

"And the guards took my surgical instruments," said Dr Rosemary. "Please may I have them back?"

"Of course," said the doge. "I'll have them left at the front desk for you. When can we start the throwing lessons?"

"We need to sort out the plague business first," I said firmly. "In the meantime, here's an exercise you can try on your own. Sneak out the way you do when you go the Academy of the Unknowns, and practise throwing a ring into the water. That'll get you used to tossing it into the sea rather than the galley, and the good doctor can fine-tune your technique afterwards. And just focus on the throwing, without worrying about the ritual words. You can add them in later."

"That's sound advice, thank you," said the doge. "I'm sorry about your having been inconvenienced by being arrested under threat of execution. That can't have been pleasant, although we're leading the way in Europe in having a purpose-built prison and I believe the cells are quite commodious."

"It was very comfortable," said Dr Rosemary.

"I got to sleep almost immediately," I said, without adding that I do that anyway, and I thought our cell was dark, damp and malodorous. "And I liked the design of the grating over the window."

The doge gave a small smile of satisfaction. "That's good to hear. We like to do things nicely."

I wondered how nice our executions would have been.

"Please see what you can do about the plague as quickly as possible," he said. "This city's prosperity depends on trade, and nobody's trading with us because they're too worried about picking up a fatal disease."

"Lightweights," I said. "And don't worry. I'm hoping to get things clarified in the next couple of days." Hoping very hard. I'm allowed a week to complete a mission, and this was now my fourth day.

Librarian Zen bowed to the doge. "Most Serene Prince. I look forward to seeing you at the next Academy meeting, and perhaps hearing more about your gondolier opera."

"Forget about the opera for the moment," I advised. "You can't go wasting time on it when there's throwing to be done."

"You're right," sighed the doge. "Maybe I shouldn't be wasting time on it anyway, if it's jejune."

"I thought Canaletto was completely out of order with that comment," said Librarian Zen sharply. "It was nothing but pretentious nonsense."

It was a measure of his annoyance that he was actually naming someone who was supposed to be Unknown. And Canaletto. That was the name of the rival gondola company that Dr Rosemary was so suspicious of. I could see his proboscis quiver.

"I suppose everyone's entitled to their opinion," said the doge.

"Maybe so, but if they're denouncing something, they won't be able to do it anonymously any more," said the librarian.

The doge gave a small laugh. "We may have to rename it the Academy of Known Unknowns." He suddenly roused himself as though he had remembered something. "But don't let me keep you. We've all got work to do. I've got legislation to pass, you've got a plague to stop. And just tell the front desk that I said they've got to return the good doctor's surgical instruments."

He gestured us towards a much grander door than the one we had come in. Just as we reached it, it opened, and in came a flunkey with a silver salver, bearing what was very definitely a cappuccino.

"Don't work too hard," I said as I put my beaked mask back on, "and remember to stop at six." The doge had the grace to blush.

Not only the door was grander, but so was the staircase, with a golden ceiling and magnificent paintings. I liked this view of the Doge's Palace much better, especially as the guards were jumping to attention rather than grabbing me and threatening me with swords. It seemed we were now on the list of honoured dignitaries entitled to use the main stair. And the staff at the front desk returned Dr Rosemary's surgical equipment right away once we said it was on the order of His Serenity.

As we came out into St Mark's Square, we could see a forlorn little queue outside the Marciana Library.

"Two seconds!" Librarian Zen called to them. "I was unavoidably detained."

"I think we were the ones who were unavoidably detained until you rescued us," I said.

"I knew that something terrible had happened to you," he said. "I had the most profound feeling of disquiet, and instinctively knew you had been taken over the Bridge of Sighs. I came as quickly as I could to try to rescue you."

I was so moved that I could hardly speak, but I managed to give him a librarianly hug, carefully tilting my head to the side to avoid putting his eye out with my beak.

He hugged me back, then said, "I really must go and open the library. In any case, I'm sure you two ladies want peace to chat about your plague strategy."

TEN

I gave a laugh that even to my ears sounded a little forced.

"I've no idea what he's talking about," I said to Dr Rosemary. "He's usually very sharp, but it's easy to make a slip of the tongue."

"Come off it," said Dr Rosemary. "I don't think there's any point in pretending any more, do you? I worked it out the minute you snorted when the doge talked about throwing like a girl."

"But you snorted as well," I said.

"Exactly," said Dr Rosemary. "So let's just admit we're two women masquerading as men."

"I thought you *were* a man," I said. "When you snorted, I thought you were a man who was being an ally."

Dr Rosemary snorted again. "That's likely!"

"Yes it is," I said. "What about Librarian Zen?"

"Yes, what about him?" she asked with sudden interest. "Are you and he an item?"

"What?" I spluttered. "Why on earth would you say that?"

"Because you've obviously been seeing him, and that was a pretty passionate embrace, and there was all that stuff about his instincts telling him you were in trouble."

"That was not a passionate embrace, that was a comradely hug," I told her. "We're colleagues. I'm a librarian."

"Explains a lot," she said, without explaining what she meant by that. "We need to talk this through. Why don't we go and get a coffee – it's freezing out here in the fog."

"There's a good coffee shop near the Campo Santa Maria Formosa," I said.

"I know it," said Dr Rosemary. "We can go by the back alleys.

Fewer people to scream at the sight of us."

The waiter was unfazed by not one but two doctors. We took off our beaked masks and settled into our chairs.

"Two ristrettos and two pastries, please," said Dr Rosemary.

"Actually, I'd prefer tea," I said. We had been through quite a stressful time, and I was in no mood to make compromises. "With milk."

The waiter gave a disdainful sniff. Once he was out of earshot, I said, "So explain to me why you're masquerading as a doctor?"

"I'm masquerading as a man," she said through gritted teeth. "I'm not masquerading as a doctor. I *am* a doctor."

"But this is 1650," I objected. "Women aren't allowed in medical schools. How could you possibly become a doctor?"

"By masquerading as a man," she said.

"You said you come from a gondoliering family," I said. "Why didn't you masquerade as a man and become a gondolier?"

"We've been through this," she said. "The strain on the musculoskeletal system from the asymmetric working. Ten times worse for women than men. I'd waste far too much time on remedial exercises. I've just always been drawn to medicine. As a doctor, you can help to make the world a better place."

The Blainer's *raison d'être*. I was impressed.

"I went off to Bologna. The student gowns are quite concealing. But because nobody thought a girl would have the nerve to try to study medicine, it never even crossed their minds. And once I graduated and got my doctor's robes, people just look at the clothes, not the person. It's been even better with the plague doctor's outfit, because I'm concealed completely."

"Yes, I've found it very useful as well," I said.

The waiter reappeared with our drinks, muttering under his breath as he set down my jug of milk, and flounced away.

"It was a real shock to find that the plague had returned," Dr Rosemary said. "I left my practice right away and came into the city centre to offer whatever help I could. And now it's turned into a complete nightmare with people blaming the Cornetto gondolas. My family's going to be destitute." Her voice cracked. "I'm going to be their only means of support – please, please don't denounce me."

I swallowed hard. "Denounce you? Goodness, why ever would I denounce you? I can't imagine ever doing such a thing."

Sometimes it's important to own up to your transgressions; at other times, not so much.

"Denounce me for not being a man. I've qualified through deception. I realise you must have done the same, but who cares about librarians? If I denounced you, people would just shrug their shoulders and let you get on with it. But I'd be banned from ever practising medicine again. And possibly executed."

"Let me tell you," I said, "about James Miranda Barry. She went off to study medicine, and they just thought she was a young lad, presumably the same as they thought about you. She graduated..." I avoided mentioning that she had graduated from Edinburgh University. Dr Rosemary knew that there was no Edinburgh Medical School right now, and it would just confuse her if I explained all this happened in the nineteenth century, "... and she passed the exams for the Royal College of Surgeons, after which she joined the army as a military surgeon."

"I've got forceps for extracting arrow heads, and a bullet extractor in my medical kit, but I've never had a chance to use them," said Dr Rosemary. "They say the army's a good way of seeing the world."

"James Miranda had an extremely distinguished fifty-year career," I said. "And she was very widely travelled – she went to the West Indies, St Helena, Malta, Corfu, Canada and South Africa."

"And nobody knew she wasn't a man?"

"Maybe a couple of people, but they never said anything. Because they knew she was helping to make the world a better place, just the same as you're doing. So rest assured, you have my full support, and I'm not going to denounce you. And I know that goes for my fellow librarian as well."

Dr Rosemary grasped my hand, saying, "Thank you from the bottom of my heart, Dr Distance-Learning," and I felt a sudden tingling. That's generally the sign indicating the focus of my mission and it was a timely reminder that Dr Rosemary and I had plague business to attend to. But she had now withdrawn her hand and was using it to dunk her pastry in the cappuccino. It was wise to fortify ourselves first, and the pastry was lovely.

"Now that we have this bond," she said through a mouthful of pastry, "I can't keep calling you 'Dr Distance-Learning'. What's your real name?"

While Librarian Zen had been well able to cope with it, I wasn't confident that Dr Rosemary could, so I decided to keep it simple.

"Call me Shona," I said.

She tried it out. "Shona. That's very unusual. But it must be nice to have such an exotic name."

"And what's yours?" I asked.

"Very plain in comparison, I'm afraid. Rosamaria."

That would be easy to remember, especially as I was still going to think of her as Dr Rosemary. We solemnly shook hands after wiping most of the pastry off them.

"One thing I wanted to ask," I said. "When you told the guards you had dealt with patients suffering from necromancy, is that something you've really done?"

"Of course not," she said. "I was just trying to frighten them. There's no such thing as necromancy. I would have thought you knew that. But tell me about this cardiopulmonary resuscitation thing you did to save His Serenity's life."

I was delighted. It's a very easy emergency procedure and the more people who know how to do it, the better. I began explaining it to her, but she said, "No, words are no good."

As a librarian, I rather took exception to this, but she was snapping her fingers and calling, "Waiter!"

After being promised a substantial tip, he agreed to be the CPR dummy. I showed Dr Rosemary how to place her hands, and to compress the chest by at least a third before letting it rise

again, and also taught her the musical accompaniment of "Stayin'
Alive", although just as "la la" since I thought the foreign lyrics
would be a bit complicated for her.

"You're not really seeing the full effect," I said, "because he's
still breathing."

"Stop breathing, and there's another ten ducats in it for you,"
Dr Rosemary told him, but he said he'd had enough and there
might be other customers. That seemed unlikely, since when
potential customers saw us, with our beaked masks on the chairs
beside us, they screamed and ran away.

But I felt he needed mollifying, so I ordered another tea and
coffee and another couple of pastries.

"Still tea with milk? Right away," he said with a look of utter
contempt.

"Why did you order that?" Dr Rosemary protested. "Nobody
drinks tea with milk. He'll think you're a complete ignoramus,
and we want people to respect doctors."

The waiter returned with our order and an ill grace. I could
hear him muttering under his breath, "This city's going to rack
and ruin. Bad enough when those arty-farty intellectuals came
in ordering cappuccinos at all hours of the day, but you expect
better of a medical man."

Dr Rosemary shot me a reproachful look. In an effort to
distract her, I said, "I'm still wondering why one of the doctors
tried to murder me."

"Well, you are quite irritating," she said.

"Irritating enough to merit murder?" I asked frostily.

She thought about this. "Yes, I think so."

"In that case, we must agree to disagree," I said even more
frostily. I took a bite of the new pastry to soothe myself, and a sip
of tea, which helped to thaw me.

She scooped some rogue pieces of pastry out of her ristretto
and said, "So you and Librarian Zen, you're definitely not?"

"Definitely not what?" I asked.

"You know," she said impatiently.

"I really don't," I said. "I mean, we're definitely not doctors, we're not gondoliers, we're not doges. But all of that's self-evident."

"Are you lovers?"

The woman was obsessed. The hug I gave him hadn't even been lingering. This is how rumours begin, and I was very glad we were in an era before social media.

"Lovers?" I said. "We most certainly are not! I've only just met the man."

"Sometimes that's all it takes," she said. "He's very good-looking."

I was astonished. I have no objection whatsoever to good-looking men. But I wouldn't have put Librarian Zen among them.

"Really?" I said.

"Really," she said. "Those lovely dark eyes, and the long eyelashes. And the dimples. You don't often see a man with dimples."

This was all news to me. I'd never noticed dark eyes and long eyelashes, and definitely not any dimples. I simply saw Librarian Zen as a fellow professional. And then I wondered whether this was some sort of failsafe mechanism. It wouldn't do to have librarians falling in love with one another, given the danger that they might then neglect their books.

And right now, I was neglecting my mission.

"Rosamaria," I said, "so far the information we have on the plague victims is that they had all recently been on a Cornetto gondola."

"That's a lie," she burst out. "It must be! How can our gondolas have anything to do with the plague?"

"There's one way of finding out," I said. "I'm going to go on one."

She stared at me. "It's my family. If anyone's going to go on one, it should be me."

"But exactly, it's your family. You've grown up with these gondolas. You're not in the best position to notice anything unusual or different about them. It needs a fresh eye."

"It's precisely because I've grown up with the gondolas that I'll notice anything unusual or different," she said. "You wouldn't have the faintest idea."

She was being very argumentative, but she sounded upset rather than aggressive.

"Why are you insisting on going?" I asked.

"Because it's my responsibility," she said. "If something my family's doing is spreading the plague, then I should be the one to take the risk. Shona, if you went, and you died, I'd never forgive myself."

I then felt obliged to forgive her for calling me irritating.

I lowered my voice. "You don't have to worry about me," I said. "I can't really explain this properly, because it's very new medication that doesn't exist here yet, but I've taken it, and it means I won't get the plague. I don't actually need the aniseed in my beak. It's just there because it's a nice smell."

She was nodding in understanding. "You may not have qualified as a doctor, but I can see that you have great medical expertise with your knowledge of anatomy and the Heimlich manoeuvre and cardiopulmonary resuscitation. You're sure this medication works?"

"I've been here for four days, lifting several more plague victims than I've had hot dinners, and I'm absolutely fine," I said. "You don't need to worry about me. You go back to the doctors' residence and start collating the information that's come in since we left. For all we know, the plague victims who were on a Cornetto gondola will turn out to be statistical outliers and it will be something else entirely that they all have in common."

"I bet there won't be any more information that's come in because that lot won't have bothered to record it," she muttered. "They'll be up in the reception room eating and drinking, and just leaving the bodies to stack up in the hall for us to deal with when we get back. Amazing how it's always the women who have to do all the work, even when they don't know we're women."

"So true," I said, and we both dunked our pastries a bit more in a companionable way.

"I'll take you to my brother's gondola and introduce you," she said.

I shook my head. "We can't do that if we're trying to replicate what happens to an ordinary passenger," I said. "We don't want him behaving any differently from usual. Just tell me where he's likely to be, and I'll find him." I gave her an encouraging smile. "It's all going to be fine. The plague's probably got nothing at all to do with your family's gondolas. And if it does, we'll find out what it is and put it right."

"I'm sorry I said you were irritating," she said, passing me what was left of her pastry. "I mean, you are a lot of the time, but you're also very kind, and I'm excited to try out cardiopulmonary resuscitation."

As apologies went, I thought that was pretty fulsome.

We handed over a more than generous tip to the waiter, who was still muttering about the decline in social standards, put our masks back on and went out. There were quite a few people around and I expected to be met with the usual screams. But there was no reaction. They all had their backs to us and were lining the canal, apparently riveted by something.

And there, through the mist, we saw it, the funeral gondola, black and gold, with its four silent hooded gondoliers, the black curtains fluttering in the cool breeze, and atop everything, the anti-Cornetto banner.

People were no longer screaming when they saw it. Instead, they seemed to be treating it as a public information message.

A small child laboriously spelled out the letters. "Mamma, does it mean that if I go on a Cornetto gondola, I'll die?" she asked.

"Exactly right, dear," said the mother. "The Cornetto gondolas are what are known as plague ships. You must never, ever go near one."

"I won't, Mamma," the child promised. "Not ever."

I could hear Dr Rosemary gulping back furious sobs under her mask. "This is dreadful," she muttered. "This will ruin us, if we're not ruined already."

I patted the back of her goatskin overcoat. "I'm about to go on a Cornetto gondola," I said, "and will get to the bottom of it. Stop worrying."

She clutched my hand. "Thank you. I'll go back to the residence and start collating. If you go first right, then over the bridge, then take the next alleyway, go over the third bridge after that, and then take the second lane to the left – that'll take you to my brother. Good luck."

I followed her instructions, although it was a bit tricky to work out what qualified as an alleyway and what was a lane, and found myself in a small square, with a gondola sitting waiting at the wooden berth. The gondolier leaned, slouching on his oar, and I was very disappointed. I had thought Dr Rosemary's brother had taken my exercises to heart. And then I saw that this wasn't someone tall and gangly, but medium-sized and slightly podgy. He was talking to two men lounging against the wall.

Since business was so bad, Dr Rosemary's brother had probably got fed up and gone home, leaving the berth for another member of the extended Cornetto family.

But even when it seems superfluous, I always have Miss Blaine's stricture about never assuming at the back of my mind.

As I approached, I called, "Is this a Cornetto gondola?"

The gondolier straightened up. "No, Doc, you're quite safe, we're Canalettos."

Dr Rosemary had obviously got confused between her bridges, alleyways and lanes and misdirected me. Either that, or I had made a wrong turning – unlikely given my excellent sense of direction. Dr Rosemary had her suspicions about the Canalettos, as yet unproven, but I certainly hadn't liked the way Academician Canaletto had spoken to the doge, even if he had got a bit nicer after the cardiac arrest.

"No, thank you," I said. "It's a Cornetto gondola I want."

The two men onshore had also straightened up. I try not to judge by appearances, but I didn't like the look of them. They had the appearance of neds, cunning and brutish. Their eyes were suspiciously close together.

"You want a Cornetto gondola? Nah, Doc, you really don't," said one of them.

"Haven't you heard?" said the other. "Going on a Cornetto gondola's seriously bad for your health. I would have thought you knew that, being a medical man."

"As a medical man, I know nothing of the kind," I said. "I deal in facts, not unsubstantiated speculation."

"You calling me a liar?" he growled.

"By no means," I said. "I couldn't call you a liar unless I knew you were deliberately telling an untruth. I'm calling you a purveyor of unsubstantiated speculation."

The pair of them started moving towards me. At last, I thought, an opportunity to redeem myself in the martial arts stakes. There was enough room in the square for my Shaolin kung fu combat skills.

There must have been something about my stance (a low wide squat with my hands on my waist) that gave them pause. They paused.

Then the first one said in a pleasanter tone, "Our gondolas are much more comfortable than the Cornetto ones, and our prices much more reasonable. Where do you want to go, Doc? We'll get you there in half the time."

I didn't move. "I can see from what you're wearing that you two aren't gondoliers," I said. "I prefer to deal with the organ grinder rather than the monkeys."

"You calling us monkeys?" growled the other ned.

"By no means," I said again. "I'm using a form of metalepsis, which is a figure of speech."

He took another step towards me.

"If you want to get mollocated, fine by me," I said.

"I don't know any of these posh words you're using," he growled. "What does 'mollocated' mean?"

I beamed beneath my mask. "Come a bit closer, and you'll find out."

There was a sudden whistle from the gondolier, and the duo turned and went over to him. They were quite far away and muttering to one another, but fortunately I have excellent hearing.

"What do you think you're doing?"

"Getting you a fare."

"That's not how you get fares."

"Are you telling us our job?"

"Your job isn't to get fares."

"We're trying to stop him going on a Cornetto gondola."

"Why?"

"So we get the business."

"We still need people on Cornetto gondolas."

I was tempted to shout, "Why?" at this point, but I didn't want them to know they'd been overheard. Instead, I shouted, "Excuse me, but I really do want to get a Cornetto gondola. Could you give me directions?"

The gondolier shouted back, "Down that alleyway, over the bridge, and then second lane on the right."

"Thanks," I called back, setting off and hoping the difference between alleyways and lanes would be more obvious this time.

I found myself in another small square, with another gondola waiting at the wooden berth. And this time there was no doubt about the gondolier. Tall and gangly, with a thin moustache and an expression of intense concentration, he was reaching backwards with his palm upwards, stretching his pectoral muscle exactly as I had told him.

"Hello," I called. "You're the ideal patient."

Startled, he almost fell off the gondola. And when he saw who it was, he was even more startled.

"It's surely not forty days since you were detained on the plague island?" he said.

"It was an administrative mix-up. His Serenity himself annulled it." I felt a little uneasy. Had the doge been distracted by his cappuccino and forgotten? "You mean you haven't heard?"

"I'm afraid I haven't," he said. "But that doesn't mean there hasn't been an announcement. I've lost track of time and everything else. I've just been focusing on my exercises."

"That's really good to hear," I said. "And how are you getting on with rotating through your spine and hips when you're working?"

His face crumpled. "I haven't had any work since I saw you last. I've got no customers because everyone thinks they're going to get the plague if they go on a Cornetto gondola. The whole family's facing insolvency and starvation."

"Now, now," I said encouragingly. "Not the whole family. Your sister's doing very well. Medicine's a lucrative profession."

He took a step backwards and the gondola tipped alarmingly. "You know? About … her?"

"Well, obviously," I said. "We've got to know one another quite well through being medical colleagues." There was no need to tell him that we'd got to know one another in the condemned cell, and that I wasn't actually medically qualified. "And I'm here to help. I'd like you to take me on a gondola trip, and I'm going to check to see if there's anything going on that might be causing the plague. If there is, we'll find a way of getting rid of it."

"You make it sound so simple," he sighed.

"Most things are," I said. "People just like to complicate them. So let's go, payment in advance." I fished in my pouch and extracted a couple of coins. "These do you?"

His eyes widened. "Are you sure? This would more than make up for the previous lack of customers."

In answer, I handed the coins over. I was sure my reasonable expenses would stretch to paying a bit over the odds for a gondola ride, especially if it helped the Cornetto family avoid insolvency and starvation.

He put out his hand to help me on board and I was about to tell him I was quite capable of getting on by myself when I realised it was part of the service. He deposited me in the passenger cabin, a black wool canopy over a wooden frame, and then took his place standing at the stern, setting the oar in the oarlock, and propelling us away from the berth.

In the twenty-first century, gondoliers like you to stay where you're put, but I had an investigation to carry out. I figured that Dr Rosemary's brother would be able to cope since the enclosed passenger cabin in his time period allowed for all sorts of goings-on, and I would be comparatively motionless. I got down on my hands and knees and began to examine my surroundings. I was particularly excited to detect the eight requisite types of wood that gondolas are made of: elm, fir, oak, larch, lime, cherry, mahogany and walnut. On my very first mission, I met a beautiful Russian heiress with a genius for woodwork. I hadn't seen her since, but I very much hoped she had managed a trip to Venice. She would have loved building gondolas.

But there was nothing I could see that was out of the ordinary, no sign of any contamination or flea-ridden rats. And Dr Rosemary's brother, dutifully rotating through his spine and hips as he rowed along, was obviously in great form, even better now that he was doing his exercises so assiduously.

"I have a question," I called. "How are all your gondolier relatives?"

"They're all very well, thank you," he said. "Apart from being quite depressed about the impending insolvency and starvation."

That was peculiar. Dying of the plague from a Cornetto gondola seemed to affect only the passengers and not the gondoliers.

"Is there anything that gondoliers do that's different from everyone else?" I called.

"Yes," he said, "asymmetrical working."

I couldn't see how strain on the musculoskeletal system would protect you against the plague. But I recognised that I wasn't medically qualified; I would have to check it with Dr Rosemary.

"Thanks anyway," I called. "There's absolutely no sign of your gondola being plague-ridden, which is good in one way, totally baffling in another. We might as well go back now."

On the return journey, I opened the wool covering on the passenger cabin so that I could sit and enjoy the view. I felt slightly guilty about taking time just to be a tourist when there was a mission to accomplish, but right now there wasn't anything else I could do. I couldn't see a great deal because of the mist, only a series of not terribly clear shapes, but they were different shapes from the ones you see in Morningside, which made it interesting.

When we got back to the wooden berth and Dr Rosemary's brother helped me out, he said, "Was it just my imagination, or did you notice it as well?"

"Notice what?" I asked.

He sighed. "So it's just me being paranoid. Sorry, all this trouble with the plague is getting to me. I kept thinking we were being followed."

"By what?" I asked. "A dolphin? They're very friendly, although it's important not to hit them on the nose with your oar."

"I know," he said. "I'm always very careful not to do that. No, I thought we were being followed by another gondola. It seemed to be lurking round corners. But if you didn't see anything, there was obviously nothing there. I can't be thinking clearly."

"You've been under a lot of pressure," I said kindly. "The mind can play tricks on us in these situations. Take it easy, apart from with the exercises. You're doing very well with them, but it's essential to make them part of your daily routine."

"It would be pointless to be given exercises designed to make me better and then not do them," he said.

Another Blainer-in-the-making. I was impressed by the attitude of the Cornetto brother and sister, and I very much hoped that collating accurate information on the outbreak of plague would offer some means of helping the family's collapsing enterprise.

We parted with good wishes on either side, and I set off for the doctors' residence. I had got to the second lane on the left and was just about to cross the bridge when two figures loomed out of the doorway where they had been lurking, each grabbing one of my ankles and tugging, so that I toppled into the canal. As I fell, I could see the stern of a gondola, with a medium-sized and slightly podgy gondolier standing on it, holding the oar without it being in the oarlock. It seemed an unwise rowing technique, and then I realised he was shoving the oar downwards to keep my head underwater.

This was exactly what had happened to Librarian Zen. I had been right – these weren't common or garden footpads; they were assassins. Librarian Zen hadn't been able to think of anyone with a grudge against him apart from Librarian de' Pazzi in the San Marco Library in Florence, but we had pretty well ruled him out. And he certainly had no grudge against me that would account for this second attack. One of the doctors, whether Oregano, Parsley or Marjoram, had tried to murder me, but I couldn't think why they would want to murder Librarian Zen.

As the oar jabbed at me again, I suddenly had a flash of intuition. This was the Canaletto gondolier and his two ned mates, and they were indiscriminately pouncing on people and trying to drown them. I couldn't think of a good reason why, but it really wasn't the time to try to come up with theories.

I remembered Librarian Zen's technique. He had seized the oar, pulling his assailant into the canal while simultaneously propelling himself on to dry land, and seeing off the other two with a couple of elbow strikes. I engaged my core. The two neds were holding me down on the edge of the paving stones by my ankles, but it was a matter of a moment to tense my feet and get purchase. At the same time, I tugged on the oar, dragging the gondolier into the water, and began to rise upwards. But then I found myself falling back into the canal with a splash.

The two neds had obviously recognised Librarian Zen's technique and had let go of me in order to avoid another lot of elbow strikes. The gondolier was floundering about, and they reached out to help him ashore.

"Quick!" he spluttered. "We need to finish him off. He's seen too much."

"He can't have gone far," growled a ned. "We'll get him."

The three of them leaped on to the gondola, the neds picking up two spare oars, and they began ramming them randomly into the canal with the aim of shoving me underwater.

"There!" shouted a ned. "I see him!"

The gondola moved with amazing speed and an oar whacked the water. They must have thought they had seen my head, but they were wrong. I had discovered that I could use my beak as a snorkel. Quietly and with as little disturbance of the water as I could manage, I paddled on my back under the bridge where my beak was concealed in the shadows among some vegetation.

They were getting closer, and if they struck me amidships with an oar, I'd give myself away by flailing and spluttering.

They were being chillingly methodical, sweeping the oars across and through the narrow waterway. I couldn't move from my hiding place without creating ripples that would reveal where I was.

And then I felt a sudden surge of water that pushed me further into the stonework of the bridge. Something was coming in the opposite direction, fast. There was going to be a collision between the Canaletto gondola and the incoming one, and I would be collateral damage between the two.

I feared I was about to be skewered with the full set of gondola construction material: elm, fir, oak, larch, lime, cherry, mahogany and walnut. But the thing that passed me was smooth and warm. And it was whistling and clicking in an extremely annoyed manner. I could feel the approaching gondola pitch and rock amid the unexpected waves. Panicked shouting suggesting that the two neds had fallen into the passenger cabin, and the gondolier was fighting to keep his craft afloat as it swirled around in the dolphin's wake.

"Bloody stupid fish!" he shouted after it, and I had to stop myself telling him that a dolphin wasn't a fish, but a mammal.

In any case, it was my friend the dolphin I wanted to communicate with. The neds on the gondola were so preoccupied that I felt I could get away with a few clicks and whistles.

"Thank you very much! That was a nasty moment," I communicated, and got back a faint reply, "It's a pleasure. That gondolier's the worst for hitting me on the nose."

The nose-hitter had now unfortunately regained control of the gondola.

"At least we know the doctor's safely drowned by now," growled a ned. "He couldn't have survived that tidal wave."

"Shall we look for the body?" asked the other.

"No way," said the gondolier. "It could have been swept miles away by now. I just want to finish this job and get home."

Slowly and carefully, the gondola was now passing me. I was quite safe with nobody now jabbing oars in my direction. My pouch had a threaded leather band on it which I managed to loop over the ornamental bit of iron at the stern. I clung to the pouch and let the gondola pull me along, only my snorkel-beak visible above the water line. I was confident the gondolier would keep looking forward and wouldn't notice the added weight.

If I had had time to plan ahead, I would have checked whether there were any small mirrors in my pouch, and then I could have turned my beak into a periscope as well as a snorkel. But it's easy to be wise after the event. All I could do was let myself be towed along, the dense network of canals making it impossible for me to work out where we were going.

At last we stopped and berthed. I was able to unhook my pouch and dodge round the stern on the nearside, still concealing my presence. The two neds were grumbling about something being heavy and the gondolier was telling them to get on with it, The gondola bounced around a bit as the neds dragged something ashore.

I waited until I heard their footsteps fade and then I carefully hauled myself out of the canal. Delightful as the waterways of Venice were, I was getting a bit sick of being in them. I was outside a building, not residential, not a church, not a doge's palace, and I had a very odd sensation. Beyond the aniseed, I could smell something else. It was the same thing I had smelled during the dissection, something unexpected and yet oddly familiar. I still couldn't work out what it was.

Keeping close to the building, and ducking down to avoid the windows, I reached the corner just in time to see a ned disappearing through a side doorway, helping to carry something weighty. The daylight was beginning to go, and the mist was still swirling, so I edged round the building until I reached the doorway. The smell, by no means unpleasant, was getting stronger, and I had an unsettling feeling that I should know what it was. The door wasn't completely closed, and I chanced going in. I could see men hunched over large lectern-like structures covered in small wooden boxes, and others beside big wooden Heath Robinson-style contraptions with flat wooden plates and a range of odd-looking handles. A worker struggled past me carrying a bulky covered container and set it down beside a man who took off the lid and scooped out a thick sticky substance. He spread it on the flat surface in front of him, and began methodically rolling a pair of hemispherical leather balls over it.

I suddenly realised what he was doing and what the smell was. He was "working up" printer's ink before it was transferred on to the type. This was a printworks. And beyond the man with the ink, I could see others hard at work with needle and thread and leather. They were making books. Beautiful books. I could hardly contain my excitement. Next to letting me visit Signori Chepman and Myllar in Edinburgh, Miss Blaine couldn't have sent me anywhere more perfect.

I was beginning to walk towards the printers and bookbinders so that I could admire their skill close up when I heard an anguished whisper close by.

"Psst! Doc! They'll see you! In here."

It was the growly ned. One of the trio who had recently tried to murder me. I went into automatic defence mode, about to send my assailant flying. Two things stopped me. First, I couldn't risk causing any damage to the publishing house. Miss Blaine would never forgive me, and I would never forgive myself. Second, the ned was showing no signs of attacking me and in fact was looking rather obsequious. That seemed very odd, but perhaps he had had an epiphany and had seen the error of his ways. Or perhaps he was trying to lull me into a false sense of security.

He gestured for me to follow him behind a curtain. Unlulled, and ready to go back into defence mode, I followed him.

I was completely unprepared for what was behind the curtain.

ELEVEN

I didn't initially realise that there were five people in the alcove. The three standing in front of me I already knew. The two neds and the gondolier. What surprised me was that they didn't seem to recognise me. I was extremely damp, which I thought would have been a giveaway.

"Oh, goodness, Doctor," whispered the gondolier. "Did you fall in the canal?"

It was tempting to say, "No, I was thrown in the canal", but that would have given the game away.

The whispering suggested that they didn't want to be heard, which gave me an idea. I'm very good at charades, so I put my finger to my mouth as though warning them to keep quiet, and mimed tripping and plunging into water. They then mimed being sad, although they didn't do it very well.

The gondolier tried miming something that I couldn't work out at all, so I mimed for him to speak very softly.

Keeping a respectful distance, he whispered, "Sorry, Doc, we weren't expecting you so soon. We got delayed; we had to deal with one of your colleagues. He won't bother us any more. But as you can see, we've only just got started."

He stood aside and indicated. That was when I saw the other two. One of them was crouched on the ground, two open containers of thick sticky ink in front of him, one black, one red. Beside him were a couple of wooden stamps, just like the ones Librarian Zen had given me to stamp the hands of those getting an hour's reading of the popular books.

The person beside him was lying on the ground. He was mainly in a sack, and extremely dead. This was what the growly ned had been helping to carry into the building. And the man with the red and black ink had been busy stamping circles on his face and torso, as though he was issuing library books.

Things were beginning to fall into place. It was a Burke and Hare situation, only about two hundred years earlier. Burke and Hare became murderers so that they could sell the cadavers to Edinburgh University's medical school for dissection. This lot were doing exactly the same, drowning their victims, but with the added twist of pretending that they had succumbed to the plague.

The doctors had said that all of their predecessors had died during the previous outbreak, so they were having to work out what to do all over again. But that was complete baloney. They had concocted this pandemic themselves, and the black and red spots were just added colour. Dr Rosemary had been absolutely right when she said the plague victims were textbook cases. In real life, they would have been covered in hideous boils. But in the textbook illustrations she had seen, they would have been covered in flat black and red ink spots, just as the deceased beside me was.

I wondered whether Marjoram, Parsley or Oregano was behind the dastardly plot. Or perhaps they were all in it together.

And then I realised the implication of what the gondolier had said to me, *Sorry, Doc, we weren't expecting you so soon.* They had mistaken me for one of the trio, who must now be on his way here to see what was going on. I couldn't be discovered. Leaving aside the deceased, that was four potential attackers, five when the doctor turned up, and while that was reasonably manageable, there were all of the printing and book-binding workers, who might or might not have been in on it. I can only do so much. It was time for me to make a swift exit.

Using my miming skills, I gave them a big thumbs-up with both thumbs, and then waved goodbye.

"But Doc—" the gondolier began in a whisper.

I put my finger over my masked mouth to indicate silence, and slipped out the way I'd come in.

It was virtually dark now, and I wasn't at all sure where I was. Being dragged along in the slipstream of the gondola with only my beak above water hadn't given me a great sense of my surroundings. I could be wandering around the city's lanes and alleyways for days without success, since if I tried to ask passers-by for directions, the majority would scream and run away. I had little faith that they would believe me if I told them the plague was a hoax. But time was of the essence, as this was already day four of my mission.

It struck me with renewed vigour that I didn't have the faintest idea what my mission was. I had assumed – no, I hadn't assumed, I had deduced – that it was to bring back an accurate account of a hitherto-unknown outbreak of plague in Venice in 1650. But if there actually wasn't an outbreak of plague in Venice in 1650, that would explain why it was unknown. So here I was, more than halfway through my allotted time, having to completely rethink what I was supposed to be doing.

I was about to send a plea to Miss Blaine for instructions when I decided to change course. At times in the past, I've wished for prior guidance or written instructions, and this has generally resulted in the pain in my big toe. Miss Blaine expects her girls to work things out by themselves.

In the dimness, I saw a gondola approaching and flattened myself against the wall to try to blend in, in case it was bringing the doctor to his appointment in the printworks. I wouldn't know which doctor it was, since we all looked the same in our PPE, but I could easily get him in a chokehold and literally unmask him.

I was in a quandary. If that wasn't part of my mission, I would be wasting valuable time. But if a Blainer's job was to make the world a better place, unmasking the doctor responsible for a massive medical fraud was probably justifiable.

I scanned the gondola as it got closer. The black wool coverings on the passenger cabin were open and there was nobody inside. The gondolier was tall and gangly with a thin moustache.

I stepped out towards the canal and waved. The gondola pulled up.

"Hello," I said to Dr Rosemary's brother. "What are you doing here?"

"Nobody was passing where I was berthed, so I thought I'd come out and see if I could pick up any fares," he said. "But of course the minute they see it's a Cornetto gondola, they just leg it."

"Well, I would very much like a lift," I said. "Back to the doctors' residence, please."

"Of course," he said.

As he helped me on board, he did a double-take and said, "You're all wet."

"Yes, about that," I said, going into the passenger cabin. I kept the wool coverings open so that I could keep chatting to him. "I think you were right about a gondola following us. I was heading back home after our excursion, and I'd made it to the second lane on the left, just before the bridge, when I was set on by two neds who had obviously been waiting for me."

"That's terrible," he said. "But what's that got to do with you being wet and us being followed?"

I had to remember that not everybody was blessed with my quick wits, and needed to have everything spelled out. He was very nice, but his sister was obviously the brighter one in the family. I had now worked out the whole terrible plot, but it would be too complicated to explain to him if he couldn't make even the most obvious connections. It was going to be much easier to share my insights with Dr Rosemary.

"Oh look," I said, in order to distract him, "a dolphin."

Quickly and skilfully, he steered us closer to the side of the canal.

"Hello again. I like this one," the dolphin clicked, pointing its nose at Dr Rosemary's brother. "He always slows down and gives us plenty of room to pass. How are you?"

"Fine, thanks to you," I clicked back.

"Great, see you around," it whistled, and sped off.

"That's really good fun, trying to copy the sound a dolphin makes," said Dr Rosemary's brother. "I'll give it a go as well." He began clicking his tongue.

I shuddered. "Please," I said. "Don't ever say that in front of a dolphin or it will get very upset."

"Good one!" he said. "I like that, pretending that the noise means something."

Definitely not the brightest. But he was good at gondoliering, and delivered me safely to the residence, where I handed over another couple of coins.

"Thank you for hiring me," he said. "It's very encouraging, even though it's only briefly postponing my future of insolvency and starvation."

"I said I was going to help, and I will," I said firmly. "I'm pursuing some very promising lines of enquiry."

"That's good," he said, although I could tell he didn't believe me. "Give my best to Rosamaria."

It was as I was walking up the steps to the loggia that I realised I was even closer to exposing the villainy than I had thought. All I had to do was check which doctor was missing, and he would be the one behind the fake outbreak of plague.

Removing my mask, I went into the reception room and found Dr Rosemary.

"Has anyone gone out?" I asked.

"Yes, all of them," she said.

"Together?"

"No, separately."

"Did they say where they were going?" I asked. It would be very useful if one of them had said he was off to the printworks.

"They didn't say, and I didn't ask," she said. "Why, what's going on?"

"At least one of our colleagues is a very, very bad person," I said. "There is no plague in Venice."

Dr Rosemary gave me a look of bitter disappointment. I recognised it from the look I had seen Marcia Blaine teachers give pupils who were cast in the same mould as Dr Rosemary's brother.

"I know you're not a doctor," she said, "but I thought you had a rudimentary grasp of medical matters. I can assure you there is plague in Venice, and I have a storeroom full of its victims."

There was no point in arguing. This was a case of show, don't tell. I fetched Dr Oregano's towel from my room, then went to the dining table and picked up the balsamic vinegar.

"Come with me," I said, leading the way to the storeroom.

I wished I had put my mask back on because it was definitely easier viewing the deceased through the portholes. I would just have to squint to avoid seeing them too clearly.

"This gentleman," I said. "How do you know he's a plague victim?"

Dr Rosemary sighed. "Because of the black and red boils and pustules, of course."

"Watch this," I said. I dipped the edge of the towel in the balsamic vinegar and began rubbing at the nearest red spot.

"What are you doing?" cried Dr Rosemary. "You'll release more contagion!" And then she stopped abruptly as she saw the red spot disappearing.

"You have a go," I said, handing her the towel and indicating a body covered in black spots. She hesitated, and then set to it with sudden determination. The black spot she was working on started to dissolve.

She grabbed the balsamic vinegar from me, and began dabbing at other black and red spots on other bodies, with the same result.

"Printer's ink," I said briefly. "Let's go back upstairs and I'll explain it all."

I sat her down and reminded her of what her dissection had revealed. "I'm confident that if you dissect the other bodies, you'll find they've all died of drowning and not the plague, since there is no plague."

"But ... why?" she asked. "I don't understand."

I relayed the story of Burke and Hare, careful not to specify the date or the university.

"I still don't understand," she said.

Apparently she was more like her brother than I realised. "One of our doctors is inducing neds to drown people so that he has a ready supply of bodies to dissect. Obviously a sudden spate of drownings would look suspicious, so he's got them to pretend that the bodies are plague victims."

She rubbed her hand across her brow. "Sorry, I'm still not following this. First of all, there isn't a university in Venice, so there aren't loads of students wanting to do dissections. Second, I'm the only person who's actually done a dissection. I can't imagine why the others would pay for bodies to dissect, since they've just been lounging around showing no sign of wanting to get involved. And third, the bodies have been getting moved by funeral gondola to the quarantine island so that they can get buried, so they haven't been available for dissection at all. We've seen it with our own eyes."

This was awkward. I was forced to concede that she could be right.

"My basic point still stands," I said. "These people haven't died of the plague, they've been drowned."

"Why do you say they've been drowned? That was only one body, and the person could have fallen into the canal by accident. The others could have died from a range of natural causes."

At least now I could rely on hard facts, which she wouldn't be able to argue with. "Librarian Zen was set upon by a bunch of footpads – at least, that's what he thought they were. They tried to drown him, but fortunately he's extremely resourceful, and he escaped."

"I don't see what that's got to do with anything," she muttered.

"Exactly the same thing happened to me," I said. "I'd just been checking your brother's gondola – he sends you his best, by the way – and you're right, it's immaculate, absolutely no signs of plague. He thought we were being followed by another gondola, and I didn't notice, having been seduced by the misty scenery at that point."

"He thought you were being followed by another gondola?" she said sharply.

"Yes, and it's my belief it hid just round the corner, and when I went round the corner on foot, that's when the supposed footpads set upon me and tried to drown me."

"A Canaletto gondola," she said slowly.

"Exactly right," I said. "I met them earlier and they were at pains to tell me that it was a Canaletto gondola and not a Cornetto one."

"So this is absolutely nothing to do with doctors and dissections," she burst out. "This is the Canalettos who are trying to frame us. They're murdering our customers and claiming they died of the plague, which they somehow contracted from our gondolas."

"That too is a plausible theory," I said cautiously, not wanting to show that I had got it slightly wrong, and Rosemary had got it slightly right. It was obvious now: the Canalettos were bumping off the Cornetto customers to put the Cornetto company out of business. "Of course, I can't swear to whose gondola Librarian Zen was on."

"I'll bet you a million ducats that it was one of ours," she said heatedly.

If I lost, I didn't think Miss Blaine would consider that an acceptable expense, and it was more than likely that she disapproved of gambling in the first place. "You could be right," I said. "And we can always check with him."

"And you're telling me that one of my *colleagues*," she spat out the word, "is involved in this?"

I considered it. I felt a bit wrong-footed by the way she had demolished my Burke and Hare theory. "The group in the printworks thought I was the person they were meeting because of my plague doctor outfit, and they certainly called me 'Doc'," I said. "It's only the five of us who wear this stuff. And remember, someone in here tried to murder me."

"When I find out which one of them it is, I won't *try* to murder them, I'll succeed," she declared.

I reminded her of the Hippocratic Oath, and she said that if this other doctor had ignored it, that entitled her to ignore it as well.

"But we don't know which one it is, and it's getting late," I said. "Who knows when they'll be back? If you're going to murder someone, you need to be clear-headed. A good night's sleep will do you a power of good."

She was going to argue, but I pointed out that we had no idea how long it would be before the others came back, and that she would be getting progressively sleepier, with poorer reaction times.

We wished each other goodnight, and went to our respective bedrooms. I was glad to change into my nightshirt, since my PPE still wasn't quite dry. For a second time, I lugged the wooden chest across the room to block the door and stop anyone trying to murder me during the night. I got into bed and wondered how I could go about identifying which of Dr Oregano, Dr Parsley and Dr Marjoram was our villain, and how I could stop Dr Rosemary from murdering him. And then I fell asleep and had disturbing dreams about dissection.

I awoke to the realisation that this was day five of my mission, and I was no longer entirely clear what that mission was. It certainly seemed to have very little to do with plague. But my first task of the day was to unmask a rogue doctor. When I went into the reception room, I found all four doctors already there, breakfasting on cappuccino and pastries brought by the woman who did.

"Afternoon," said Dr Rosemary acidly. I could understand that she was raring to go on the unmasking, but it's important to get a good night's sleep.

I sat down to join them, grabbing a pastry to dunk in my cappuccino. My preferred breakfast involves porridge, but I accept that missions involve making sacrifices.

Dr Marjoram looked at me gloomily. "So neither of you got executed. Our young colleague's been explaining that anonymous denunciations are no longer allowed, and you've got some sort of ducal dispensation for breaking quarantine because of your plague research."

Was that disappointment in his voice? Had he hoped that my execution would save him the bother of trying to murder me again?

"Yes, it all worked out very well," I said. "I was a bit delayed in getting home, and I was disappointed that nobody was here apart from your young colleague. I thought perhaps we could have had a wee celebratory prosecco."

That last wasn't true, since I never drink when I'm on a mission.

"Where were you, by the way?" I asked ingenuously.

"I was out at the opera," he said.

"That sounds fun," I said. "What was the opera?"

"No idea," he said.

I exchanged glances with Dr Rosemary. That was suspicious. He looked like our man.

"It was very good, whatever it was," he said. "At the Teatro San Cassiano. I didn't really like the music, but I liked what they did on stage. The new technology is amazing. There was a marvellous thunderstorm, with flashes of lightning and real rain, and they had a god sitting on a cloud, and boats that grew wings and flew, and a ballet performed entirely on horseback. Oh, and a chorus of singing plants."

It was a nice touch, claiming not to know what he had seen, the sort of thing an innocent man would say. His lengthy description proved nothing. He could have heard about it from a friend. But I still had two other suspects.

I took a swig of cappuccino and innocently asked Dr Parsley, "Were you at the opera as well?"

"I went for a walk," he said. "I'm a firm believer in the great Hippocrates' dictum that walking is man's best medicine."

"You went for a walk?" I said, sounding surprised. "I always find that awkward with the way people scream when they see me."

"I obviously didn't go out in my plague outfit," he said.

Dr Rosemary and I exchanged glances again. A plague doctor

going out without his PPE: did that imply he knew there wasn't a plague to protect himself against?

"And where were you?" I asked Dr Oregano as I ate the remaining piece of pastry.

He looked at me as though I was a piece of particularly noxious algae polluting the canals.

"Absolutely none of your business, Dr Distance-Learning. Don't be so inquisitive."

A third exchange of glances. If he had nothing to hide, why wouldn't he tell me? But this wasn't getting us anywhere. And then my disturbing dreams gave me an idea.

"That was incredibly useful getting the dissection workshop with your young colleague. Informative and practical," I said to Dr Oregano. I turned to Dr Rosemary. "But I have to say, Doctor, no offence, you're quite young and you did only go to the University of Bologna."

Dr Rosemary, unaware of what I was up to, gave me a look of fury, which was useful since all of the others saw it as well.

"I would really appreciate it if we could all go down to the storeroom and you three could show me how it's done."

Dr Oregano slammed his cappuccino cup down on the table. "You really are the most impertinent fellow it has ever been my misfortune to meet. We're not running a nursery school here for your benefit. Now get back down to your post and record the bodies coming in."

"We're run off our feet here dealing with this dreadful disease, but suddenly we're expected to drop everything for the benefit of this unqualified foreigner," said Dr Parsley to nobody in particular.

"The closer we get to those bodies, the more likely we are to find that marjoram's completely useless against the plague," said Dr Marjoram gloomily.

I drained my cappuccino cup. "I'm so sorry, I realise now what a thoughtless request it was," I said, sounding as contrite as I possibly could. "You're all busy, important men and your time is at a premium. But it's exactly because of your importance that I asked. Your young colleague is all very well for showing me the basics, but I'm really anxious to learn, and to learn from the best." I leaned forward earnestly. "You'll all have gained different sorts of expertise in your respective universities, and it would be so interesting for me to see the differences in technique. I'm sure I can pick up different tips from all of you."

"Are you indeed?" snapped Dr Oregano. "You think you can learn something from graduates of the Universities of Genoa and Perugia that you can't learn from me? Although of course you can – you can learn how to do it wrong."

"How dare you, sir!" gasped Dr Parsley.

"Leave it, Doctor. He's not worth it," said Dr Marjoram gloomily. "You just have to ignore it."

Dr Oregano jumped to his feet. "Gentlemen, there's only one way to settle this. We will go to the storeroom, we will each dissect a body, and then it will be evident to all which of us is the best doctor."

My plan had worked. Except Dr Parsley and Dr Marjoram stayed exactly where they were.

"Might I remind you," said Dr Oregano in a silky tone, "that I am in charge here, which includes being in charge of your salaries."

"Hang on," I said, briefly diverted from my task of uncovering the villain, "does that mean I get a salary?" I didn't see why Miss Blaine should be underwriting my gondola trips and coffee shop bills if she didn't have to.

"Of course you don't get a salary," Dr Oregano snapped. "What would you get a salary for? You're not qualified." He clapped his hands as though calling a rowdy class to order, not something that was ever necessary in my school. "Gentleman. The storeroom. Now."

Reluctantly, the two doctors got to their feet, and all five of us put on our plague outfits and went downstairs to the storeroom, where Dr Oregano assigned them each a body.

"Ready, steady, go," he said.

"Oh, goodness," said Dr Marjoram with an embarrassed laugh, "I've forgotten to bring my surgical instruments. I'll just go upstairs and get them."

Now I knew exactly who our villain was. And I definitely wasn't going to let him slip upstairs and then sneak out from the loggia on to the nearest gondola.

"I'll come with you," I said.

"Absolutely no need," he said, flapping a dismissive hand at me. "I know where I left them. I won't be a moment."

"Nevertheless," I said, "Hippocrates said walking is man's best medicine." I winced at the non-inclusive language. "A quick sprint up and down the stairs is just what I need."

I did a little jog on the spot so that Dr Marjoram would realise he couldn't outrun me. I followed him upstairs, and we went into his room. This was the most dangerous moment. He had tried to murder me once, and now he could attack me with any one of his surgical instruments, or two if he was reasonably ambidextrous.

The most likely, I thought, were the knife and the hacksaw. The moment he attacked me, the priority would be to disarm him.

"Ah, here it is," he said, moving his carelessly flung nightshirt to reveal the box on a chair. He picked it up, and I tensed, waiting for the moment when he would open it. He put it under his arm, walked past me and set off downstairs. This wasn't at all what I had expected. I followed him, warily.

"I was all for starting without you," said Dr Oregano scornfully. "But your colleague here insisted that it was only fair to wait until you got back, so that we could all start at the same time. Well, Dr Distance-Learning, are you ready to watch a masterclass in dissection?"

I absolutely wasn't. But the great thing about being back in my PPE was that they couldn't see if I wasn't looking.

"And again," he said. "Ready, steady, go."

The three doctors raised their surgical knives in unison and brought them down on their respective cadavers. I closed my eyes briefly, which in retrospect was a mistake. I felt someone push past me, gasping, "Stuffy. Need air."

By the time I opened my eyes, there were two doctors in the hallway. One was reaching for the door handle, the other was grabbing at the hem of his goatskin overcoat in a bid to stop him. The first doctor lashed out with his surgical knife, but the second nimbly dodged away without letting go of the coat.

The escaping doctor then tried to get out of his coat, but his hands were too clumsy in their gloves to undo the fastenings, and he was hampered by the knife. He threw it on the ground and started to take his gloves off, but by that time, I was back in action, and quickly immobilised him with a well-judged wrist lock.

"Get his mask off," I instructed the other doctor, who I deduced was Dr Rosemary. She complied. And revealed that the absconder, red-faced and wheezing, was Dr Parsley.

Dr Oregano and Dr Marjoram had abandoned their dissecting to join us.

"What on earth is going on?" asked Dr Oregano.

"This man," I said, still keeping Parsley in an armlock, "is not a doctor."

"Don't be ridiculous," said Dr Oregano. "You're the one who isn't a doctor. Even though this man's degree is merely from the University of Perugia, he's still classified as a doctor."

"No he's not," I said. "Ask him a medical question."

"Doctor, would you use boiling oil to cauterise a wound?" asked Dr Marjoram.

"Tell this madman to unhand me!" panted Parsley. "I don't know why he's making these absurd allegations."

"Why don't you just answer the question?" asked Dr Rosemary.

"Because the situation is outrageous!" he snarled. "I am a graduate of the medical school of the University of Perugia, and it's an insult to ask me to prove it!"

"It's not exactly a difficult question," said Dr Marjoram. "Boiling oil to cauterise a wound, yes or no?"

"This is absurd!" moaned Dr Parsley.

"Answer, Doctor," said Dr Oregano in a voice that would have done credit to a Marcia Blaine prefect asking a third-year to hand over their cigarettes.

"Oh, all right! Yes, boiling oil to cauterise a wound."

There was a moment's silence. Then, "Wrong choice," said Dr Rosemary. "We stopped using boiling oil years ago. You're not a doctor, and I'm going to denounce you."

"You can't do that," sneered Dr Parsley. "Anonymous denunciations aren't allowed any more. You told us that yourself."

"I have no intention of being anonymous," said Dr Rosemary. "I am going to proclaim from the rooftops what you, a Canaletto, have done to try to destroy my family's business."

"Oh no!" Parsley groaned. "I've been captured by Cornettos!"

"Just one Cornetto," I said. "I'm helping out of solidarity – I don't have a family connection."

"Would someone please explain what's going on?" asked Dr Oregano, confusion replacing his usual arrogance.

"That could take a while," I said. "I suggest we all go back upstairs to the comfy seats, but we need to do something to restrain the fake doctor."

"There are lots of spare sacks here," said Dr Marjoram. "We could put him in one of those."

Manoeuvring Parsley through the wrist lock, I attempted to get him to stand in a sack until we realised that meant we would have to carry him upstairs. We threw the sack over his head instead, securing it round his waist with a belt, and propelled him upstairs. We attached him to a chair with more belts, and Dr Rosemary, showing admirable surgical skills, carefully cut out two eyeholes in the sack so that he could observe the proceedings.

"Right," I said, once we were all seated, "the first thing to say is that there is no plague in Venice."

Dr Marjoram turned to Dr Oregano. "This is the sort of thing that happens when you take in unqualified people who know nothing about medicine. Just as well we're here to spread terror among the population, or they wouldn't take it seriously."

As though addressing a particularly dull primary school pupil, Dr Oregano said to me, "We've just been in the storeroom preparing to dissect several plague victims."

"I'm afraid Dr Distance-Learning is right," said Dr Rosemary. "Those textbook black and red spots – they're nothing more than printer's ink."

"The victims were drowned and then stamped with ink," I said.

"What? Drowned?" exclaimed Dr Oregano.

"What? Stamped with ink?" stuttered Dr Marjoram.

"I'm sorry I didn't manage to drown you," Parsley snarled at me through the sack. "I was suspicious of you from the start, the way you just turned up. You followed me, didn't you, that night when I went down to report to the Canaletto team?"

"Was that what you were doing? I did wonder why you were wandering out in the middle of the night," I said. "I didn't know it was you, of course, because you were wearing a spare mask without your trademark parsley in it."

"Yes, that was clever of me," he said proudly. "That was always my strategy when I went out on Canaletto business. I was a herbless doctor."

"You're not a doctor, you're a Canaletto," I said.

"No I'm not," he protested. "I'm not a family member, I'm just a tiny cog. I was forced into it – yes, that's it, I was coerced. I never wanted to get involved. I'm a victim."

"Not as much of a victim as all these people who got drowned," I said severely. "And I don't believe your story for a moment. I think you're in it for the money, which suggests you're in a job that doesn't pay well. You've been playing a part here, and you've had to sound plausible in front of these doctors. I think you're one of these non-singing actors who gets to prance around the stage at the Teatro San Cassiano."

Dr Marjoram peered at him closely. "I think you're right. I'm sure I've seen this fellow on stage dressed as a shepherd."

Parsley looked sulky. "I did pretty well," he said. "I had you all fooled. Until now. Just because I guessed wrong about the boiling oil to cauterise wounds. It could so easily have gone the other way."

"Luckily, it didn't," I said briskly. "And we'd have quizzed you some more – you couldn't guess them all correctly. Anyway, as you've heard, two of us here are planning on publicly denouncing you."

"I'm denouncing him as well," said Dr Oregano. "Coming in here, pretending to be a doctor."

"If everyone else is denouncing him, I suppose I'd better denounce him too," said Dr Marjoram gloomily.

"That's four of us now. The only thing that can save you—"

"Hang on," said Dr Rosemary. "I don't want him saved."

"That's a nice way to talk about a former colleague," said Parsley plaintively.

"Doctor, you've heard this man tell us he is a tiny cog," I said. "Wouldn't it be better to go for the big wheel? I suggest that we offer to let him go back to the Teatro San Cassiano in return for information."

"That depends on the quality of the information," said Dr Rosemary.

"There," I said to Parsley. "It's all down to you. Sing like a canary."

He peered nervously at me through the eyeholes in the sack. "I'm generally a non-speaking role at the Teatro. They've never wanted me to sing like a canary. I'm not sure I would know how."

"Just tell us what the Canalettos are up to," I said.

"I don't know much, being a cog," he said. "But the Canalettos are worried about there not being enough gondola business to go around. Their main rival company is the Cornettos, so they decided to get rid of them by pretending that anyone who went on a Cornetto gondola died of the plague."

"The fiends!" burst out Dr Rosemary.

"I know you're upset," I told her. "But our priority is getting information out of this pretend doctor. It doesn't help to have constant interruptions."

She murmured an apology.

"Please go on," I said to Parsley.

"There's a whole network of us," he said self-importantly. "The others are just doing manual work such as drowning and stamping. But when the doge established the rapid response team to deal with the outbreak of plague, the Canalettos hired me. They thought it would be good to have someone on the inside to make sure the medics didn't suspect anything about the cause of death as the bodies came in. We knew they'd be so busy fighting the plague that they wouldn't waste time checking my credentials."

"I never imagined that anyone could be so corrupt as to claim a medical qualification from the University of Perugia that they weren't entitled to," snapped Dr Oregano.

"By the way," said Dr Marjoram to me. "You don't have any medical expertise. How did you know he wasn't a doctor?"

"I didn't know it was him," I admitted. "I just knew it was one of you four. But ironically, he was the one who gave me the idea of testing you all when he mentioned Hippocrates. It reminded me of the doctor's Hippocratic oath, promising to do no harm, and I thought that didn't sit well with a doctor trying to murder me. But tell me, what do you use to cauterise wounds instead of boiling oil?"

"You really do know nothing," sighed Dr Oregano. "Egg yolk, oil of roses and turpentine, of course." He glared at Parsley. "And I see it now. You were the one who suggested that the bodies be left undisturbed in the storeroom, and then suggested that our young colleague be the one to look after them. You knew that we, with our far greater experience, would have discovered the fraud immediately."

"You were about to start dissecting the bodies and you didn't realise," I reminded him, annoyed by the unjustified criticism of Dr Rosemary. He subsided, muttering.

"Go on," I said to Parsley. "We want the full story."

"I'm part of a city-wide network," he boasted. "Whenever a Cornetto gondola picked up a passenger, a Canaletto gondola would trail it. When the passenger disembarked, they would be grabbed, drowned and taken to the printworks to be stamped. Then they were left near where they came ashore, and all that people knew was that they had last been seen on a Cornetto gondola and now had the plague."

Dr Rosemary became quite abusive at this point, using language more suited to a gondolier than a clinician. I was quietly and modestly congratulating myself that I had worked out the whole plot unaided, and now Parsley was confirming it in his laborious way.

"This is outrageous!" Dr Rosemary shouted. "I'm off right now to denounce the Canalettos."

"Take it easy," I said. "We need to go carefully. All we've got is an uncorroborated statement from a tiny cog. If you, a Cornetto, start denouncing the Canalettos, it will just be dismissed as *your* family's attempt to undermine a rival. What you need to do right now is get all Cornetto gondolas grounded so that there are no more murders. Don't worry, that's just a temporary measure while I go to seek expert advice on how to proceed."

I stood up and smoothed down my goatskin overcoat. My hand brushed over the half-book in its protective compostable bag and my fingers tingled. "I'll be back as soon as I can. Keep an eye on your former colleague."

"You said you'd let me go back to the Teatro San Cassiano," whined Parsley.

"I did, but I didn't say when," I pointed out. "Just sit still and behave yourself."

And with that, I went off to see Librarian Zen. He greeted me warmly, and, as quickly and concisely as I could, I outlined the situation, including his own brush with death at the hands of the Canaletto thugs.

He listened attentively, and once I had finished, said, "And you say the Canalettos are responsible? Oh no, Librarian Macaroni Mona Lisa Glissando. That's quite impossible."

TWELVE

"Excuse me, Librarian Zen, but do you disbelieve me?" I asked.

"Never!" he protested, visibly shocked. "That would imply I thought you were telling an untruth. I'm merely observing that you're entirely incorrect."

"Maybe I didn't explain it properly," I said. "I'll go over it again."

"No need," he said. "You were very clear, and I followed it all. But both Canaletto and Cornetto are good friends of mine, and good friends of each other. It's quite impossible that Canaletto would do anything like this."

I blinked. Canaletto had been the offensive intellectual in the Academy of the Unknowns, who had had a go at the doge.

"I could easily imagine him doing lots of things like this," I said. "I thought he was thoroughly unpleasant."

"Ah, no, that's the son," said the librarian. "A complete wastrel who capitalises on the family name. I suspect he only got into the Academy through bribery. But we really need to get this sorted out." He went over to a reader who was hunched over a chained volume on the table of the most popular reads. "Let me interrupt you," he said pleasantly.

"Oh, please don't, Librarian," said the reader. "I'm enjoying this book tremendously, and according to the hourglass, I've still got fifteen minutes left."

"How would you feel about three uninterrupted hours? To be taken whenever you like. But right now, I need you to go and ask Signor Cornetto and Signor Canaletto to come and join me."

The reader sprang up and sprinted off down the stairs. A

short time later, he returned with two elderly gentlemen, both wearing long serviceable brown wool gowns with no pretensions to fashion. They visibly recoiled at the sight of me in my PPE.

Librarian Zen hurried over to greet them. "Don't worry, gentlemen, there's no danger to your health. The only problem is if you dislike the smell of aniseed."

"Not at all," said the first elderly gent, who turned out to be Signor Cornetto.

"It's most pleasant," said the second, Signor Canaletto, nodding at my proboscis.

Librarian Zen took us to an anteroom where we could talk without disturbing the readers. The elderly gents were charming, amiable and appalled to hear my story.

"I don't understand how you haven't heard about this already," I said.

"What we've heard about is the plague," said Signor Cornetto.

"And at our age, it's wiser to stay in if there's plague going around," said Signor Canaletto. "It's a great relief to hear there isn't any."

"We've been working from home, trying to come up with ways of keeping the business going, and that's taken up all our time, given the lack of customers," said Signor Cornetto.

"I thought of introducing an incentive scheme of free cappuccinos before 11am, but right now, I simply don't have enough ready cash to finance it," sighed Signor Canaletto.

"An excellent idea," said Signor Cornetto. "I thought of something similar with pastries, but again, it wasn't economically feasible."

"We're all facing insolvency and starvation," said Signor Canaletto. "But the worst thing is these terrible rumours."

"They're not rumours, Signor Canaletto," I said firmly. "The fake doctor has admitted that he was hired by your firm, and I have first-hand experience of Canaletto employees trying to drown me. I also saw these same employees overseeing the red and black stamping of someone they'd just murdered." I couldn't put it any more plainly than that. "With library stamps," I added, bringing home the full horror to my colleague, who winced.

"I don't understand it," faltered Signor Canaletto, grasping Signor Cornetto's hand. "My old friend, you know I would never do anything to harm your business."

Signor Cornetto patted Signor Canaletto's hand. "Of course I know. Just as I would never do anything to harm yours. Gondoliers are brothers."

Something outside the window caught my eye.

"Then how do you account for that?" I asked, ushering them over to have a look. There, sailing unhurriedly down the canal, was the black funeral gondola of doom, with its banner proclaiming "Take a Cornetto Gondola and Die".

Signor Cornetto gasped. "I've never seen anything like it!"

"Nor have I," said Signor Canaletto. "What do you make of it?"

"Difficult to tell from this distance, especially with everything painted black, but I would say no larch," said Signor Cornetto. "And definitely no elm."

"Your eyesight's better than mine," said Signor Canaletto. "I spotted the lack of elm, of course, but I think you're right about the larch. And I wonder – the cherry?"

"I wonder about that too," said Signor Cornetto. "And as the good doctor has just said, how do you account for it?"

"There's no accounting for it," said Signor Canaletto. "A non-Venetian gondola in Venice."

"You mean it's not a Canaletto gondola?" I said.

The pair of them burst out laughing.

"A Canaletto gondola?" wheezed Signor Cornetto. "Good gracious, no!"

"Oh dear," said Signor Canaletto. "It makes you wonder why we go to all that bother of craftsmanship when people mistake an eyesore like that for the real thing."

"What?" I said.

"What?" said Librarian Zen.

The two elderly gentlemen continued studying the gondola as

it continued on its way.

"It's a very good counterfeit, I grant you," said Signor Canaletto.

"Very good," agreed Signor Cornetto. He turned to us. "You two gentlemen obviously can't tell the difference. Perhaps most people couldn't."

"But the pair of us have been in this business so long," said Signor Canaletto. "We can tell right away."

"Anyway, old friend, there's a mystery here, and we need to get to the bottom of it," said Signor Cornetto.

"We do indeed," said Signor Canaletto. "And this is how I think we should go about it."

He outlined his plan, we all approved it, and the reader was yet again dragged away from the book he was enjoying so much to go on another errand, with the promise of another three hours of uninterrupted reading. Soon we were organised, and I set off with the two elderly gentlemen. Librarian Zen reluctantly felt that he had to stay and keep the library open after it had been closed for so long when he was in the Doge's Palace.

Signor Canaletto walked briskly ahead in the direction of Dr Rosemary's brother's gondola. Signor Cornetto and I sauntered slowly after him for a while before breaking off and taking up our positions. We had to wait for what seemed like an age before there was any sign of activity, but suddenly there it was, and it was exactly the activity we wanted to see. The neds sneaking into the square and lying in wait.

A few moments later, Signor Canaletto, fresh from his trip on the Cornetto gondola, came along the lane. He was dressed as me, and he was heading for the bridge.

With my super-acute hearing, I picked up on what the neds were saying in their place of concealment.

"It's him! That interfering doctor!"

"You're right. I can smell the aniseed. We'll finish him off properly this time."

I stayed where I was in my own place of concealment, since they weren't talking about me, but about Signor Canaletto, with whom I had changed clothes in the library. He was about the same height as me, and walked almost as briskly as me, although I noticed that his left shoulder was leading, and his former oar hand trailed behind slightly. I was sure it would go unnoticed by everyone else, just as Librarian Zen and I had been unable to tell the gondola of doom wasn't local and didn't include the full complement of eight types of wood.

As soon as the neds started approaching Signor Canaletto, we made our move. I dealt with the pair of them in short order, leaving them sprawling on the paving stones, while Dr Rosemary's brother, who had helpfully followed his recent fare, wrestled the gondolier on shore.

Signor Canaletto tore off his – my – beaked mask. "What is the meaning of this outrage?" he roared. "Gondolier, I can't believe you're mixed up in this! You are summarily dismissed, and you will never work for my company again."

"Oh, your company, is it?" sneered the gondolier. "Not for much longer."

That was the point at which Signor Cornetto said, "How dare you talk to your boss like that?" and thumped him on the nose.

"This is far too complicated for us to deal with," said Dr Rosemary's brother. "This is something that needs to go before the doge."

There was an attempted escape at this point, but I helped Dr Rosemary's brother to subdue the gondolier, and Signor Cornetto and Signor Canaletto, whose years of operating a gondola had left them with an impressively vice-like grip, each took hold of a ned.

We dragged them off to the Doge's Palace where Dr Canaletto, once again wearing the beaked mask, briefly had to pretend to be me for the benefit of the guards, so that he, Dr Cornetto, Dr Rosemary's brother and I were allowed up the grand staircase, the guards taking charge of the prisoners.

The doge greeted us warmly and invited us to take a seat, although there was no word of a cappuccino. I hoped that meant he was taking my advice on not overdoing it seriously.

"I've got great news, Your Electedness," I told the doge. "La Serenissima is now plague-free, thanks to your rapid response team. You can take full credit for it. Get that news out to the populace and your trading partners as soon as you like, and I can guarantee that it, and you, will be very popular."

"Very popular?" he asked eagerly.

"This is the news we have been praying for," said Signor Cornetto.

"The people will praise your name for all time," said Signor Canaletto.

The doge, blushing slightly, summoned a gofer and issued instructions for a proclamation.

"What's happening to the prisoners?" I asked slightly nervously.

"They'll be interrogated by the Council of Ten," said the doge, and I shuddered. The Council of Ten was a sinister state security organisation that made the Spanish Inquisition look like the teddy bears' picnic.

"So how's the gondoliering?" asked the doge politely. I saw that like most heads of state, he had been well trained in the art of small talk.

"Terrible," said Signor Cornetto.

"Awful," said Signor Canaletto.

"Too many gondolas, too few passengers," said Signor Cornetto. "Both of our family businesses are at risk of collapse, so we're facing insolvency and starvation."

"I'm sorry to hear that," said the doge. "I'm never on a gondola myself, with not being allowed out except on ceremonial occasions. I have my own galley."

"Yes, we've seen it," said Signor Cornetto.

"We saw it when you—" began Signor Canaletto.

I could tell he was about to say something about the disastrous Marriage of the Sea ceremony, possible even "when you threw the ring like a girl", so I quickly interrupted with, "I believe you've got all sorts of marvellous carvings on your galley, lions and hydras and sirens and dolphins. I saw a dolphin the other day.

Marvellous creatures. Very friendly. Although I believe they have trouble with gondoliers smacking them on the nose with their oars."

"Disgraceful!" snapped Signor Canaletto. "That's the sort of thing that gives our profession a bad name. There's absolutely no excuse for it. They wouldn't dare try it with crocodiles."

"Crocodiles," I said, to prevent any return to the galley conversation, "now there's an interesting reptile. Did you know their jaws are configured in such a way that they can't actually chew, so they have to swallow stones to help them digest their food?"

"How very interesting," said the doge, a phrase I imagined he had used many times on many occasions.

I was just preparing to explain the difference between crocodiles and alligators (crocodiles have pointy snouts, while alligators have wide ones; alligators like fresh water, crocodiles prefer a mixture of fresh and salt) when a door opened, and a figure dressed all in black glided in. He oozed menace. He had a black beard and black moustache and black hair under his square black cap, which gave full focus to his glittering, darting eyes. I didn't need to be told that this was a member of the Council of Ten.

"Most Serene Prince," he said, bowing low, and it turned out he had quite a squeaky voice, which rather detracted from the menace. "It's all been a bit disappointing."

"Oh dear," said the doge. "Have they all died before managing to confess? I do wonder whether you need to be a little less enthusiastic."

"It's not that," squeaked the councillor. "We never got a chance to do anything – we couldn't shut them up. We had to threaten to cut their ears off to make them stop."

"How frustrating for you," said the doge. "And what do you have to report?"

"A dreadful plot against the state; one of our citizens conspiring with a foreign power to take over our transport infrastructure.

The situation is so grave that we felt unequal to dealing with it, and are bringing it to you, Most Serene Prince."

"Really?" said the doge, looking a lot less serene. He obviously preferred to delegate.

"We now have the felon in custody, along with his foreign collaborator," squeaked the councillor. "You need to hear their confessions and determine what's to be done with them."

"I do?" said the doge.

"You do. They're just outside." The councillor oozed back to the door and opened it. The guards brought in two men. One kept his head down, as though he was deeply embarrassed by his situation. He was wearing simple breeches and a smock. Smocks are seldom high fashion, but if ever a smock was ill-fitting, this was the one. The other man, wearing a stylish lace collar over his silk doublet, had a positive swagger, as though the guards were a ceremonial escort. He looked condescendingly round the room, taking us all in: the doge, Librarian Zen, me, Signor Cornetto and finally Signor Canaletto.

"Hello, Papa," he said.

THIRTEEN

Signor Canaletto gaped at him. "You! What are you doing here?"

"A silly misunderstanding, Papa," he said. "I'm glad to have the opportunity to explain things to His Serenity." He gave the doge another nod. "Most Serene Prince, it won't have escaped your notice that the gondola industry is sinking fast." Parsley wasn't the only punster in town.

"Actually, it has – escaped my attention, that's to say," the doge stammered, "I can't remember the last time I took a gondola. I have my own galley, you see."

"Indeed, I think we all know about your galley and the rings – that is, the things one finds under its floorboards," said Canaletto junior with an unpleasant smirk. I found myself wishing someone would turn him into a dolphin so that he could be smacked on the nose. But someone as unpleasant as him didn't deserve to be something as adorable as a dolphin. He would be better as a crocodile, being smacked on the nose by St Theodore.

"Some people here," he continued with a sideways glance at Signori Cornetto and Canaletto, "insist on clinging to tradition, which is just another way of saying they're hopelessly out of touch with the modern age."

Signor Cornetto gave Signor Canaletto's arm a sympathetic squeeze.

"There was only one thing to do," Canaletto junior went on. "Rationalise the number of gondola companies."

This time it was Signor Canaletto giving Signor Cornetto's arm a sympathetic squeeze, but Signor Cornetto didn't even notice.

"Wretched boy!" he roared. "You attempted to destroy the

time-honoured company of Cornetto?"

"*Scusi*! May I speak?" It was the man in the ill-fitting smock, waving his arm to get attention. I registered something odd about the way he was talking.

"Shut up!" snarled Canaletto junior. "Nobody wants to hear from you."

"I do," said the doge unexpectedly. He gave a quick nod to the bloke from the Council of Ten, who in an instant shoved a wad of material into Canaletto junior's mouth while simultaneously pushing him to the ground and keeping him there by means of sitting on him. I could see these councillors knew their stuff.

"Speak," said the doge, the invitation obviously aimed at the main in the ill-fitting smock, since Canaletto junior was no longer able to say a word.

"Thank you," said the smock man. "Apologies if I haven't quite understood everything, but I don't speak Venetian." That was what I registered as odd – he was speaking heavily accented Italian.

"We can understand you," said the doge. "That's what matters."

"The plan was not to destroy the Cornetto company, but the Canaletto company," said smock man. "That is why we built the beautiful big gondola with the message 'Take a Cornetto Gondola and Die', so that people knew Cornetto gondolas were the best gondolas."

"You're from Naples!" I burst out.

I expected my deduction to cause some excitement, but instead there was something of an awkward silence until Librarian Zen said, "Yes, we can tell from his accent."

Strange noises were emerging from Canaletto junior, who finally managed to spit out the wad of material and yell, "Don't be stupid! That message means that anyone who takes a Cornetto gondola dies! That's the company we were destroying!"

The councillor retrieved the material and skilfully shoved it back in Canaletto junior's mouth while continuing to sit on him. I wondered whether he might offer masterclasses.

Smock man gave Canaletto junior a look of serious disapproval. "You mean you've been murdering Cornetto customers? That wasn't the plan. The family won't be happy to hear you've made such a bad mistake."

He ferreted in the pocket of his smock and produced a sheet of paper. "Here," he said, giving it to the doge. "You can see he's got it completely wrong."

As the doge read it, we could see the horror on his face.

"Get them out of here," he managed to say to the councillor. "I need time to decide what to do with them."

With the panache I so admired, the councillor lugged Canaletto junior to his feet and shunted him out of the door, the guards following on with smock man.

"Most Serene Prince?" asked Librarian Zen. "What's happened?"

"Here." With a shaking hand, the doge held out the sheet of paper to him.

"Oh dear," said the librarian as he read it. "This is very bad." He turned to Signor Canaletto. "Your son—"

"He's no son of mine!" hit out Signor Canaletto. "I repudiate him completely."

"That's probably wise," said Librarian Zen. "This document outlines a dreadful plot against our republic. If you'll allow me a little latitude, from what the individual previously known as your son was saying, I can extrapolate what he thought was happening, and then tell you what was actually happening."

I settled back in my chair to listen, although Signori Cornetto and Canaletto looked quite tense.

"The young man seems to have been concerned about his inheritance—" Librarian Zen began.

"I'll give him concerned," Signor Canaletto again interrupted. "I'm cutting him off without a ducat." I felt that while the doge was still thinking of what to do with the criminal, it was unfortunate to be talking about cutting things off in case it gave him any ideas.

"He was anxious to ensure your family business was a going concern, so he decided to get rid of his rivals by suggesting that anyone who travelled in a Cornetto gondola would die of the plague."

"He did more than suggest it," I said. "We've got a storeroom full of bodies to prove it."

I quickly outlined what had been going on for the doge's benefit.

After a moment's consideration, he said, "What dreadful ongoings. It's good, though, being able to announce that there isn't any plague."

"Indeed so," said Librarian Zen. "I can't think of an announcement that would be more popular."

The doge beamed.

"However, the young man needed funding for his scheme—"

"Because he's a spendthrift who squanders everything I give him on fine clothes, fine wine and highly dubious women," snapped Signor Canaletto.

"And bribing members of the Academy of the Unknowns to nominate him as a member," said the doge, adding hastily, "So I've heard. I obviously don't know anything about the Academy of the Unknowns, as I'm not allowed out except on ceremonial occasions."

"Quite," said Librarian Zen. "Anyway, the young man became involved with a very unsavoury family in Naples who offered to underwrite the plan."

"Foreigners," muttered the doge, since this was two hundred years before Italy was unified.

"They misunderstood the brief, since their Venetian wasn't very good, and built a gondola that they thought was an advertising campaign for the Cornetto company," said the librarian.

Signor Canaletto and Signor Cornetto snorted almost as loudly as Dr Rosemary and I had snorted over the "throws like a girl" line.

"A Neapolitan family building a gondola. That explains everything," said Signor Canaletto.

"Precisely," said Signor Cornetto. "Not the first idea what they were about. No elm, no larch, and I'm sure you're right about the cherry."

"Sorry, are you saying the funeral gondola that's been sailing up and down was actually made in Naples?" I asked.

"Well, obviously," said Signor Canaletto. "Rubbish like that certainly wasn't made here."

"But how did it get here?" I asked.

Signor Cornetto looked at me as though wondering whether I was serious. "It sailed," he said.

"But Naples is on the wrong side of the country," I said. "It must be a thousand nautical miles away."

Signor Cornetto shrugged. "People who live in ports are seafarers."

It still struck me that the four guys on the funeral gondola were pretty impressive if they'd managed to row that thing all the way down the Tyrrhenian Sea, round the toe and heel of Italy, and up the Adriatic to Venice.

A discreet cough from Librarian Zen, and he resumed his account. "With the Neapolitans bankrolling everything, the young man duly hired a squad of ne'er-do-wells, a mixture of thugs and out-of-work actors and set about murdering Cornetto passengers."

Signor Canaletto distractedly ran his fingers through his hair. "I don't understand," he said. "He could never have imagined that I would condone any of this."

"I'm afraid," said Librarian Zen, "that he intended you to be a plague victim as well, after which he planned to take over the company. What saved you was staying indoors, otherwise you might have been drowned."

"I blame his mother," growled Signor Canaletto. "She's always spoiled him."

"Mothers!" said Signor Cornetto, shaking his head sympathetically.

"What he didn't realise," said Librarian Zen, "was that the

Napolitano family's plans were completely different from his."

"Yes, we heard," I said. "They thought he was murdering Canaletto customers, and boosting the Cornetto business with that ridiculous slogan of theirs, but of course he could never have become the boss of that because it wasn't his family."

"He wasn't going to become the boss of anything," said Librarian Zen drily, holding up the sheet of paper. "In fact, he was due to become a plague victim as well, with the Napolitano family gaining control of the Venetian gondola industry."

The doge gasped. "Foreigners! Coming up here and taking our jobs!"

"Exactly," said Librarian Zen. "It's thanks to the good doctor here that we've uncovered this iniquitous plot."

"Doctor," said the doge, turning to me with a catch in his voice, "first you save my life, then you save Venice's way of life."

"Honestly, I'm just glad to be able to help," I said.

"But you haven't really," objected Signor Cornetto. "We're still in exactly the same position of having too few passengers, which means both Canaletto and myself are facing insolvency and starvation."

Signor Canaletto nodded vigorous agreement. I thought this particularly churlish given that I had apparently saved his life as well by stopping the evil plan before his son murdered him. But I didn't let that deflect from my *raison d'être* of being helpful.

"The solution," I said, "is to get more passengers."

"And how do we do that?" scoffed Signor Cornetto. "Conjure them up out of thin air?"

"We don't want to do that," said the doge in alarm. "That's necromancy, and Librarian Zen tells me I'm responsible for setting the exact penalty for it. I really don't like that part of the job."

"It's nothing to do with necromancy," I said. "It's perfectly simple – you need to develop Venice as a tourist destination. All these travellers from antique lands who come here to trade – make the place more attractive to them, and they'll stay for longer, and tell their friends and relations."

It was Signor Canaletto who did the scoffing this time. "How can we make La Serenissima more attractive? It's already the most beautiful city in the world."

You clearly haven't seen Edinburgh, I thought. We have glorious architecture, verdant hills and parks, a castle, an extinct volcano, and yes, we have a canal as well.

"It's nothing to do with the surroundings," I said. "You need to give them something to do. Music always cheers people up." I paused to think of the gloomy strains of Leonard Cohen, and since I was in Baroque Italy, the slithering melancholy of Gesualdo. Neither of them guaranteed to cheer people up by any direct route. But I decided to keep these caveats to myself, lest introducing exceptions weakened my argument. I repeated, with renewed authority, "Music always cheers people up."

"I'm writing an opera," said the doge shyly. "It's about gondoliers, brothers called Marco and Giuseppe. There's a back story featuring Don Alhambra del Bolero—"

I really had to get him off this idea or there would be a dreadful musical collision.

"No, Your Electedness," I said, "the city can't afford to have you skimping on your vital civic duties to write an opera. And if it got performed, you would never know whether it was any good, or whether people were just saying it was because you're the most important man in Venice. No, what you want to do is become a patron of the arts, encouraging other people to write operas. It would mean lots of evenings out. You could go to all the performances of the operas you commissioned. If you wrote your own opera, you'd only be able to attend the premiere or people would think you were a terrible egotist."

I could see him beginning to waver.

"A patron of the arts," he said, almost to himself. "To commission an opera. An opera at the Teatro San Cassiano. Oh, yes – that would be so much better than all the dreary stuff we have to put up with in St Mark's every day. These old fogeys, Gabrieli and Monteverdi. All very earnest and worthy, and dull, so dull. Not much of a tune to get your teeth into. But an opera! People would come for miles for an opera."

I thought it better not to mention that Monteverdi composed three operas, in case it dimmed his enthusiasm. Instead, I said quickly, "If you like, Your Electedness, I can call in by the Ospedale della Pietà just down the road. They take in orphans, and give them the most wonderful musical education. I'm sure they'd be able to recommend a few who would write really good operas. Obviously it's entirely your decision and I wouldn't dream of trying to influence you. But I'm pretty sure nothing says 'popular' more than supporting musical orphans."

"Popular," murmured the doge dreamily. Then, rousing himself, "Yes, those poor unfortunate orphans. I would like to give them a chance in life."

"Speaking of giving people a chance, have you decided what to do with the prisoners?" I asked.

"Something to do with boiling oil, I hope," grunted Signor Canaletto, obviously still aggrieved after hearing that his son had planned to murder him.

"In my medical capacity, I can tell you that boiling oil is old-fashioned, and the preferred materials are now egg yolk, oil of roses and turpentine," I said.

"That doesn't sound very lethal," said Signor Canaletto.

"We don't necessarily want it to be lethal," I said. "It can be very popular to temper justice with mercy."

"It can?" asked the doge with interest.

"Public executions are very popular," said Signor Canaletto.

"They are?" asked the doge, showing faint signs of stress. "Which would you say is more popular?"

"If you will allow me to distinguish between the two," said Librarian Zen smoothly. "Public executions are very popular among the baying, bloodthirsty mob. However, that sort of person will be distracted fifteen minutes later, probably by grappa, and have forgotten the whole thing by the next day. But a wise and benevolent ruler wins the respect of the higher echelons of society. That ruler can expect to be chronicled as such in the annals of history, and to be immortalised in murals and frescoes alongside personifications of virtues such as justice, charity and fortitude."

"The sort of people who would be impressed by justice tempered with mercy," said the doge. "Are they the sort of people who might be members of, oh, I don't know, just choosing something at random, the Academy of the Unknowns? They wouldn't think that someone tempering justice with mercy was an idiot?"

"Absolutely not," I said. "They'd be really impressed. It's not an organisation I'm familiar with, obviously, but it sounds very sophisticated. Not the sort to allow, for example, a convicted felon to be a member."

That clearly resonated. The doge withdrew into a corner with Librarian Zen where they engaged in an earnest conversation. I would have been interested in listening in, with my excellent hearing, but Signori Canaletto and Cornetto were anxiously asking whether I really thought more people would come to Venice.

"Absolutely no doubt about it," I said. "And what's Venice got that's different? Gondolas. And an opera about gondoliers will have a subliminal message. It'll make everyone want to take a gondola trip."

"We've been thinking of laying people off, but we might even have to hire some more," said Signor Cornetto.

"But where from?" asked Signor Canaletto.

"I'll tell you who you should get," I said. "Those four chaps who rowed the funeral gondola from Naples to Venice. They obviously know what they're doing and they're not afraid of hard work."

The two business owners looked at one another.

"That's true," said Signor Cornetto. "That gondola's rubbish, but there was no problem with their rowing technique."

"We'll need to train them up in where everything is, which canals are dead ends, who sells the best coffee," said Signor Canaletto.

"I had a very nice hot drink and pastry in a new place just by the Campo Santa Maria Formosa," I said. "You should add that to the list."

We were interrupted by the guards returning with Canaletto junior and smock man, who had been summoned by the doge.

"You," said the doge to smock man, "are being deported."

"*Scusi*," said smock man in Italian, "can you speak more slowly? It's hard to follow your language."

"You're going back where you came from," said the doge, enunciating every word very clearly. "*Capeesh?*"

"*Sì*," said smock man, looking pleased to have understood.

"How did you get here?" asked the doge.

"On the big boat with the four rowers," he said.

"Then that's how you're going back," said the doge.

Signor Canaletto coughed to attract the doge's attention and bowed low. "Most Serene Prince," he said, "My colleague and I would like to keep the four rowers here, if that's possible. They could be useful when the tourists arrive for the opera."

"Of course," said the doge. "Anything to support the opera." He returned to addressing smock man. "You're taking the boat back on your own. Careful to stick to your own shipping lane. And I've got a message for you to pass on to the Napolitano family. If they ever, *ever* try to interfere with our most serene republic again, they'll wake up to find a crocodile's head on their pillow. Attached to the rest of a very live crocodile."

"*Sì*," said smock man, nodding enthusiastically. This was definitely the sort of language he understood.

"And now for you," said the doge to Canaletto junior. "Your father was keen for you to be executed, but I'm known for tempering justice with mercy. At least, I am now."

The wad of material was still in Canaletto junior's mouth, but he managed to convey utter boredom with his eyes.

"We're preparing to become an international centre for opera, and you will have a central role, as a cleaner in the Teatro San Cassiano."

Canaletto junior raised his eyes heavenwards in an "is that all you've got?" sort of way.

"Also, as a convicted felon, you will have your membership rescinded of any club or organisation in the city," the doge said.

Canaletto junior's eyes bulged. His face went puce and there were alarming gurgling noises as he tried to speak through the gag. The doge signalled for it to be removed.

"You can't do that!" Canaletto junior yelled.

"I can," said the doge, sounding almost surprised. "I can do what I like. I'm the doge." He looked over to Librarian Zen, who discreetly mimed applause.

"And lastly," said the doge, "you're banned from drinking coffee for thirty days."

"What?" Canaletto junior's voice was a whisper now. "No – that's impossible. I'll die if I don't have coffee."

"You'll die if you do," said the doge matter-of-factly. "Right, that's all, Take them away."

We could hear Canaletto junior shrieking imprecations all the way down the back stairs.

"Most Serene Prince," said Canaletto senior admiringly, "when you refused to have him executed, I thought you were going easy on him. I see I was mistaken."

"I'm not the pushover people assume," the doge said.

As we left down the grand staircase, Signori Canaletto and Cornetto were positively bubbling with enthusiasm.

"If anyone can turn this place into a tourist destination, it's His Serenity," said Signor Canaletto.

"Let's go and find those four rowers and get them learning their canals," said Signor Cornetto.

There was another forlorn queue of would-be readers outside the library, and Librarian Zen raced off to let them in. I made my way the short distance along the Riva degli Schiavoni to the Ospedale della Pietà to commission the opera. What I hadn't mentioned in the Doge's Palace was that it specialised in the musical education of girls. The music scene was so male-dominated that I felt some adjustment was required. Of course, there were always a few male allies around – in fifty years, Vivaldi would be a violin teacher there, and write loads of pieces for the orchestra to play.

I was introduced to a music teacher who assured me there was no problem about commissioning an opera from a suitable student, and asked for my specifications.

I remembered Dr Marjoram's description of the opera he had seen, with thunderstorms, a god on a cloud, boats that grew wings and flew, a ballet on horseback, a chorus of singing plants. It was all very well having a spectacle like that, but I wanted people to focus on the singing.

"I'd like it to be about two heroes, please, gondoliers – perhaps you could actually call it *I Gondolieri*, but their names don't matter, so long as they're not Marco and Giuseppe, and they're not brothers. Maybe they're professional rivals, but they're in love with two sisters who reconcile them."

I thought that sounded as silly as an opera plot should be, and would give sufficient opportunities for duets, trios and quartets.

"That seems clear enough," said the music teacher. "We've got a very good student, Francesca della Pietà, who'll make a marvellous job of it. Anything else?"

"Yes," I said. "Could we have a small singing role for a gondolier from each of Venice's main companies, Cornetto and Canaletto?"

"Of course," she said. "Francesca won't give them anything too taxing. Is that it?"

I supposed I had to give the audience something if they were used to dramatic displays. "One last thing," I said. "I'd like a chorus of dancing dolphins."

"Real dolphins or people dressed as dolphins?" the music teacher asked.

I wondered whether she'd taken leave of her senses. "Real dolphins can't sing," I pointed out.

"They can whistle and click," said the music teacher. "Fascinating rhythms. I'm sure Francesca could develop a very interesting chorus based round that. Our students always enjoy a chance to be innovative."

I opted for real dolphins, approved the relevant paperwork, and told the teacher to send the bill to the doge. As I walked back to the doctors' residence, I felt quite sad that I wouldn't hear the opera, since my week's mission was almost up.

And then in sudden alarm I realised that I still had no idea what my mission was, and therefore couldn't complete it. What if I was just left here? It would be nice to hear the opera, but that would scarcely be compensation for not being back in Morningside Library. And I was getting a little tired of the carb-heavy food.

Miss Blaine? I sent out in the mist. *Just a hint would be good. This is quite late on day five.* Nothing. I pulled my overcoat round me more tightly against the evening chill, and felt the contour of the poor half-book. I understood Dr Rosemary's motive in severing it, but I was still shocked by her action. And now that the city would be attracting quantities of visitors, there was no need for the Cornettos to seek other business opportunities. The book's fate seemed such a tragic waste.

When I reached the residence, everything was much as I had left it. Parsley was still sitting there tied to his chair with a sack over his head, although someone – I suspected Dr Rosemary – had cut another hole for his mouth and had been feeding him fried sardines. The woman who did had obviously been again, since the doctors were sitting at the table tucking into risotto blackened with cuttlefish ink. It looked horrible.

I went over to Parsley and untied him. "As promised, you're free to go," I said. "They'll be glad to see you and your fellow malefactors back at the Teatro San Cassiano, since rehearsals will be starting soon for a new opera. Just try to stay out of trouble in future."

"I will," he promised, heading for the loggia and freedom. "Thank you, Dr Distance-Learning."

"So is everything sorted now?" asked Dr Oregano.

"It is," I said. "You can all return to your own medical practices.

The wicked man who fabricated the outbreak of plague has been punished, and Venice is facing a golden age of music and tourism. However, it's been a long day. I'll wish you all goodnight."

As I got into bed, I was only too aware that the morning would bring day six of my mission, a mission that was still unidentified. What I had said to Dr Oregano was quite wrong. Everything was very far from sorted.

FOURTEEN

When I got up in the morning, the doctors were sitting at the table in their everyday medical robes with their cappuccinos and pastries, two packed bags beside them. I was still in my PPE, those being my only clothes apart from my nightshirt, although I decided to carry my beaked mask rather than wear it.

"I'd better drink this quickly and get back to my own practice," said Dr Marjoram gloomily. "That scrofula won't cure itself."

"Yes, I should get back to my practice as well," said Dr Rosemary, a little too quickly.

Dr Oregano leaned back in his chair and surveyed the large, airy reception room with the elegant loggia beyond. "I'm going to suggest to the doge that I stay in this building as head of the rapid response team," he said. "I'll tell him you never know when there might be another outbreak of plague and it's best to be prepared."

"You're going to move your practice here?" said Dr Marjoram. "But it's miles away from your current surgery. What about your patients?"

"The walk will do them good," said Dr Oregano carelessly. "Isn't that what Hippocrates always says?"

When breakfast was finished, we all shook hands and promised to meet up soon for a reunion. I felt almost as gloomy as Dr Marjoram, wondering whether I would find myself available for reunions for the foreseeable future.

"My brother's come to pick me up," said Dr Rosemary. "Can we give you a lift?"

"That would be lovely," I said, following her to the loggia and the steps to the canal, my gloom deepening as I realised I had no idea where to go.

I cheered up slightly as we reached the gondola to see her brother practising rotating through his spine and hips.

"These exercises are great," he said when he saw me. "Is there any chance you could teach them to the rest of the family?"

I gave him a wobbly smile. "Maybe. I'm not quite sure of my commitments at the moment," I said.

He waited until we were settled in the passenger cabin, the black wool canopy pulled aside so that we could see out.

"Where to?" he asked.

I politely waited for Dr Rosemary to give her destination first.

She bit her lip. "Home, I suppose," she muttered.

"Don't you want to call in on your medical practice and see how it's doing?" I asked.

"I don't have a medical practice," she said in a low voice. "I've only just graduated. I was about to look for somewhere in Venice when I heard about the plague and came to see how I could help."

Again, the Blainer's motto. Was there any way I could help her? In an instant, I had it.

"Dr Oregano!" I said.

Despite herself, she giggled. "Dr Oregano – have you been calling us all after the herbs we use? Doctor Oregano, Doctor Parsley, Doctor Marjoram, Doctor Rosemary? That's brilliant – we should have called you Doctor Aniseed. I'm going to start using those names, too. Anyway, what about Dr Oregano?"

"You can take over his practice, since he's abandoning it to head up the rapid response team. That will save his patients having to walk for miles to get to him," I said.

"But then he won't have any patients," said Dr Rosemary.

"I think that will suit him very well," I said. "I don't think we need to worry about him – he's the type that always lands on their feet. He'll get the doge to pay him a substantial retainer for keeping a lookout for the plague. And with his posh new premises, I'm sure he'll attract plenty of posh new patients."

"Go for it," said her brother. "I've had some of his current patients in the front of my gondola, and they don't think much of him."

"I'll do it," said Dr Rosemary with determination. "Thank you, Shona."

"Shona?" said her brother. "What an unusual name – so exotic. Anyway, where can we drop you?"

It was a good question. Perhaps if Miss Blaine was going to abandon me in seventeenth-century Venice, I could do good by joining Dr Rosemary's practice and teaching remedial exercises to asymmetric gondoliers. And then I thought of the Marciana Library, a place of sanctuary and solace. If I was going to end my days here, how better than by assisting Librarian Zen, and ensuring that nobody turned up with a secret stash of fried sardines?

"St Mark's Square, please," I said to Dr Rosemary's brother.

"Near the Marciana Library?" asked Dr Rosemary. "Where Librarian Zen works? Perhaps we could call in and say hello."

"You're not supposed to talk in libraries," I said severely. It would be restful working in an era before small children in libraries were allowed to whoop and chatter to their hearts' content.

"I'll say hello very quietly," she promised.

Perhaps it was the mention of libraries, but I suddenly felt a tingling in my right hand as it rested over the poor half-book. The non-plague victims had been given a decent burial: why should a defunct book be given less? It was dreadful to think of the saturated pages at the bottom of a canal.

"You really can't remember where you threw the other half of the book?" I asked Dr Rosemary.

She shook her head. "Just somewhere between the doctors' residence and the library."

"So it must be somewhere on this route?" I persisted. "Can't you concentrate and try to jog your memory?"

She looked around helplessly. "I wasn't paying attention at the time. And with this mist, it's difficult to focus on anything."

"Please, just try," I urged.

She leaned over the side of the gondola, peering into the water as though it was possible to see all the way to the bottom. As she looked, she began unconsciously to whistle tunelessly to help her concentrate.

"Hold on," said her brother. "I'm just going to pull into the side to let it pass."

I expected to see a gondola, but instead, a dolphin barrelled alongside. My dolphin. It pulled up in front of us.

"I thought I heard someone whistling my name," it clicked. "Great to see you again, and the nice gondolier as well."

It must have a very unfortunate name if it sounded like Dr Rosemary's off-key whistling, but I was too polite to say that. I had better pretend that it had been intentional.

"Yes, thank you for coming so promptly," I clicked back. "We dropped something in the canal, half a book, and now we can't find it."

"You wouldn't believe the stuff people drop in here," whistled the dolphin. "Cooking pots, shoes, candlesticks. Not many books, though. Give me a minute." It disappeared under water.

Dr Rosemary and her brother were staring at me.

"Were you..." Dr Rosemary began, "...were you *communicating* with that dolphin?"

"I was," I admitted. "It's actually not that hard. The grammar is quite basic."

"Goodness," she breathed admiringly.

I find praise a bit embarrassing. "I had the finest education in the world," I said in explanation.

The dolphin popped up again, balancing a small black rectangle on its nose.

"This it?" it clicked.

"Sorry, no," I whistled. "We're looking for something in very damp red silk, probably frayed at the edges."

Doctor Rosemary peered over to see what I was discussing with the dolphin.

"That's it!" she cried. "That's it!"

I retrieved the dry half-book from my pocket, the deep red of the silk clearly visible through the protective recyclable, compostable and waterproof bag.

"No," I reminded her, "it doesn't have a black cover. It's red, like this."

"But I wrapped it in cloth covered in pitch to stop it getting wet," she said.

"What?" I said.

"Pitch," said her brother. "It's black stuff that we put on the hull of our gondolas so that the water doesn't get in."

"And I always carry some cloth covered in pitch for patients – marvellous for weeping sores," said Dr Rosemary.

The dolphin was listening intently, its head on one side but still keeping the black rectangle perfectly balanced. "What are they saying?" it asked.

"I think you might have found it," I clicked shakily, stretching out a hand for the rectangle. A moment later, I had unwrapped the pitch-covered cloth to reveal the other half of the book, safe and dry.

"Dolphin, you're wonderful," I told it.

"I know," it whistled. "Got to go. Things to do, turtles to see." With a farewell splash, it shot off down the canal.

"Please," I said to Dr Rosemary's brother, "get us to the library as quickly as possible."

I raced up the Marciana steps, Dr Rosemary at my heels, and signalled to Librarian Zen to come out of the reading room to join us so that our conversation wouldn't annoy the readers. I reckoned they were already annoyed enough by the number of times the library had been closed.

"Ladies," he said, "what can I do for you?"

Dr Rosemary was practically simpering. I scrutinised the librarian. He was smiling and yes, there were the dimples, which I hadn't noticed before, but he still did nothing for me beyond being a valued and trusted colleague.

"Here," I said, handing him both halves of the book. He gave a gasp of amazement, then gently and carefully put the two halves together.

"Can it...?" I found myself hesitating, afraid of the answer, "... can it be saved?"

"I don't know," he said. "We need to get it to the printworks." It was the quiet, urgent, voice I've heard people using when they say, "We need to get him to the hospital."

I ran into the reading room and clapped my hands loudly. "Everybody out," I called in the voice that could reach to the furthest edge of the playground during my schooldays. "The library's closing early today."

"It's only just opened," protested a reader.

"Ssh," I said. "No talking. You should know the rules by now."

It seemed an eternity before Dr Rosemary, Librarian Zen, the two halves of the book and I were in her brother's gondola, although it was probably only about ninety seconds.

"Step on it!" I shouted.

"Step on what?" her brother asked anxiously. "Is it a new exercise?"

More valuable time being lost.

"Just go as fast as you can, to the printworks," I yelled and practically fell off my seat as we took off at speed. I've seen the Venice boat race on television, much more exciting than the Oxford and Cambridge one. It had first appeared on the sporting calendar before the thirteenth century. And at this rate, Dr Rosemary's brother was going to win it.

When we reached the printworks, Librarian Zen had barely crossed the threshold when a large, powerful-looking man rushed over to greet him.

"Librarian," he said, grasping Zen's hand in his own vast paw.

"Publisher," said Zen. I could sense the kinship between the two, forged through a mutual devotion to books.

"And this," Zen went on, indicating me, "is not a doctor, but my colleague from Edinburgh, Librarian Macaroni Mona Lisa

Glissando."

"Edinburgh, city of literature!" said the publisher, bowing to me. "You're most welcome, Librarian. We have the deepest respect here for Walter Chepman and Androw Myllar."

"As do we for Aldus Manutius," I said, bowing back. If I was going to be left in Venice, it might not be too bad.

"And we also have a doctor and a gondolier with us," said the librarian as Dr Rosemary and her brother hovered behind us.

"We make no judgements here," said the publisher. "Please, come in."

The printers and bookbinders were all hard at work, some deploying the presses, others typesetting, still more creating wood-cuts, or stitching and embroidering, while apprentices ran between them, replenishing supplies. The publisher pulled aside a curtain to usher us into a quiet space, the very space where I had seen a supposed plague victim being stamped, only the other night.

The publisher frowned, and bent down to pick up two small wooden items off the floor, one covered in tell-tale black ink, the other in red.

"No idea what these are doing here," he said in surprise, showing them to Librarian Zen. "More your department, I would have thought."

"Indeed," said Zen grimly, pocketing the library stamps. At least there was no doubt about the publisher's surprise: he had no involvement in the sordid business.

"The place is so hectic that we use this alcove for visitors," he said. "Otherwise you run the risk of your robes getting covered in ink or being sewn into a book cover. So, Librarian, to what do I owe the honour?"

"A most delicate matter," said Zen. "One that I fear is beyond anyone's capabilities to remedy. We have a book – that is, we have a dismembered book."

"How did it come to be dismembered?" asked the publisher.

Behind me, I could practically feel the heat radiating from Dr Rosemary's face.

"That, I'm afraid, must remain a mystery," said the librarian. "It may be too late, but we felt we had to bring it even if there was an infinitesimal chance of saving it."

"Let's see it," said the publisher.

Wordlessly, Librarian Zen handed over the two halves. The publisher sucked in his breath, then lifted one half to study its edge intently and then the other.

"It's bad," he said briefly. "Very bad. But something may be possible; it's a very clean cut, almost surgical."

Dr Rosemary was overcome by a fit of coughing and had to be slapped on the back by her brother.

"And it's not from here," he said. Very gently, as though he was touching a single rose petal, he opened one of the halves and his eyes widened. "This is from an antique land. It's a different system from ours."

So it was game over, I thought sadly. Android versus iOS. Impossible to merge the two. Librarian Zen gave a heartfelt sigh, having reached the same conclusion, though probably not using the same analogy.

"Thank you for your time, Publisher," he said. "I feared it was a lost cause, but you'll understand – I had to try."

The publisher put a hand on his shoulder. "Now, Librarian. There are no lost causes, only lost confidence. You've done all you can; now it's down to me. Go home and try to get some rest. I'll see you in the morning."

I could see it was a struggle for Zen to keep his emotions in check. He swallowed hard, nodded and turned away.

"One more thing, Publisher," I said. "This alcove has been used for non-work purposes. I've witnessed it myself. How might that happen?"

His face darkened. "I don't know. But I'm going to find out." He summoned the foreman who went back into the printroom and returned a short time later, dragging a young apprentice by the ear.

"Well now, young man," said the publisher in an affable tone, which was arguably more scary than if he had shouted, "perhaps you'll explain what's been going on?"

"It was my cousin, sir," said the apprentice. "It was at night, when there weren't any visitors, so I didn't think it would do any harm. He's an actor, sir, with a non-speaking role at the Teatro San Cassiano. He said he and his friends needed somewhere to learn their lines."

"An actor with a non-speaking role needing somewhere to learn his lines?" said the publisher in the same affable tone.

There was a pause.

"Oh," said the apprentice. "That doesn't really make sense."

"I told you we should never have hired this one," said the foreman.

"Please, sir," wailed the apprentice, "don't fire me. All I've ever wanted to do is work with books. I love it here. You don't even need to pay me. I'll find another job that pays, which I can do in my spare time."

The publisher turned to me, raising an eyebrow.

"How could you think of firing such an enthusiastic lad?" I asked. "Yes, he's made a mistake, but he was trying to help a family member. And the situation has now resolved itself – I guarantee it won't happen again."

"I'd probably have fired you," the publisher said to the trembling apprentice. "You can thank the librarian here for persuading me not to."

"Thank you, Librarian," gasped the apprentice, whose ear was still in the foreman's grip. "Being a librarian must be almost as good as being a publisher."

"Take him away before I change my mind," I said to the foreman, trying to make it sound like a joke, and the apprentice was duly dragged back to the printroom.

"Librarian Macaroni Mona Lisa Glissando," said Librarian Zen. "We must leave, and let the publisher get on with his work."

That was, of course, the most important thing, but I was glad to have found that the printworks had no direct involvement in Canaletto junior's terrible fraud.

The journey back to St Mark's Square was slower and silent, although I noted that Dr Rosemary seemed to be sitting closer to Librarian Zen than was absolutely necessary.

There was a small disgruntled queue outside the library, but the librarian waved them away.

"We're closed until further notice," he told them wearily.

Once the four of us were in the reading room, Dr Rosemary said, "Now what?"

"We wait," said Librarian Zen. "And we pray."

FIFTEEN

It was now day seven of my mission or, to put it another way, the first day of the rest of my life in Venice.

We had all slept in our clothes on the floor of the reading room, although I had been kept awake for quite a while by Dr Rosemary chatting to Librarian Zen.

"Shona told me about an army doctor who was a woman, but nobody knew," she said. "I thought I might like that, but I wouldn't really like the war part. I've got forceps for extracting arrow heads, and a bullet extractor in my medical kit, but I'm sure I could use them for other things."

"They might well be useful for repairing damaged books," said Librarian Zen thoughtfully.

"The main reason I liked the sound of the army was the travel. I've only been as far as Bologna, and I'd love to see other places."

"You don't need war as an excuse to travel," said Librarian Zen. "You can travel for any number of reasons. To visit libraries, for example. The new Mazarine Library in Paris is wonderful. You could visit medical libraries, and advise on what medical books we should have here."

"But I'm about to take on a medical practice. I can't do both."

"Of course you can. His Serenity is very supportive of field trips that help to keep Venice preeminent among the cities of the world. These will be even more important now we're going to be a tourist hub – and the tourists will want to be reassured that they'll get the best medical care, hence the need for the best medical library. His Serenity knows you now – if you liked, we could put in a joint bid for a travel grant and visit libraries together."

"I'd love that," said Dr Rosemary. "It's so exciting going to places where they have roads."

"Excuse me," I said, "people trying to sleep here."

They kept it down a bit, but they didn't stop talking, and eventually I nodded off from sheer exhaustion. From the snoring on the other side of me, Dr Rosemary's brother had had no such trouble.

Now, in the cold light of the misty morning, I was bleary-eyed and half-asleep and wanted nothing more than a hot drink and a pastry.

"Librarian," said Zen, slight surprise in his voice, "we're due at the printworks."

I couldn't believe that I'd forgotten. It showed how sleep-deprived I was. I hastily followed the others to the gondola. Nobody was urging Dr Rosemary's brother to go faster this time. It was as though we wanted to postpone the moment when the publisher would tell us there was no hope. But eventually we reached the printworks, Librarian Zen valiantly leading the way.

Nobody came to meet us. There was an unnatural calm in the printroom. At the far end, we could see the publisher stooped over a workspace.

I felt Librarian Zen's fingers interlock with mine. "Come on," he said quietly. "No point in prolonging it."

Just as we reached the publisher, he straightened up, flourishing a volume covered in exquisite red silk.

"We've done it!" he roared, and the entire printroom erupted in applause. He sank back on to the wooden stool, wiping his brow with a nearby cloth.

"It was touch and go," he said. "Twice I thought we'd lost it for good. But we kept going, and here you are."

Librarian Zen took the restored book with trembling fingers. "We'll never be able to thank you enough," he said. "How much do we owe you?"

"No charge," said the publisher heartily. "It was a privilege."

We were all in a daze as we went back to the gondola. I think it was Dr Rosemary's brother who suggested we stop somewhere for a cappuccino and a pastry, and I recommended the place by the Campo Santa Maria Formosa. For once, I felt I needed a coffee.

The waiter looked at us with utter scorn as we walked in and ordered.

"Sorry," said Librarian Zen in an undertone, "I'm afraid this is my fault. I came in a few days ago with a bunch of people, and we all had cappuccinos even though it was well after 11am."

I didn't mention having milk with my tea.

While we were waiting to be served, Librarian Zen reverently opened the book.

"Librarian Macaroni Mona Lisa Glissando, let's see whether our language skills are up to this," he said.

We started reading our way down the stylised Chinese calligraphy.

"It looks," he said, sounding a little puzzled, "like recipes, but I can't quite—"

The waiter arrived at this moment with the cappuccinos and pastries, and Librarian Zen hastily put the book away to avoid anything damaging it.

I was in a quandary. There hadn't been an outbreak of plague in Venice in 1650, so I wasn't rewriting the accepted history of the time. And in that case...

But first, I would have to explain myself. And risk getting myself locked up in an asylum. I looked around. There were no other customers in the shop, and the waiter had wandered off, clearly hoping that we would do the same. I took a deep breath.

"I'm not who you think I am," I said.

Dr Rosemary wrinkled her brow. "I know you're not a doctor, but you mean you're not a librarian either?"

"She's a librarian," said Librarian Zen with a smile. "It's not the sort of thing you can fake."

"Yes, I'm a librarian, but – I know this is going to be hard for you to understand – I come from the future. It's a thing called time travel. This is the seventeenth century, but I come from the twenty-first."

Dr Rosemary and her brother were looking at me open-mouthed as though I was talking complete gibberish. But Librarian Zen nodded and said, "I wondered whether it might be something of the sort."

That encouraged me. I hoped he would do as I asked, even though it went against all our librarianly impulses.

"This book," I said, "was brought to Venice by a traveller from an antique land, who wanted to present it to the doge as a business opportunity. Dr Rosemary here—"

Dr Rosemary giggled and whispered to her brother, "She's calling me by my herb instead of my name."

"The doctor here," I said, "got hold of the book out of concern for her family, hoping that they could capitalise on this opportunity if their gondola business collapsed."

"So now we don't need it, should we give the book to His Serenity?" asked Dr Rosemary's brother.

"Absolutely not," I said. "I'm going to give you some information from the future that you must promise never to reveal. These are recipes for ice cream."

"What's ice cream?" said Dr Rosemary, a reasonable question under the circumstances.

"It's something the Chinese invented over a thousand years ago," I said. "It's a very cold dessert involving dairy products. And your country is going to become world-famous at making it."

"Ah," said Librarian Zen.

"I've heard of a man in Florence who's invented something with ice and eggs and honey," said Dr Rosemary.

"A man in Florence! That can't be up to much," said her brother.

"What he's done is just a variation on sorbet, flavoured ice, and Marco Polo brought the recipe for that to Venice in 1295," I said. "I'm talking about proper ice cream, made with milk and cream and sugar."

"That sounds delicious," said Dr Rosemary's brother. "So why aren't we taking the book to His Serenity?"

"Because we're not due to become world-famous yet," said Librarian Zen. "Am I right, Librarian Macaroni Mona Lisa Glissando?"

"Always," I said with a comradely smile. "If you could keep the book under wraps until 1680, that would work well."

"I won't say it's going to be easy," he said. "Of course I want to make every book available to everyone."

"As do I," I agreed. "Apart from the one I mentioned to you."

"Then there we are," he said. "You have your book in a locked cupboard, and I shall have this in a locked cupboard. Along with the octavos, which are available on request, but I'll keep this safely at the back where nobody can see it until the appropriate time."

"Thank you for being so understanding," I said.

"Librarians always understand," he said.

Cappuccinos and pastries consumed, we went back to St Mark's Square. And as we got there, the mist suddenly cleared and the sun shone out of a brilliant blue sky. It was my first proper view of La Serenissima, and it was gorgeous. If I wasn't going back to Morningside, this was a good second best.

"If you don't mind," I said, "I'm going to go off for a swim and take in the sights. I'll catch up with you later."

"I'll go and lock the book in the cupboard," said Librarian Zen.

"I'll go and open my medical practice," said Dr Rosemary.

"I'll go and look for customers," said Dr Rosemary's brother.

I had ended up fully clothed in a canal so many times that I was quite used to it. I put on my beaked mask to stop my hair getting wet, much better than those horrible rubber bathing caps we had to wear at school, and eased myself into the water. Given the beak, the easiest thing to do was to float on my back. As I drifted along past the Doge's Palace, I reflected once again how practical it was not being hampered by my DMs. It had been quite a frantic week, and it was delightful to be able to relax and enjoy my surroundings.

There was a sudden flash, and something landed on the end of my proboscis. I squinted to see what it was. It was golden. It looked like a ring. A golden ring. And then I gasped as I was seized by a hideous abdominal cramping, exactly the sort I experienced when I was due to be transported back to Edinburgh. But that was impossible, as I hadn't completed my mission. The abdominal cramping continued. This was definitely it – I was going home.

But there was a gold ring on my proboscis. A gold ring that I now realised had been thrown by the doge, the ring he was supposed to throw when Venice married the sea – and that wasn't due to happen for weeks. What was he going to do? What was I going to do? I would be in Edinburgh with a seventeenth-century ring that I wasn't supposed to have. I couldn't keep it. I could take it to the National Museum of Scotland, but how would I explain where I'd got it? I could scarcely claim to have dug it up in the back green. What if I got charged with theft, and extradited to Italy to stand trial? I couldn't help it; I let out an anguished whimper.

An instant later, the water churned around me.

"Sorry, I didn't quite get that. Were you calling me?" asked the dolphin.

"Please," I whistled feebly as the cramping continued, "could you get me to shore?"

The dolphin glided under me, and I was gently carried to the Doge's Palace, where the doge stood waiting anxiously.

"You've got my ring," he said.

"Only because you threw it," I managed to say. "Why did you do that?"

"I'd been practising with the wooden rings, but I'd used them all up, so I thought I'd practise with the real ring," he said.

"You'd used them all up because they sank," I said. "Didn't it strike you the same thing would happen with the real ring?" The populace was right; he was an idiot.

"Sorry," he muttered, leaning forward and removing it from my proboscis.

"Keep that safe, and order some more wooden rings," I said. "And book some throwing lessons with Dr Rosemary."

I suddenly remembered I had news for the dolphin. "A music student at the Ospedale della Pietà is writing an opera and it's going to have a chorus of dancing dolphins," I told it. "I hope you'll audition for it, and ask your friends as well."

I had barely finished the sentence when I was whirled through an icy vortex and arrived back in Edinburgh winded and breathless.

"Good heavens, girl, whatever's the matter?" said Miss Blaine. "Do you require the Heimlich manoeuvre?"

"Thank you, no," I gasped. "I'm just back from my mission."

"Then stop slouching and sit up straight," said Miss Blaine.

I was still in the ice cream parlour, in my own clothes, wearing my trusty DMs, which were perfect so long as I wasn't immersed.

"Miss Blaine," I said, "did I complete my mission? What was I supposed to be doing? I helped establish Venice's first female doctor. And I got an opera commission for Francesca della Pietà, the first step in boosting Venice's tourist industry. And I reassured the populace that there wasn't an outbreak of plague. Or was it the book, salvaging the book with the ice cream recipes?"

"Everybody talks about the Chinese inventing gunpowder," said Miss Blaine. "But that was centuries after they invented ice cream. Did you know the Chinese invented ice cream?"

"Of course, Miss Blaine," I said.

"But the best ice cream is Italian," she said.

She looked at her bowl, which was empty, and signalled to a waitress.

"Another two of these, if you would be so kind."

"Right away," said the waitress. "What was it, toffee fudgy wudgy?"

"Certainly not," said Miss Blaine. "Plain vanilla. That is all that is required."

ACKNOWLEDGEMENTS

I am hugely grateful to all of the readers and reviewers who take an interest in Miss Blaine's Prefect and her missions, and to the following, who have helped ensure the success of Shona's visit to Venice:

Sara Hunt and all at Saraband, especially editor Ali Moore;

Iain Matheson;

Al Guthrie;

Gavin Routledge;

Michael Daniell;

Martin Gray;

Yvonne Morley-Chisholm;

Luca's Café, Morningside;

The Muriel Spark Society coffee police;

Dame Muriel Spark, especially for her Venetian novel, *Territorial Rights*;

and Alistair, who could almost be a dolphin.